Some news and thoughts in no order: ¶This issue came together quickly and went to press quickly. Some of our regular contributors, like Lawrence Weschler, are not present only because the speed of this production process, and the stripped-down production values, didn't allow for us to indulge some of our inclinations and regular features. ¶This is the first paperback McSweeney's Publishing has put out in more than two years. We thought it best to go back to our origins, for many reasons, chief among them financial. Given the elaborate shapes of previous issues, we have frankly been losing lots of money fulfilling our subscriptions. Each copy of Issue 7, for example, cost $5 to ship to subscribers, in postage alone. Factor in the actual cost of printing and we're wondering why we didn't do the math sooner. ¶This issue contains twelve very straightforward works, mostly stories, all of them urgent in some way. We love these stories. ¶To submit work for the print version, send manuscripts to: 826 Valencia Street, San Francisco, CA, 94110. Please include email address and phone number, and allow many months for a response. Our reading periods are sporadic, and we don't have a paid reading staff, and can't guarantee a speedy return of correspondence. We really do the best we can, and we appreciate your submissions, and your patience. ¶This April, McSweeney's opened the 826 Valencia Writing Project, a nonprofit tutoring center in the Mission district of San Francisco. 826 Valencia is designed to help students age eight to eighteen develop and improve writing and communication skills of all kinds. We offer drop-in tutoring, afterschool workshops in everything from comics creation to SAT prep, field trips, and assistance with student publications. We support local teachers in any way we can and are always open to new ideas. ¶We are just getting started, but so far it's been fantastic. We spent six months getting the building ready—it used to be a weightroom—doing much of the construction work ourselves, and finally we opened to no fanfare at all. While the students were slow to trickle in, the place is now swirling with activity, from 11am to 9pm, every single day. We almost can't believe it, how we wanted kids to come in and learn and goof around, to share the building with us, and after a few months, there they are. The space is theirs as much as it is ours, and the storefront's open to everyone, so feel free to come by. It's always full, always loud. It's a good space. ¶We have a terrific group of tutors—amazingly qualified and energetic—drawn primarily from the huge and generous writing and publishing community of the Bay Area. These volunteers include: Mandy Field, Chad LeJeune, Eleni Sotos, Kiara Brinkman, Charles Koppelman, Brie Mazurek, Julie Landry, Alicia Anka, Jennifer King, Nicole Miller, Kate Pavao, Ian Stewart, Jeni Paltiel, Rachel Chalmers, Pamela Smith, Julie Bennett, Maya Hazarika, Chris Colin, Matt Ness, Jon Sung, Leslie Hamanaka, Renata Ewing, Margaret Berry, Aimee Goggins, Aimee Male, John Borland, Abigail Jacobs, Amanda Eicher, John McMurtrie, Sarah Gault, Amie Nenninger, Kate Kudirka, Laurel Newby, Sam Silverstein, James Daly, Natalie Linden, Roderick Simpson, Jennifer Birch, Eric Hellweg, Gabriel Roth, Mathew Honan, Janelle Brown, Arne Johnson, Jenny Traig, Todd Pound, Katherine Covell, Taylor Jacobson, Chloe Cockburn, Leora Broydo Vestel, Lee Konstantinou, Cynthia Wood, Jason Roberts. ¶And the students have been astounding. One of them, a steely-eyed chess prodigy named Stephen, has at presstime begun a story titled "The Fat Man That Can't Fit into a Boat." Another story, written by Phoebe, twelve years old and one of our most frequent visitors, concerns her travels with her pirate-uncle Starzen, who takes her on a three-hour trip in a rowboat, to Thailand, where they meet up with creatures Phoebe calls *"them crazy swimmin' elephants!"* ¶Many of the stories written by our younger visitors involve nautical themes, because directly in front of the writing lab is our new store, where we sell quality pirate supplies at reasonable prices. The store's proceeds pay the rent at 826 Valencia, *in toto*, because we expected and have been correct in thinking that people were sick of having to drive all the way to the mall to buy swabbing mops, planks and millet. ¶Behind the store and the writing lab are our new editorial offices, where we assemble all the McSweeney's books and journals, with our full-time staff of two and the help of many outstanding interns. ¶These three pieces—the publishing, the lab, the store—interact in wonderful and unexpected ways that can't be explained here. We feel very thankful for the life that exists at 826 Valencia each day, the noise it generates and the kids who come in to learn or laugh or, for some, to sit and read quietly in our richly-appointed Morroccan-style library nook. For more information, please visit www.826valencia.com, or come by sometime. ¶Editorial assistance for this issue and with McSwys generally was provided by the following volunteers: In San Francisco: Justin Gallagher, Andrew Leland, Suzanne Kleid, Dave Kneebone, Alan Thuma, Matt Dorville, Pamela Smith, Gabe Koplowitz, Tommy Wallach, Kate Addiego & Ieva Aldins. In New York: Ted Thompson, Jason Kellermeyer, Krista Overby, Anthony Mascorro, Chad Albers, Becky Hayes, Aaron Bleyaert, Michael Hearst, Joshua Camp, Allison Devers & Joe Pacheco. Contributing editors: Lawrence Weschler, John Warner. Editors at large: Sean Wilsey, Lee Epstein. Friends from Way Back and Always: Diane Vadino, Todd Pruzan, Mieka Strawhorn. Website Man: Michael Genrich. Brooklyn Store Leader and Events Coordinator: Scott Seeley. San Francisco Store Leader and Events Coordinator: Yosh Han. Vice President of McSwys Operations Emeritus: Julie Wright. New Managing Editor: Eli Horowitz. Educational Director of 826 Valencia: Ninive Clements Calegari. President of McSwys Publishing: Barb Bersche. President of McSwys Publishing Emeritus: Sarah Min. Editor: Dave Eggers.

The back cover painting, *Garden Variety* (60 x 76, oil on canvas), is by Scott Greene. Greene is represented by the Catharine Clark Gallery in San Francisco. See more at www.scottmgreene.com.

WILLIAM T. VOLLMANN..............*Three Meditations on Death*. 7
Vollmann walks among the bones under Paris, watches coroners pick apart corpses and examines the fate that awaits us, in all its unvarnished, decaying ordinariness. Rattling but gorgeously written.—*Suzanne Kleid*

A.M. HOMES............................*Georgica* 27
Sand. Sex pants. Condoms. Stake-out. Lifeguards. Self-insemination. Desperation. Night-vision goggles. Breaking and entering. Mommy. Swan bites. Drunk driving. Wise grandmother. Friendly cop. This story makes me wonder if I'm ready.—*Dave Kneebone*

NATHANIEL MINTON.................*A Threefold Cord* . . . . , , 53
So strange and good. Is this some kind of fable, or is the mom really dying? The photographer is breathing through a tube? It all seems impossible, but then it's all for real.—*Eli Horowitz*

K. KVASHAY-BOYLE....................*Saint Chola* 65
I've never been a Muslim girl in junior high going through puberty. All the same, by the time I finished Boyle's story, I felt like I would have no problem shooting the shit with Shala M. Sawy. This story makes you pump your fist in triumph—for me, it's like watching *Revenge of the Nerds*, late at night, all alone.—*Gabe Koplowitz*

GABE HUDSON............................*Notes from a Bunker Along Highway 8*. 81
Gabe Hudson updates and expands the Cold War delusion and paranoia of Donald Barthelme's "Game" for the semi-contemporary landscape of Desert Storm. He treats general topics like War, Spirituality, Homosexuality and America as if they were symbols, albeit fat, slippery symbols that don't signify as you'd expect, creating a comic and surreal moral shitstorm. This story is fucking hilarious.—*Andrew Leland*

DENIS JOHNSON...............................*Soul of a Whore* 127
Eugene O'Neill meets Greek drama meets, of course, Denis Johnson. The characters are blurred in mystery and seem suspiciously connected through fate or destiny. This is a play you read and cannot wait to see performed on stage.—*Matt Dorville*

VAL VINOKUROV........................*Talking Fiction: What is Russian Skaz?*. 169
Why have I never heard of *skaz* before? This is not the Russian Lit of all those skipped lectures in college. Vinokurov is tapping into something big here, a genre as classic as Gogol and as contemporary as *Trainspotting*.—*Dave Kneebone*

ISAAC BABEL ....*Salt*. 181
"Salt" enjoys a glory seemingly reserved for poems, and rarely attained by prose: many people know it by heart.—*Jorge Luis Borges*

DOUG DORST............................*A Long Bloodless Cut* · 185
This story begins with a rotting human head, and then later there's the part with the grenade in the mouth. It gets better each time I read it.—*Eli Horowitz*

ELLEN MOORE............................*Gateway to the West* · . . . . · 199
A quiet gem, this one. Nothing louder than a shaky washing machine; just muffled voices, grunting patients, missed concerts.—*Alan Thuma*

JEFF GREENWALD ....*My New Best Friend*· 213
The Maoist guerillas won't be the biggest danger on this Himalayan pilgrimage.—*Brian McMullen*

ROY KESEY ....*Pacazo*. . . . . , , 243
Kesey nails the cognitive and moral overload of an American abroad, and the result is a story where the tactile world—taxis, sweat, and lizard shit—crowds and buzzes.—*Andrew Leland*

All recommendations except one are from McSwys 2002 interns.

THREE MEDITATIONS
ON DEATH

by WILLIAM T. VOLLMANN

I.
CATACOMB THOUGHTS

DEATH IS ORDINARY. Behold it, subtract its patterns and lessons from those of the death that weapons bring, and maybe the residue will show what violence is. With this in mind, I walked the long tunnels of the Paris catacombs. Walls of earth and stone encompassed walls of mortality a femur's-length thick: long yellow and brown bones all stacked in parallels, their sockets pointing outward like melted bricks whose ends dragged down, like downturned bony smiles, like stale yellow snails of macaroni—joints of bones, heads of bones, promiscuously touching, darkness in the center of each, between those twin knucklespurs which had once helped another bone to pivot, thereby guiding and supporting flesh in its passionate and sometimes intelligent motion toward the death it inevitably found—femurs in rows, then, and humerii, bones upon bones, and every few rows there'd be a shelf of bone to shore death up, a line of humerii and femurs laid down laterally to achieve an almost pleasing masonry effect, indeed, done by masonry's maxims, as interpreted by Napoleon's engineers and brickmen of death, who at the nouveau-royal command had elaborated and organized death's jetsam according to a sanitary aesthetic. (Did the Emperor ever visit that place? He was not afraid of death—not even of causing it.) Then there were side-chambers walled with bones likewise crossed upon bone-beams; from these the occasional skull looked uselessly out; and every now and then some spiritual types had ornamented the facade with a cross made of femurs. There had been laid down in that place, I was told, the remains of about six million persons—our conventional total for the number of Jews who died in the Holocaust. The crime which the Nazis accomplished with immense effort in half a dozen years, nature had done here without effort or recourse, and was doing.

I had paid my money aboveground; I had come to look upon my future. But when after walking the long arid angles of prior underground alleys I first encountered my brothers and sisters, calcified appurtenances of human beings now otherwise gone to be dirt, and rat-flesh, and root-flesh, and green leaves soon to die again, I felt nothing but a mildly melancholy curiosity. One expects to die; one has seen skeletons and death's heads on Halloween masks, in anatomy halls, cartoons, warning signs, forensic photographs, photographs of old SS insignia, and meanwhile the skulls bulged and gleamed from walls like wet river-boulders, until curiosity became, as usual, numbness. But one did not come out of the ground then. Bone-walls curled around wells, drainage sockets in those tunnels; sometimes water dripped from the ceiling and struck the tourists' foreheads—water which had probably leached out of corpses. A choking, sickening dust irritated our eyes and throats, for in no way except in the abstract, and perhaps not even then, is the presence of the dead salutary to the living. Some skulls dated to 1792. Darkened, but still not decayed, they oppressed me with their continued existence. The engineers would have done better to let them transubstantiate. They might have been part of majestic trees by now, or delicious vegetables made over into young children's blood and growing bones. Instead they were as stale and stubborn as old arguments, molds for long dissolved souls, churlish hoardings of useless matter. Thus, I believed, the reason for my resentment. The real sore point was that, in Eliot's phrase, "I had not thought death had undone so many"; numbness was giving way to qualmishness, to a nauseated, claustrophobic realization of my biological entrapment. Yes, of course I'd known that I must die, and a number of times had had my nose rubbed in the fact; this was one of them, and in between those episodes my tongue glibly admitted what my heart secretly denied; for why should life ought to bear in its flesh the dissolving, poisonous faith of its own inescapable defeat? Atop bony driftwood, skulls slept, eyeholes downwards, like the shells of dead hermit crabs amidst those wracked corpse-timbers. This was the necrophile's beach, but there was no ocean except the ocean of earth overhead from which those clammy drops oozed and dripped. Another cross of bone, and then the inscription—

SILENCE, MORTAL BEINGS—VAIN GRANDEURS, SILENCE—

words even more imperious in French than I have given them here, but no more necessary, for the calcified myriads said that better than all poets or commanders. In superstition the carcass is something to be feared, dreaded and hated; in fact it deserves no emotion whatsoever in and of itself, unless it happens to comprise a souvenir of somebody other than a stranger; but time spent in the company of death is time wasted. Life trickles away, like the water falling down into the catacombs, and in the end we will be silent as our ancestors are silent, so better to indulge our vain grandeurs while we can. Moment by moment, our time bleeds away. Shout, scream, or run, it makes no difference, so why not forget what can't be avoided? On and on twisted death's alleys. Sometimes there was a smell, a cheesy, vinegary smell which I knew from having visited a field-morgue or two; there was no getting away from it, and the dust of death dried out my throat. I came to a sort of cavern piled up to my neck with heaps of bones not used in construction: pelvic bones and ribs (the vertebrae and other small bones must have all gone to discard or decay). These relics were almost translucent, like seashells, so thin had death nibbled them. That smell, that vinegar-vomit smell, burned my throat, but perhaps I was more sensitive to it than I should have been, for the other tourists did not appear to be disgusted; indeed, some were laughing, either out of bravado or because to them it was as unreal as a horror movie; they didn't believe that they'd feature in the next act, which must have been why one nasty fellow seemed to be considering whether or not to steal a bone—didn't he have bones enough inside his living meat? He must not have been the only one, for when we came to the end and ascended to street level we met a gainfully employed man behind a table which already had two skulls on it, seized from thieves that day; he checked our backpacks. I was happy when I got past him and saw sunlight— almost overjoyed, in fact, for since becoming a part-time journalist of armed politics I am not titillated by death. I try to understand it, to make friends with it, and I never learn anything except the lesson of my own powerlessness. Death stinks in my nostrils as it did that chilly sunny autumn afternoon in Paris when I wanted to be happy.

In the bakeries, the baguettes and pale, starchy *mini-ficelles,* the croissants and *pains-aux-chocolats* all reminded me of bones. Bone-colored cheese stank from other shops. All around me, the steel worms of the Metro bored through other catacombs, rushing still living bones from hole to hole. In one of the bookshops on the Rue de Seine I found a demonically bound volume of Poe whose endpapers were marbled like flames; the plates, of course, hand-colored by the artist, depicted gruesomely menacing skeletons whose finger-bones snatched and clawed. I spied a wedding at the Place Saint-Germain, whose church was tanned and smoked by time to the color of cheesey bones; I saw the white-clad bride—soon to become yellow bones. The pale narrow concrete sleepers of railroads, metallic or wooden fence-rails, the model of the spinal column in the window of an anatomical bookshop, then even sticks, tree trunks, all lines inscribed or implied, the world itself in all its segments, rays, and dismembered categories became hideously cadaverous. I saw and inhaled death. I tasted death on my teeth. I exhaled, and the feeble puffs of breath could not push my nausea away. Only time did that—a night and a day, to be exact—after which I forgot again until I was writing these very words that *I must die.* I believed but for a moment. Thus I became one with those skulls which no longer knew their death. Even writing this, picking my letters from the alphabet's boneyard, my *o*'s like death's-heads, my *i*'s and *l*'s like ribs, my *b*'s, *q*'s, *p*'s and *d*'s like ball-ended humerii broken in half, I believed only by fits. The smell came back into my nose, but I was in Vienna by then— whose catacombs, by the way, I decided not to visit—so I went out and smelled espresso heaped with fresh cream. The writing became, as writing ought to be, informed by choreographies and paradigms which mediated that smell into something more than its revolting emptiness. I take my meaning where I can find it; when I can't find it, I invent it. And when I do that, I deny meaninglessness, and when I do *that* I am lying to myself. Experience does not necessarily lie, but that smell is not an experience to the matter which emits it. Death cannot be experienced either by the dead or the living. The project of the Parisian workmen, to aestheticize, to arrange, and thus somehow to transform the objects of which they themselves were composed, was a bizarre success, but it could have been done with stale loaves of bread. It affected bones;

it could not affect death. It meant as little, it said as little, as this little story of mine. It spoke of them as I must speak of me. I can read their meaning. Death's meaning I cannot read. To me death is above all things a smell, a very bad smell, and that, like the skeletons which terrify children, is not death at all. If I had to smell it more often, if I had to work in the catacombs, I would think nothing of it. And a few years or decades from now, I will think nothing about everything.

II.

AUTOPSY THOUGHTS

It shall be the duty of the coroner to inquire into and determine the circumstances, manner, and cause of all violent, sudden or unusual deaths ...

California state code, sec. 27491[1]

ALDOUS HUXLEY ONCE wrote that "if most of us remain ignorant of ourselves, it is because self-knowledge is painful and we prefer the pleasures of illusion."[2] That is why one brushes off the unpleasantly personal lesson of the catacombs. But we can extend the principle: Not only self-knowledge hurts. Consider the black girl whom an investigator pulled from a dumpster one night. Her mouth was bloody, which wasn't so strange; she could have been a homeless alcoholic with variceal bleeding. But, shining the flashlight into that buccal darkness, the investigator caught sight of a glint—neither blood nor spittle sparkling like metal, but metal itself—a broken-off blade. In her mouth, which could no longer speak, lay the truth of her death. The investigator couldn't give her her life back, but by this double unearthing—the knife from the corpse, the corpse from the stinking bin—he'd resurrected something else, an imperishable quantity which the murderer in his fear or fury or cold selfishness meant to entomb—namely, the fact of murder, the reality which would have been no less real had it never become known, but which, until it was known and proved, remained powerless to do good.—What good? Quite simply, determining the cause of death is the prerequisite for some kind of justice, although justice, like other sonorous concepts, can produce anything from healing to acceptance to compensation to revenge to hypocritical clichés. At the chief medical examiner's office they knew this good—knowing also that the job of turning evidence into justice lay not with them but with the twelve citizens in the jury box:—what coroners and medical examiners do is necessary but not sufficient. Probably the black woman's family had figured that out, if there *was* any family, if they cared, if they weren't too stupefied with grief. The morgue would be but the first of their Stations of the Cross. (Afterward: the funeral parlor, the graveyard, perhaps the courtroom, and always the empty house.) Dealing with them was both the saddest and the most important part of the truth-seeker's job: as I said, knowledge hurts. Dr. Boyd Stephens, the Chief Medical Examiner of San Francisco, would later say to me: "One of the things I hoped you'd see was a family coming in here grieving. And when it is a crime of violence, when someone has her son shot during a holdup, that makes it very hard; that's a tremendous emotional blow." I myself am very glad that I didn't see this. I have seen it enough. In the catacombs death felt senseless, and for the investigator who found the black woman, the moral of death remained equally empty, as it must whether the case is suicide, homicide, accident, or what we resignedly call "natural causes." Twenty-six years after the event, a kind woman who had been there wrote me about the death of my little sister. I was nine years old, and my sister was six. The woman wrote: "I remember you, very thin, very pale, your shoulders hunched together, your hair all wet and streaming sideways. You said, 'I can't find Julie.'" She wrote to me many other things that she remembered. When I read her letter, I cried. Then she went on: "I am tempted to say that Julie's drowning was a 'senseless death' but that's not true. I learned the day she died that there are realms of life in which the measure of sense and nonsense don't apply. Julie's death exists on a plane where there is no crime and no punishment, no cause and effect, no action and reaction. It just happened." Fair enough. Call it morally or ethically senseless, at least. (I don't think I ever wrote back; I felt too sad.) Only when *justice itself* condemns someone to death, as when a murderer gets hanged or we bombard Hitler's Berlin or an attacker meets his victim's lethal self-defense, can we even admit the possibility that the perishing had a point. Principled suicides also mean something: Cato's self-disembowelment indicts the conquering Caesar who would have granted clemency, and whose patronizing power now falls helpless before a mere corpse. But most people (including many suicides, and most who die the deaths of malicious judicial *in*justice) die the death of accident, meaninglessly and ultimately anonymously discorporating like unknown skulls in catacombs—and likewise the black woman in the dumpster.

No matter that her murderer had a reason—she died for nothing; and all the toxicology and blood spatter analyses in the world, even if they lead to his conviction, cannot change that. The murderer's execution might mean something; his victim's killing almost certainly will not.

FROM THE WHITE HEARSE TO THE VIEWING ROOM

In fiscal year 1994-95, slightly more than eight thousand people died in San Francisco County. Half of these deaths could be considered in some sense questionable, and reports on them accordingly traveled to Dr. Stephens's office, but in three thousand cases the doubts, being merely pro forma, were eventually cleared, signed off by physicians—that is, explained circumstantially if not ontologically. The remaining 1,549 deaths became Dr. Stephens's problem. His findings for that year were: 919 natural deaths, 296 non-vehicular accidents, 124 suicides, ninety-four homicides, thirty mysterious cases, six sudden infant death syndromes, and eighty vehicular fatalities, most of which involved pedestrians, and most of which were accidents (there were six homicides and one suicide).[3] And now I'm going to tell you what his people did to reach those findings. In San Francisco they had a white ambulance, or hearse as I might better say, which was partitioned between the driver's seat and the cargo hold, and the cargo hold could quickly be loaded or unloaded by means of the white double doors, the inside of which bore an inevitable reddish-brown stain: anything that touches flesh for years must get corrupted. It smelled like death in there, of course, which in my experience is sometimes similar to the smell of sour milk, or vomit and vinegar, or of garbage, which is to say of the dumpster in which the murdered girl had been clumsily secreted. A horizontal partition subdivided battered old stainless steel stretchers into two and two. Because San Francisco is hilly, the stretchers, custom-welded years before by a shop just down the street, were made to be stood upright, the bodies strapped in, and rolled along on two wheels. "Kind of like a wheelbarrow in a way," one stretcher man said. This might be the last time that the dead would ever again be vertical, as they serenely travelled, strapped and sheeted, down steep stairs and sidewalks. The ambulance pulled up behind Dr. Stephens's office, in a parking lot that said AMBULANCES ONLY. Out came each stretcher. Each stretcher went through the door marked NO ADMITTANCE, the door which for those of us whose hearts still beat might better read NO ADMITTANCE YET. Inside, the body was weighed upon a freight-sized scale, then wheeled into the center of that bleak back room for a pre-liminary examination, and fingerprinted three times (if it still had fingers and skin), with special black ink almost as thick as taffy. Finally it was zipped into a white plastic bag to go into the fridge overnight.[4] If the death might be homicide, the investigators waited longer—at least twenty-four hours, in case any new bruises showed up like last-minute images on a pale sheet of photographic paper floating in the developer, as might happen when deep blood vessels had been ruptured. Bruises were very important. If the body of a man who seemed to have hanged himself showed contusions on the face or hands, the investigators would have to consider homicide.[5]

By now perhaps the family had been told. In the big front room that said ABSOLUTELY NO ADMITTANCE I heard a man say, "Yes, we have Dave. I'm so sorry about what happened to Dave." If the family came, they would be led down a narrow corridor to a door that said VIEWING ROOM. The viewing room was private and secret, like the projection-ist's booth in a movie theater. It had a long window that looked out onto another very bright and narrow room where the movie would take place, the real movie whose story had already ended before the atten-dant wheeled in the former actor. The movie was over; Dr. Stephens needed the family to verify the screen credits. They only saw the face. There was a door between the viewing room and the bright and narrow room, but someone made sure to lock it before the family came, because they might have tried to embrace this thing which had once been someone they loved, and because the thing might not be fresh anymore or because it might have been slammed out of personhood in some hideous way whose sight or smell or touch would have made the family scream, it was better to respect the love they probably still felt for this thing which could no longer love them, to respect that love by respecting its clothes of ignorance. The people who worked in Dr. Stephens's office had lost their ignorance a long time ago. They blunt-ed themselves with habit, science and grim jokes—above all, with necessity: if the death had been strange or suspicious, they had to cut the thing open and look inside, no matter how much it stank.

A Solomonic parable: Dr. Stephens told me that once three different mothers were led into the viewing room one by one to identify a dead girl, and each mother claimed the girl as hers, with a desperate relief, as I would suppose. I know someone whose sister was kidnapped. It's been years now and they've never found her. They found her car at the side of the road. My friend used to live with her sister. Now she lives with her sister's clothes. From time to time the family's private detective will show her photographs of still another female body partially skeletonized or not, raped or not, and she'll say, "That's not my sister." I know it would give her peace to be able to go into a viewing room and say (and *believe*), "Yes, that's Shirley." Those three mothers must all have given up hoping that their daughters would ever speak to them or smile at them again. They wanted to stop dreading and start grieving. They didn't want to go into viewing rooms any more. And maybe the glass window was dirty, and maybe their eyes were old or full of tears. It was a natural mistake. But one mother was lucky. The dead girl was really her daughter.

The Innocent Metermaid

To confirm that identification, someone at Dr. Stephens' office had already looked inside the dead woman's mouth, incidentally discovering or not discovering the gleam of a knife-blade, observed her dental work, and matched it to a dentist's files. Somebody had fingerprinted her and found a match; somebody had sorted through her death-stained clothes and come up with a match. Starting with flesh and cloth, they had to learn what the mothers didn't know. The meter maid didn't know, either, and I am sure she didn't want to know. A young man eased some heroin into his arm—maybe too much, or maybe it was too pure (heroin just keeps getting better and better these days). He died and fell forward, his face swelling and purpling with lividity. The meter maid didn't know, I said. Even after he began to decompose, she kept putting parking tickets on his windshield.

"I'm a Happy Customer"

A stinking corpse, pink and green and yellow, lay naked on one of many parallel downsloping porcelain tables each of which drained into a porcelain sink. The man's back had hurt. Surgery didn't help, so he took painkillers until he became addicted. The painkillers proving insufficiently kind, he started mixing them with alcohol. When the white ambulance came, there were bottles of other people's pills beside his head. He was not quite forty.

"Everything's possible," said one morgue attendant to another, leaning against a gurney, while the doctor in mask and scrubs began to cut the dead man open. "You're limited only by your imagination." I think he was talking about special effects photography. He had loaned his colleague a mail-order camera catalog.

Meanwhile the dagger tattooed on the dead man's bicep trembled and shimmered as the doctor's scalpel made the standard Y-shaped incision, left shoulder to chest, right shoulder to chest, then straight down the belly to the pubis. The doctor was very good at what he did, like an old Eskimo who I once saw cutting up a dying walrus. The scalpel made crisp sucking sounds. He peeled back the chest-flesh like a shirt, then crackled the racks of ribs, which could almost have been pork. His yellow-gloved hands grubbed in the scarlet hole, hauling out fistfuls of sausage-links—that is, loops of intestine. Then he stuck a hose in and left it there until the outflow faded to pinkish clear. Beset by brilliant lavender, scarlet, and yellow, the twin red walls of rib-meat stood high and fragile, now protecting nothing, neatly split into halves.

The dead man still had a face.

The doctor syringed out a blood sample from the cavity, sponged blood off the table, and then it was time to weigh the dead man's organs on a hanging balance, the doctor calling out the numbers and the pretty young pathology resident chalking them onto the blackboard. The lungs, already somewhat decomposed, were indistinct masses which kept oozing away from the doctor's scalpel. "Just like jello," he said sourly.

The right lung was larger than the left, as is often the case with righthanded people. Another possible cause: the dead man had been found lying on his right side, a position which could have increased congestion in that lung. Either way, his death was meaningless.

His heart weighed 290 grams. The doctor began to cut it into slices.

"This vessel was almost entirely occluded with atherosclerosis," explained the resident. "He used a lot of drugs. Cocaine hastens the onset of atherosclerosis. We get lots of young people with old people's diseases."

That was interesting to know and it meant something, I thought. In a sense, the investigators understood the dead man. I wondered how well he'd been understood before he died.

"God, his pancreas!" exclaimed the doctor suddenly. "That's why he died." He lifted out a purple pudding which spattered blood onto the table.

"What happened?" I asked.

"Basically, all these enzymes there digest blood. This guy was hemmorhagic. The chemicals washed into his blood vessels and he bled. Very common with alcoholics."

Out came the liver now, yellow with fatty infiltrations from too much alcohol. "See the blood inside?" said the doctor. "But the pancreas is a sweetbread. The pancreas is a bloody pulp. Blood in his belly. Sudden death. We got lucky with him—he's an easy one. This is a sure winner."

Quickly he diced sections of the man's organs and let them ooze off his bloody yellow-gloved fingers into amber jars. The pathology and toxicology people would freeze them, slice them thinner, stain them and drop them onto microscope slides, just to make sure that he hadn't overdosed on something while he bled. Meanwhile the doctor's knowledge-seeking scalpel dissected the neck, to rule out any possibility of secret strangulation. Many subtle homicides are misdiagnosed as accidents by untrained people, and some accidents look like murders. The doctor didn't want that to happen. Even though he'd seen the pancreas, he wanted to be as thorough as he could to verify that there was no knifeblade in the mouth, that all the meaning had come out.— "Okay, very good," he grunted. Then the attendant, who I should really call a forensic technician, sewed the dead man up, with the garbage bag of guts already stuck back inside his belly. His brain, putrefying, liquescent, had already been removed; his face had hidden beneath its crimson blanket of scalp. The attendant sewed that up, too, and the man had a face again.

"I'm a happy customer," said the doctor.

OF JOKES AND OTHER SHIELDS

If the doctor's wisecracks seem callous to you, ask yourself whether you wouldn't want to be armored against year after year of such sights and smells. Early the next morning I watched another doctor open up an old Filipino man who, sick and despondent, had hanged himself with an electric cord. I have seen a few autopsies and battlefields before, but the man's stern, stubborn stare, his eyes glistening like black glass while the doctor, puffing, dictated case notes and slashed his guts (the yellow twist of strangle-cord lying on an adjacent table) gave me a nightmare that evening. This doctor, like his colleague, the happy customer, was doing a good thing. Both were *proving* that neither one of these dead men had been murdered, and that neither one had carried some contagious disease. Like soldiers, they worked amidst death. Green-stained buttocks and swollen faces comprised their routine. They had every right to joke, to dull themselves. Those who can't do that don't last.

Strangely enough, even their job could be for some souls a shelter from sadder things. Dr. Stephens himself used to be a pediatric oncologist before he became coroner in 1968. "At that time, we lost seventy-five percent of the children," he said. "Emotionally, that was an extremely hard thing to do. I'd be dead if I stayed in that profession."

The thought of Dr. Stephens ending up on one of his own steel tables bemused me. As it happens, I am married to an oncologist. She goes to the funerals of her child patients. Meanwhile she rushes about her life. Embracing her, I cherish her body's softness which I know comprises crimson guts.

EVIDENCE

The little cubes of meat in the amber jars went across the hall to pathology and to toxicology: underbudgeted realms making do with old instruments and machines which printed out cocaine-spikes or heroin-spikes on the slowly moving graph paper which had been state of the art in the 1960s. But after all, how much does death change? Ladies in blue gowns tested the urine samples of motorists suspected of driving while intoxicated, and with equal equanimity checked the urine of the dead. Had they, or had they not died drunk? The drunken motorist who died in a crash, the drunken suicide who'd finally overcome his fear of guns (in 17th-century Germany, the authorities encouraged condemned criminals to drink beer or wine before the execution), the drunken homicide victim who'd felt sufficiently invincible to provoke his murder—such descriptors helped attach reason to the death. Meanwhile, the blue-gowned ladies inspected the tissue samples that the doctors across the hall had sent them. I saw a woman bent over a cutting board, probing a granular mass of somebody's tumor, remarking casually on the stench. If the stomach was cancerous, if the liver was full of Tylenol or secobarb, that comprised a story, and Dr. Stephens's people were all the closer to signing off that particular death certificate.

In her gloved hands, a lady twirled a long, black-bulbed tube of somebody's crimson blood. On a table stood a stack of floppy disks marked POLICE CASES. Here was evidence, information, which might someday give birth to meaning. Kidneys floated in large translucent white plastic jars. They too had their secret knives-in-the-mouth—or not. They might explain a sudden collapse—or rationalize the toxic white concentration of barbiturates in the duodenum, if the decedent's last words did not. In San Francisco one out of four suicides left a note. Some of the laconic ones might leave unwitting messages in their vital organs. "I would say that about twenty-five percent of the suicides we have here are justified by real physical illness," Dr. Stephens told me. "We had one gentleman recently who flew in from another state, took a taxi to the Golden Gate Bridge, and jumped off. Well, he had inoperable liver cancer. Those are *logical* decisions. As for the others, they have transient emotional causes. A girl tells a boy she doesn't want to see him anymore, so he goes and hangs himself. No one talked to him and got him over to the realization that there are other women in the world."

Look in the liver then. Find the cancer—or not. That tells us something.

"And homicide?" I asked. "Does that ever show good reason?"

"Well I've seen only a few justified homicides," Dr. Stephens replied. "We handle a hundred homicides a year, and very few are justified. They're saving their family or their own lives. But the vast majority of homicides are just a waste, just senseless violent crimes to effect punishment."

And accident? And heart attack, and renal failure? No reason even to ask. From the perspective of the viewing room, it is all senseless.

DEATH CAN NEVER HURT YOU UNTIL YOU DIE

On that Saturday morning while the doctor was running the hanged man's intestines through his fingers like a fisherman unkinking line, and the forensic tech, a Ukrainian blonde who told me about her native Odessa, was busily taking the top of his head off with a power saw, I asked: "When bodies decompose, are you at more or less of a risk for infection?"

"Oh, the T.B. bacillus and the AIDS virus degrade pretty quickly," said the doctor. "They have a hard time in dead bodies. Not enough oxygen. But staph and fungus grow… The dead you have nothing to fear from. It's the living. It's when you ask a dead man's roommate what happened, and the dead man wakes up and coughs on you."

He finished his job and went out. After thanking the tech and changing out of my scrubs, so did I. I went back into the bright hot world where my death awaited me. If I died in San Francisco, there was one chance in five that they would wheel me into Dr. Stephens's office. Although my surroundings did not seem to loom and reek with death as they had when I came out of the catacombs—I think because the deaths I saw on the autopsy slabs were so grotesquely singular that I could refuse to see myself in them,[6] whereas the sheer mass and *multiplicity* of the catacomb skulls had worn down my unbelief—still I wondered who would cough on me, or what car would hit me, or which cancer might already be subdividing and stinking inside my belly. The doctor was right: I would not be able to hurt him then, because he'd be ready for me. Nor would his scalpel cause me pain. And I walked down Bryant Street wondering at the strange absurdity of my soul, which had felt most menaced by death when I was probably safest—how could those corpses rise up against me?—and which gloried in removing my disposable mask and inhaling the fresh air, letting myself dissolve into the city with its deadly automobiles and pathogen-breathers, its sailboats and bookstores; above all, its remorseless *futurity*.

III.
SIEGE THOUGHTS

AND NOW, CLOSING my eyes, I reglimpse tangents of atrocities and of wars. I see a wall of skulls in the Paris catacombs. Likewise I see the skulls on the glass shelves at Choeung Ek Killing Field.[7] In place of the tight wall of catacomb skulls gazing straight on at me, sometimes arranged in beautiful arches, I see skulls stacked loosely, laid out on the glass display shelves in heaps, not patterns—although it would give a deficient impression to omit the famous "genocide map" a few kilometers away in Phnom Penh; this is a cartographic representation of all Cambodia, comprised of murdered skulls. At Choeung Ek, they lie canted upon each other, peering and grinning, gaping and screaming, categorized by age, sex and even by race (for a few Europeans also died at the hands of the Khmer Rouge). Some bear cracks where the Khmer Rouge smashed those once-living heads with iron bars. But to my uneducated eye there is nothing else to differentiate them from the skulls of Paris. The Angel of Death flies overhead, descends and kills, and then he goes. The relics of his work become indistinguishable, except to specialists such as Dr. Stephens, and to those who were there. (I remember once seeing a movie on the Holocaust. When the lights came on, I felt bitter and depressed. It seemed that the movie had "reached" me. And then I saw a man I knew, and his face was very pale and he was sweating. He was a Jew. He was really there. The Nazis had killed most of his family.) *Before* the Angel strikes, of course, the doomed remain equally indistinguishable from the lucky or unlucky ones who will survive a little longer. Death becomes apprehensible, perhaps, only at the moment of dying.

To apprehend it, then, let's approach the present moment, the fearful time when they're shooting at you and, forgetting that your life is not perfect; you crave only to live, sweat and thirst a little longer; you promise that you'll cherish your life always, if you can only keep it. Thus near-death, whose violence or not makes no difference. A woman I loved who died of cancer once wrote me: "You will not be aware of this but it is the anniversary of my mastectomy and I am supposed to be happy that I survived and all that. Actually it has been a terrible day." She'd forgotten, like me; she'd shrugged death off again, not being godlike enough to treasure every minute after all. The first time I survived being shot at (maybe they weren't shooting at me; maybe they didn't even see me), I pledged to be happier, to be grateful for my life, and in this I have succeeded, but I still have days when the catacombs and Dr. Stephens's autopsy slabs sink too far below my memory, and I despise and despair at life. Another fright, another horror, and I return to gratitude. The slabs rise up and stink to remind me of my happiness. A year before her terrible day, the one I'd loved had written: "They had to use four needles, four veins last time. I cried as they put the fourth needle in. My veins are not holding up. I vomited even before leaving the doctor's office and then spent four days semi-conscious, vomiting. I thought very seriously about immediate death. Could I overdose on the sleeping pills, I wondered... My choices aren't that many and I would like to be there to hate my daughter's boyfriends." I remember the letter before that on pink paper that began, "I know I said I wouldn't write. I lied. I've just been told this weekend that I have invasive breast cancer and will have a mastectomy and removal of the lymph nodes within the week. I am scared to death. I have three small kids... I am not vain. I do not care about my chest but I do want to live... So, tell me. This fear— I can smell it—is it like being in a war?"—Yes, darling. I have never been terminally ill, but I am sure that it is the same.

In one of her last letters she wrote me: "There was definitely a time when I thought I might die sooner rather than later—it took me awhile to believe that I would probably be okay. It still doesn't feel truly believable but more and more I want it to be the case—mostly because I want to raise my interesting and beautiful children and because I want to enjoy myself… My hair grew back to the point that I no longer use the wig."

In another letter she wrote me: "Here are the recent events in my life. I am not unhappy with them but they do not compare with being shot at and losing a friend and perhaps they will amuse you. I set up a fish tank in my study… I got the kids four fish. They named only one. I told them once they had learned to clean and change the tank and feed the fish and explain how gills work, then they could get a guinea pig. I am not into pets, preferring children. The one catfish in the tank is in great distress and swims around madly looking for a way to die."

When I close my eyes, I can see her as she looked at seventeen, and I can see her the way she was when she was thirty-four, much older, thanks in part to the cancer—bonier-faced, with sparse hair, perhaps a wig, sitting on the steps beside her children. I never had to see her in Dr. Stephens's viewing room. I never saw her body rotting. I'll never see her depersonalized skull mortared into a catacomb's wall. Does that mean I cannot envision death, her death? The six million death's heads under Paris weigh on me much less than her face, which you might call too gaunt to be beautiful, but which was still beautiful to me, which only in a photograph will I ever see again.

But—again I return to this—her death was meaningless, an accident of genetics or environment. No evil soul murdered her. I am sad when I think about her. I am not bitter.

I am sad when I think about my two colleagues in Bosnia who drove into a land-mine trap. Their names were Will and Francis. I will write about them later. At the time, because there were two distinct reports and holes appeared in the windshield and in the two dying men, I believed that they were shot, and when armed men approached I believed that I was looking at their killers. Will I had known only for two days, but I liked what I knew of him. Francis was my friend, off and on, for nineteen years. I loved Francis. But I was never angry, even when the supposed snipers came, for their actions could not have been personally intended. We were crossing from the Croatian to the Muslim side; the Muslims were sorry, and such incidents are common enough in war.

But now I open a letter from my Serbian friend Vineta, who often had expressed to me her dislike of Francis (whom she never met) on the grounds of his Croatian blood, and who after commenting in considerable helpful and businesslike detail on my journalistic objectives in Serbia, then responded to my plans for the Muslim and Croatian sides of the story (my items seven and eight) as follows: "You see, dear Billy, it's very nice of you to let me know about your plans. But, I DON'T GIVE A SHIT FOR BOTH CROATS AND MUSLIMS!" At the end of her long note she added this postscript: "The last 'personal letter' I got was two years ago, from my late boy-friend. The Croats cut his body into pieces in the town of B—— near Vukovar. His name was M——." Then she wrote one more postscript: "No one has a chance to open my heart ever again."

This is what violence does. This is what violence is. It is not enough that death reeks and stinks in the world, but now it takes on inimical human forms, prompting the self-defending survivors to strike and to hate, rightly or wrongly. Too simple to argue that nonviolent death is always preferable from the survivors' point of view! I've heard plenty of doctors' stories about the families of dying cancer patients who rage against "fate." Like Hitler, they'd rather have someone to blame. "Everybody's angry when a loved one dies," one doctor insisted. "The only distinction is between directed and undirected anger." Maybe so. But it *is* a distinction. Leaving behind Dr. Stephens' tables, on which, for the most part, lie only the "naturally" dead with their bleeding pancreases, the accidentally dead, and the occasional suicide, let us fly to besieged Sarajevo and look in on the morgue at Kosevo Hospital, a place I'll never forget, whose stench stayed on my clothes for two days afterwards. Here lay the homicides. I saw children with their bellies blown open, women shot in the head while they crossed the street, men hit by some well-heeled sniper's anti-tank round.[8] Death joked and drank and vulgarly farted in the mountains all around us, aiming its weapons out of hateful fun, making the besieged counter-hateful. Every morning I woke up to chittering bullets and crashing mortar rounds. I hated the snipers I couldn't see because they might kill me and because they were killing the people of this city, ruining the city in every terrible physical and psychic way that it could be ruined, smashing it, murdering wantonly, frightening and crushing. But their wickedness too had become normal: this was Sarajevo in the fourteenth month of the siege. Needs lived on; people did business amidst their terror, a terror which could not be sustained, rising up only when it was needed, when one had to run. As for the forensic doctor at Kosevo Hospital, he went home stinking of death, and, like me, sometimes slept in his clothes; he was used to the smell, and his wife must have gotten used to it, too, when she embraced him. (Meanwhile, of course, some people had insomnia, got ulcers or menstrual disturbances, went prematurely grey.[9] Here, too, undirected anger might surface.[10] Political death, cancer death, it's all the same.

The night after Will and Francis were killed, a U.N. interpreter from Sarajevo told me how she lost friends almost every week. "You become a little cold," she said very quietly. "You have to." This woman was sympathetic, immensely kind; in saying this she meant neither to dismiss my grief nor to tell me how I ought to be. She merely did the best thing that can be done for any bereaved person, which was to show me her own sadness, so that my sadness would feel less lonely; but hers had wearied and congealed; thus she told me what she had become. Like Dr. Stephens and his crew, or the backpack inspector at the catacombs, like my friend Thion who ferries tourists to Choeung Ek on his motorcycle, I had already begun to become that way. Sarajevo wasn't the first war zone I'd been to, nor the first where I'd seen death, but I'll never forget it. The morgue at Kosevo Hospital, like the rest of Sarajevo, had had to make do without electricity, which was why, as I keep saying, it stank. I remember the cheesy smell of the Paris catacombs, the sour-milk smell of Dr. Stephens' white hearse; after that visit to Kosevo Hospital my clothes smelled like vomit, vinegar, and rotting bowels. I returned to the place where I was staying, which got its share of machine gun and missile attacks, and gathered together my concerns, which did not consist of sadness for the dead, but only of being scared and wondering if I would eat anymore that day because they'd shot down the U.N. flight and so the airport was closed and I'd already given my food away. Death was on my skin and on the other side of the wall—maybe my death, maybe not; trying to live wisely and carefully, I granted no time to my death, although it sometimes snarled at me. Ascending from the catacombs I'd had all day, so I'd given death all day; no one wanted to hurt me. But in

Sarajevo I simply ran; it was all death, death and death, so meaningless and accidental to me.

I wore a bulletproof vest in Mostar, which did get struck with a splinter of something which rang on its ceramic trauma plate, so to an extent I had made my own luck, but Will, who was driving, discovered that his allotted death was one which entered the face *now*, diagonally from the chin. His dying took forever (I think about five minutes). Vineta said that I had been cowardly or stupid not to end his misery. I told her that journalists don't carry guns. Anyhow, had I been in his seat, my bulletproof vest would have done me no good.

The woman I loved simply had the wrong cells in her breast; Vineta's boyfriend had fought in the wrong place at the wrong time, and perhaps he'd fought against the Croats too ferociously or even just too well.[11] For the woman I loved, and for me in Sarajevo, the Angel of Death was faceless, but Vineta's tormenting Angel of Death had a Croatian face; she hated "those Croatian bastards." Vineta, if I could send the Angel of Death away from you, I would. Maybe someone who knows you and loves you better than I can at least persuade your Angel veil his face again so that he becomes mere darkness like the Faceless One of Iroquois legends, mere evil chance, "an act of war," like my drowned sister's Angel; and then your anger can die down to sadness. Vineta, if you ever see this book of mine, don't think me presumptuous; don't think I would ever stand between you and your right to mourn and rage against the Angel. But he is not Francis. Francis was good. I don't like to see him stealing Francis's face when he comes to hurt you.

The Angel is in the white hearse. Can't we please proceed like Dr. Stephens's employees, weighing, fingerprinting, cutting open all this sad and stinking dross of violence, trying to learn what causes what? And when the malignity or the sadness or the unpleasantness of the thing on the table threatens to craze us, can't we tell a callous joke or two? If I can contribute to understanding how and why the Angel kills, then I'll be, in the words of that doctor who swilled coffee out of one bloody-gloved hand while he sliced a dead body with the other, "a happy customer." Hence this essay, and the larger work from which this is extracted. For its many failures I ask forgiveness from all.

NOTES

[1] Medical Examiner's Office, City and County of San Francisco, *Digest of Rules and Regulations* [pamphlet], June 1996.

[2] Aldous Huxley, *The Perennial Philosophy* (San Francisco: Harper Colophon Books, 1970 repr. of 1944 ed.).

[3] Medical Examiner's Office, City and County of San Francisco, annual report, July 1, 1994—June 30, 1995, pp. 9, 36.

[4] Stylists frown upon the passive construction. But I fail to see what could be more appropriate for dead bodies.

[5] For this information on ante- and postmortem contusions I have, as so often, relied on Lester Adelson, *The Pathology of Homicide: A Vade Mecum for Pathologist, Prosecutor, and Defense Counsel*, Springfield, Illinois: Charles C. Thomas, 1974.

[6] Fresh death or old death, it was not my death, and I shrugged it off. In the catacombs they were so anonymous, with such clean carapaces, that it seemed they'd all died "naturally." At the medical examiner's office, some had died accidentally or strangely, a few had ended themselves, like that old man who'd hanged himself with the electric cord, and every now and then the odd murder case was wheeled in. Looking into the hanged man's stare, I'd felt a little creepy. But to protect me from it, Dr. Stephens had established the doors marked NO ADMITTANCE and POSITIVELY NO ADMITTANCE. As I sit here now, trying to refine these sentences, the only dead thing I can see is a spider glued to my windowpane by its withered web. For the most part I see cars in motion on the wide road, glorious trees, people walking down the sidewalk. The doughnut stand where a juvenile homicide occurred a couple of years ago now glows with sugar and life. I remain as yet in the land of the living, and will not believe in my death.

[7] I went there twice, and the second was more horrifying than the first. Here those technical-political details don't matter.

[8] For a description of this place, see "The Back of My Head," in *The Atlas* (p. 5).

[9] Fanon found these psychosomatic symptoms in Algeria, and mentions that they were very common "in the Soviet Union among the besieged populations of towns, notably in Stalingrad" (*The Wretched of the Earth*, pp. 290-93).

[10] For one of Fanon's patients, an Algerian who survived a mass execution conducted by the French because "there's been too much talk about this village; destroy it," the Angel of Death wore everyone's face: "You all want to kill me but you should set about it differently. I'll kill you all as soon as look at you, big ones and little ones, women, children, dogs, donkeys . . ." (op. cit., pp. 259-61).

[11] Martin Luther King insisted in his funeral for victims of the Birmingham bombing that "history has proven over and over again that unmerited suffering is redemptive. The innocent blood of these little girls may well serve as the redemptive force that will bring new light to this dark city" (King, *Testament of Hope,* p. 221; "Eulogy for the Martyred Children," September 1963). As for me, I don't believe that such redemption occurs very often.

GEORGICA

by A.M. HOMES

A PHOSPHORESCENT DREAM. Everything hidden under cover of night becomes abundantly clear, luminescent.

Hiding in the dunes, she is a foot soldier, an intruder. The sand caves in around her. What was so familiar by day is inside out, an X-ray etched in memory. The sands of Main Beach are foreign shores. With her night-vision goggles she scans the horizon. At first there is just the moon on the water, the white curl of the waves, the glow of the bath-house, the bleached parking lot. Far down the beach Tiki torches light figures dancing. Closer, there is a flash, the flick of a match, a father and daughter burst out of the darkness holding sparklers. Thousands of miniature explosions erupt like anti-aircraft fire.

"More," the little girl shouts when the sparkler is done, "more."

"Do you think mommy is home yet?" the father asks, lighting another one.

Checking her watch, she feels the pressure of time; the window of opportunity is small, twelve to twenty-four hours. Ready and waiting, her supplies are in a fanny pack around her waist, the car is parked under a tree at the far edge of the lot.

She has been watching them for weeks, watching without realizing she was watching, watching mesmerized, not thinking they might mean something to her, they might be useful. Tall, thin, with smooth muscled chests, hips narrow, shoulders square; they are growing, thick-ening, pushing out. Agile and lithe, they carry themselves with the casualness of young men, with the grace that comes from attention, from being noticed. These are hardworking boys, summer-job boys, scholarship boys, clean-cut boys, good boys, local boys, stunningly boyish boys, boys of summer, boys who every morning raise the American flag and every evening lower it, folding it carefully, beautiful boys. Golden boys. Like toasted Wonder Bread; she imagines they are warm to the touch.

She checks to be sure the coast is clear and then crosses to the tall white wooden tower, a steeple at the church of the sea.

She climbs. This is where they perch, ever ready to pull someone from the riptide, where they stand slapping red flags through the air, signaling, where they blow the whistle, summoning swimmers back to shore. "Ahoy there, you've gone too far."

She puts out supplies, stuffing condoms into the drink holders. She suspects they think the town is providing them as a service of some sort; she waits to read an angry letter to the editor, but no one says anything and they are always gone, pocketed, slipped into wallets, a dozen a day.

Carefully, she climbs back down the ladder and repositions herself in the sand. Crawling forward, the damp sand rubs her belly, it slips under the elastic waist band of her pants and down her legs, tickling.

It began accidentally; fragments, seemingly unconnected, lodged in her thoughts, each leading to something new, each propelling her for-ward. At cocktail parties, in the grocery store, the liquor store, the hardware, the library, she was looking, thinking she would find some-one, looking and seeing only pot bellies, bad manners, stupidity. She was looking for something else and instead she found them. She was looking without realizing she was looking. She had been watching for weeks before it occurred to her. An anonymous observer under the cover of summer, she spent her days sitting downwind, listening to their conversations. They talked about nothing—waves and water, movies, surfing, their parents and school, girls, hamburgers.

She found herself imagining luring one home. She imagined

asking for a favor—could you change a bulb? but worried it would seem too obvious.

She could picture the whole scenario: the boy comes to her house, she shows him the light, he stands on a chair, she looks up at his downy belly, at the bulge in his shorts, she hands him the bulb, brushing against him, she runs a hand up his leg, squeezing, tugging at his Velcro fly, releasing him.

They have a mythology all their own.

She caught herself enjoying the thought—it was the first time she'd allowed herself to think that way in months.

Now, she catches herself distracted, she puts her goggles back in place, she focuses. A cool wind is blowing the dune grass, sand skims through the air, biting, stinging, debriding.

A late-night fortune hunter emerges from the darkness, creeping across the parking lot, metal detector in hand. He shuffles onto the beach, sweeping for trinkets, looking for gold, listening on his headphones for the tick-tock of Timex, of Rolex. When he gets the signal he stops and with his homemade sifter scoops the sand, sifting it like flour, pocketing loose change.

She hears them approaching, the blast of a car radio, the bass beat a kind of early announcement of their arrival. Rock and roll.

A truck pulls into the parking lot, they tumble out. This is home plate. Every morning, every night, they return touching base, safe. Another car pulls in and then another. Traveling in packs, gangs, entourages, they spill onto the sand. And as if they know she is out there, they put on a show, piling high into a human pyramid. Laughing, they fall. One of the boys moons the others.

"Are you flashing or farting?"

Pawing at the sand with their feet, they wait to figure out what comes next.

There is something innocent and uncomplicated about them, an awkwardness she finds charming, adolescent arrogance that comes from knowing nothing about anything, not yet failing.

"We could go to my house, there's frozen pizza."

"We could get ice cream."

"There's a bonfire at Ditch Plains."

They piss on the dunes and are off again, leaving one behind—

"See ya."

"Tomorrow," he says.

The one they've left sits on the steps of the bathhouse, waiting. He is one of them—she has seen him before, recognizes the tattoo, full circle around his upper arm, a hieroglyph. She has noticed how he wears his regulation red trunks long and low, resting on the top of his ass, a delicate tuft of hair poking up.

A white car pulls into the parking lot. A girl gets out. The light from the parking lot, combined with the humidity of sea, fills the air with a humid glow which surrounds them like clouds. They stand, two angelic figures caught in her cross hairs. They walk hand in hand down to the beach. She trails after them, keeping a safe distance.

The night-vision glasses, enormously helpful, were not part of her original scenario. She bought them last weekend at a yard sale, at the home of a retired colonel. "They were mine, that's the original box," the colonel's son said, coming up behind her. "My father gave them to me for Christmas, they were crazy expensive. I think he wanted them for himself."

"Is there some way I can try them?"

He led her into his basement, pulling the door closed behind them. "I hope I'm not frightening you."

"I'm fine," she said.

"We unwrapped on Christmas Eve, my father turned off all the lights and made me try. I remember looking at the Christmas tree, weaving around the room, watching the lights move and then tripping, going down hard and starting the new year with two black eyes like a raccoon."

"May I?"

He handed her the glasses, she reached out, feeling her way forward, their hands bumped. There was something terrifying about this unfamiliar dark; she stared at the glowing fish tank for comfort.

"The on button is between the eyes." She flipped them on and suddenly she saw everything—ice skates, an old rowing machine, odd military memorabilia, a leaf blower, hammers and saws hanging from pegs. She saw everything and thought that in a minute she was going to see something extra, something she shouldn't see, a body in a clear plastic bag, slumped in the corner, a head on a stick, something unforgivably horrible. Everything had the eerie neon green of a horror movie, of information captured surreptitiously.

"If you're interested I'd be happy to throw in a bayonet and a helmet," he said, handing her one of each.

The boy and his girl are on the sand, making out. There is something delicate, tentative, in how they approach each other. Kissing and then pulling back, checking to see if it's okay, discovering how it feels, a tongue in the mouth, a hand on the breast, the press of a cock against the thigh.

He lifts her shirt, exposing an old-fashioned white bra. She unhooks it for him. Her breasts are surprisingly large, his hands are on them, not entirely sure what one does, his lack of skill endearing. She feels the urgency of their desire. Without warning she finds herself excited.

He takes his sweatshirt off and lays it on the sand. They are one atop the other. She imagines the smell of him, suntan lotion, sweat and sand, she imagines the smell of her—guacamole, fried onions, bbq, stale cologne. She either works in a local restaurant or as a baby sitter: formula, vomit, sour milk, stale cologne.

He rises for a minute, unzips his pants. His erection, long and lean, throbs in the moonlight. The girl takes it in her mouth. The boy kneels frozen, his head thrown back, paralyzed by sensation, while the girl bobs up and down, like one of those trick birds drinking from a water glass.

She becomes alarmed, hopes they don't keep at it, not wanting to waste her shot.

"The condom, put on the condom," she is thinking out loud.

And then finally, he pulls away, falls back on the sand, reaches into his pocket, locating it. He has trouble rolling it on—the girl helps. And then the girl is upon him, riding him, her bazoombas bouncing, floating like dirigibles. The boy lies back flattened, devastated, his arms straight up, reaching.

As soon as the condom is on, she feels her body opening. As soon as the girl is upon him, she is upon herself, her hands down her pants, warming to the touch. She wants to be ready. She is watching them and working herself. This is better than anything, more romantic, more relaxing than actually doing it with someone. This way, she can focus on her fantasies, on the sensations.

It ends abruptly. When they are done they are embarrassed, overwhelmed, suddenly strangers. They scramble for their clothing, hurry to the car and are gone—into the night.

She waits until the coast is clear and then rushes toward the spot, finds it and switches on her other light, a head-mounted work light, like a miner's lamp. She plucks the condom from the sand, holding the latex sheath of lust, of desire, carefully. The contents have not spilled, that's the good news, and he has performed well— the tip is full, she figures it's 3-4 cc's. Working quickly, she pulls a syringe—no needle— from her fanny pack and lowers it into the condom. She has practiced this procedure at home using lubricated Trojans and a combination of mayonnaise and Palmolive dish detergent. With one hand, she pulls back on the plunger, sucking it up. Holding the syringe upright, capping it, taking care not to lose any, she turns off her lights and makes a beeline back up the beach to her car.

She has tilted the driver's seat back as far as it goes, and put a small pillow at the head end for her neck—she always has to be careful of the neck.

She gets into the car, and puts herself in position, lying back, feet on the dash, hips tilted high. She is upside down like an astronaut prepared to launch, a modified yoga inversion, a sort of shoulder stand, more pillows under her hips, lifting her. The steering wheel helps hold her in place.

She is wearing sex pants. She has taken a seam ripper and opened the crotch, making a convenient yet private entry. She slips the syringe through the hole. When she's in as far as she can go, she pushes the plunger down—blast-off.

Closing her eyes, she imagines the sperm, stunned, drunken, in a whirl, ejaculated from his body into the condom and then out of the condom into her, swimming all the while. She imagines herself as part of their romance.

After a few minutes, she takes a sponge—wrapped in plastic, tied with a string—and pushes it in holding the sperm against her cervix.

Meditation. Sperm swimming, beach sperm, tadpole sperm, baby whale sperm, boy sperm, millions of sperm. Sperm and egg. The egg launching, meeting the sperm in the fallopian tube, like the boy and girl meeting in the parking lot, coupling, traveling together, dividing, replicating, digging in, implanting.

She has been there about five minutes when there is a knock at the window, the beam of a flashlight looking in. She can't put down the window because the ignition is off, she doesn't want to sit up because it will ruin everything—she uses her left hand to open the car door.

"Yes?"

"Sorry to bother you, but you can't sleep here," the police officer says.

"I'm not sleeping, I'm resting."

The officer sees the pillows, he sees the soft collar around her neck—under the dim glow of the interior light, he sees her.

"Oh," he says. "It's you, the girl from last summer, the girl with the halo."

"That's me."

"Wow. It's good to see you up and around. Are you up and around? Is everything all right?"

"Fine," she says. "But I have these moments where I just have to lie down right then and there."

"Do you need anything? I have a blanket in the back of the car?"

"I'll be all right, thank you."

He hangs around, standing just inside the car door, hands on his hips. "I was one of the first ones at the scene of the accident," he says. "I closed down the road when they took you over to the church—it was me with the flares who directed the helicopter in."

"Thank you," she says.

"I was worried you were a goner. People said they saw you fly through the air, like a cannonball. They said they'd never seen anything like it."

"Umm," she says.

"I heard you postponed the wedding," he says.

"Canceled it."

"I can understand, given the circumstances."

She is waiting for him to leave.

"So, when you get like that, how long do you stay upside down?"

"About a half hour," she says.

"And how long has it been?"

"I'd say about fifteen minutes."

"Would you like to get a cup of coffee when you're done?"

"Aren't you on duty?"

"I could say I was escorting you home."

"Not tonight, but thanks."

"Some other time?"

"Sure."

"Sorry to hear about your grandmother—I read the obituary."

She nods. A couple of months ago, just after her ninety-eighth birthday, her grandmother died in her sleep—as graceful as it gets.

"That's a lot for one year, an accident, a canceled wedding, your grandmother passing."

"It is a lot," she says.

"You a birder?" he asks. "I see you've got binocs in the back seat."

"Always on the lookout," she says.

In a way she could see going for coffee, she could see marrying the local cop. He's not like a real cop, not someone you're going to worry isn't going to make it home at night. Out here she'd worry that he'd do something stupid—scurry up a telephone pole for a stuck cat.

He's still standing in the door.

"I guess I'd better go," he says, moving to close the car door. "I don't want to wear your battery down." He points at the interior light.

"Thanks again," she says.

"See you," he says, closing the door. He taps on the glass. "Drive carefully," he says.

She stays the way she is for a while longer and then pulls the pillows out from under, carefully unfolds herself, brings the seat back up and starts the engine.

She drives home past the pond, there is no escaping it.

* * *

He was drunk. After a party he was always drunk.

"I'm drunk," he'd say going back for another.

"I'm drunk," he'd say when they'd said their goodbyes and were walking down the gravel driveway in the dark.

"I'll drive," she'd say.

"It's my car," he'd say.

"You're drunk."

"Not really, I'm faking it."

An old Mercedes convertible. It should have been perfect, riding home with the top down in the night air, taken by the sounds of frogs, the crickets, Miles Davis on the radio, a million stars overhead, the stripe of Milky Way, no longer worrying what the wind was doing to her hair—the party over.

It should have been perfect, but the minute they were alone there was tension. She disappeared, mentally, slipping back into the party, the clinking of glasses, bare-armed, bare-backed women, men sporty and tan, having gotten up early and taken the kids out for donuts, having spent the afternoon in action; tennis, golf, sailing, having had a nice long hot shower and a drink as they dressed for evening.

"Looking forward to planning a wedding?" one of the women had asked.

"No." She had no interest in planning a wedding. She was expected to marry him, but the more time that passed, the more skittish they both became, the more she was beginning to think a wedding was not a good idea. She became angry that she'd lost time, she'd run out of time, that her choices were becoming increasingly limited. She had dated good men, bad men, the right men at the wrong time, the wrong men a lot of the time.

And the more time that passed, the more bitter he became, the more he wanted to go back in time, the more he craved his lost youth.

"Let's stay out," he'd say to friends after a party.

"Can't. We've got to get the sitter home."

"What's the point of having a babysitter if you're still completely tied down?"

"It's late," they'd say.

"It's early, it's very early," he'd say.

And soon there was nothing left to say.

"You're all so boring," he'd say, which didn't leave anyone feeling good about anything.

"Good night," they'd say.

He drove, the engine purred. They passed houses, lit for night, front-porch lights on, upstairs bathroom light on, reading light on. He drove and she kept a lookout, fixed on the edges of the road, waiting to catch the eyes of an animal about to dash, a dog or cat, a whole family of raccoons out for adventure, the shadow of a deer about to jump.

When he got drunk, he'd start looking for a fight. If there wasn't another man around to wrestle with he'd turn on her.

"How can you talk incessantly all night and then the minute we're in the car you have nothing to say?"

"I had nothing to say all night either," she said.

"Such a fucking depressive—what's wrong with you?"

He accelerates.

"I'm not going to fight with you," she said.

"You're the kind of person who thinks she's always right," he said.

She didn't answer.

Coming into town the light was green. A narrow road, framed by hundred-year-old trees, a big white house on the left, an inn across the way, the pond where in winter ice skaters turned pirouettes, the ceme-tery on the far side, the old windmill, Episcopal church, all of it deeply picturesque.

Green light, go. Coming around the corner, he seemed to speed up rather than slow down, he seemed to press his foot harder into the gas. They turned the corner. She could tell they weren't going to make it. She looked at him to see if he had the wheel in hand, if he had any idea what he was doing, if he thought it was a joke. And then as they picked up more speed, as they slipped off the road, between two trees, over the embankment, she looked away.

The car stopped and her body continued on.

*　*　*

She remembers flying as if on a magic carpet, flying the way you might dream it, flying over water, sudden, surprising, and not entirely unpleasant.

She remembers thinking she might fly forever, all the way home.

She remembers thinking to cover her head, remembers they are by a cemetery.

She remembers telling herself—This is the last time.

She remembers when they went canoeing on the pond. A swan came charging towards the boat like a torpedo, like a hovercraft, skimming the surface, gaining on them. At first they thought it was funny and then it wasn't.

"Should I swing my paddle at him? Should I try and hit him on the head? Should I break his fucking neck? What should I do?" he kept asking, all the while leaving her at the front of the boat, paddling furiously, left, right, left, right.

Now something is pecking at her, biting her.

There is a sharp smell like ammonia, like smelling salts.

She remembers her body not attached to anything.

"Can you hear us?"

"Can someone get the swans out of here?"

Splashing. People walking in water. A lot of commotion.

"Are you in pain?

"Don't try to move. Don't move anything. Let us do all the work."

She remembers a lot of questions, time passing very slowly. She remembers the birds, a church, the leaf of a tree, the night sky, red lights, white lights in her eyes. She thinks she screamed. She meant to scream. She doesn't know if she can make any noise.

"What is your name?

"Can you tell me your name?"

"Can you feel this?"

"We're going to give you some oxygen."

"We're going to set up an IV, there may be a little stick."

"Do these bites on your head hurt?"

"Follow this light with your eyes."

"Look at me. Can you look at me?"

He turned away. "We're going to need a med-evac helicopter. We're going to need to land on that churchyard up there. We're going to need her stable, in a hard collar and on a board. I think we may have a broken neck."

She thinks they are talking about a swan, a swan has been injured.

"Don't go to sleep," they said, pinching her awake. "Stay with us."

And then she is flying again. She remembers nothing. She remembers only what they told her.

"You're very lucky. You could have been decapitated or paralyzed forever."

She is in a hospital far away.

"You have a facet dislocation, five over six—in essence a broken neck. We're going to put you in a halo and a jacket. You'll be up and around in no time."

The doctor smiled down at her. "Do you understand what I'm saying?"

She couldn't nod. She tried to but nothing happens. "Yes," she said. "You think I'm very lucky."

In the operating room, the interns and residents swab four points on her head. "Have you ever done this before?" they asked each other.

"I've watched."

"We're going to log roll you," the doctor told her. And they did.

"Get the raised part at the back of the skull and the front positioning pin lined up over the bridge of the nose, approximately seven centimeters over the eyebrows with equal distance between head and the halo all the way around."

"How are your fingers? Can you move your fingers?"

She does.

"Good. Now wiggle your toes."

"You don't want it too high—it pitches the head back so she just sees sky—and you don't want it too low because then she's looking at her shoes," the doctor said. He seemed to know what he was talking about.

"Feel my finger on your cheek—sharp or smooth?"

"Sharp."

"Let's simultaneously tighten one anterior and its diagonal opposite posterior."

"Thanks. Now pass me the wrench."

"Close your eyes, please."

She doesn't know if they're talking to her or someone else. Someone looked directly down at her, "Time to close your eyes."

She is bolted into a metal halo, which is then bolted into a plastic vest, all of it like the scaffolding around a building, like the Statue of Liberty undergoing renovations. When they were done and sat her upright—she almost fainted.

"Perfectly normal," the doctor said. "Fainting. Dizziness." He tapped her vest—knock, knock.

"What am I made out of?"

"Space-age materials. In the old days we would have wrapped you in a plaster cast. Imagine how comfy that was. I assume you didn't have your seatbelt on?"

"Do these bites on your head hurt?" one of the residents asked.

"What bites?"

"Let's clean them, put some antibiotic on, and make sure she's up to date on tetanus, etc. " The doctor said. "Get some antibiotics on board just be to sure, you never know what was in that water."

"Where am I?"

"Stonybrook," the resident said as though that meant something.

"Did someone say something about a swan?" she asks.

They don't answer.

Her grandmother is the first one who comes to see her. Ninety-seven years old, she gets her cleaning lady to drive her over.

"Your parents are in Italy, we haven't been able to reach them. The doctor says you're very lucky. You're neurologically intact."

"He was drunk."

"We'll sue the pants off them—don't worry."

"Did anything happen to him?"

"Broke a bone in his foot."

"I'm assuming he knows the wedding is off."

"If he doesn't, someone will tell him."

"Does that come off for bathing?" her grandmother points at the plastic vest.

"No. It's all bolted together."

"Well, that's what perfume was invented for."

* * *

Her girlfriends come in groups.

"We were fast asleep."

"We heard the sirens."

"I thought something exploded."

"He broke a bone in his foot?" she asks.

"His toe."

There is silence.

"You made the papers," someone says.

In the late afternoon, when she's alone, the innkeeper arrives.

"I saw it happen, I water the flowers at night right before bed. I was outside and saw your car at the light. Your fellow had the strangest expression on his face. The car surged forward, between the trees, it went out over the water and then nose down into the muck. I saw you fly over the windshield, over the water. And he was standing up, pressed against the steering wheel, one hand in the air like he was riding a bucking bronco, his foot still on the gas, engine gunning, blowing bubbles into the water. I dialed 911. I went looking for you." He pauses. "I saw you flying through the air but I couldn't see where you landed."

A human gyroscope, a twirling top. She landed at her grandmother's house, a big old beach house on the block leading down to the ocean. She landed back in time, in the house of her youth. She sat on the porch, propped up in a wicker chair. Her grandmother read her stories of adventure and discovery. At night when she was supposed to be sleeping, her mind wandered, daydreaming. She dreamt of a farmhouse by the water, of a small child hiding behind her skirt, a dog barking.

It was a summer in exile; off the party lists. No one knew which side to be on, there was talk of a lawsuit, "too ugly for summer," friends told her.

"To hell with them," her grandmother says. "I never liked any of them, their parents, or their grandparents. You're a young woman, you have your own life, what do you need to be married for? Enjoy your freedom. I never would have married if I could have gotten out of it. " She leans forward. "Don't tell anyone I told you that."

At ninety-seven her grandmother sets her free.

At the end of the season her parents come home from Italy. "Pretend it never happened," her mother says. "Put yourself out there and in no time you'll meet someone new."

In the morning, she goes back to the beach, her hair smells of salt, her skin tastes of the sea, the scent of sex is on her, a sweet funk, a mixed drink, her and him and her, rising up, blending.

She goes back down to the beach, proud, walking like she's got a good little secret. As soon as she sees him, she blushes.

He doesn't know she is there, he doesn't know who she is, and what would he think if he knew?

She watches as he squirts white lotion from a tube, filling his hand with it, rubbing the hand over his chest, his belly, up and down his arms, over his neck and face, coating himself. He lubricates himself with lotion and then shimmies up the ladder and settles into the chair—on guard.

If he knew, would he think she was a crook, stealing him without his knowledge, or would he think it was nice to be desired, had from this strange distance?

Another boy, older, walks barefoot down the warm boards of the bathhouse, his feet moving fast and high, as if dancing on hot coals. She stays through the morning. He is not the only one, there are others. It is a constant low-key sex play, an ever-changing tableau.

This year they have new suits, their standard Speedos replaced with baggy red trunks. Beneath their trunks, they are naked, cock-sure, tempting, threatening. It is always right there, the bulge, enjoying the rub of the fabric, the shrinking chill of the sea.

She watches as they work, as they sweep the deck of the bathhouse, set up umbrellas, how they respond to authority—taking direction from the man with the clipboard. Before settling on two or three of the strongest, most dominant, she watches how they play with each other. She chooses the one with the smoothest chest, and another with white hair, like feathers fanning out, crawling up his stomach, a fern bleached blond.

Standing high on a sand dune, one of the boys wraps his towel around his waist and, tugging from under, pulls his bathing suit off. He tugs a wet suit on and the towel falls away. Raising his arms up high, he stretches, preening, and then adjusting. Striding to the edge of the water, he slides his feet into his fins and disappears into the surf.

They are becoming themselves, as she is losing herself.

It's not like she's been alone for the whole year—she's dated. "I have a friend. We have a friend. He has a friend. The friend of a friend. He has four children from two marriages, they visit every other Saturday. He's a devoted father. I know someone else, a little afraid of commitment, good looking, successful, never married. And then there's the widower—at least he understands grief."

The man from two marriages wants her to wear a strap-on dildo and whack him with a riding crop. The one afraid of commitment is impotent. Even that she doesn't mind until he tells her that it is because of her. The widower is sympathetic. She confesses her desire for a family, for children. He becomes determined to get her pregnant. "Don't worry," he says. "I'll put a bun in the oven." He comes before they even begin. "It's not for lack of trying," he says.

And then there's the one who never wants children, "I would never want to subject someone so innocent to the failings of my personality," he said. And she agreed.

The idea of them causes her gut to tighten.

The heat is gaining, the beach swelling with the ranks of the weekenders. It is Friday afternoon, they hit the sand acting as if they own it.

A whistle blows downwind, the boys grab the float and are into the water. "It's no game," the head honcho says, as they pull someone out, sputtering.

Two cops in dark blue uniforms walk onto the beach and arrest a man lying on the sand. They take him away in handcuffs and flipflops, his towel tossed over his shoulder. She overhears an explanation. "Violated an order of protection, stalking his ex-girlfriend. She saw him from the snack bar and dialed 911."

The temperature goes up.

She is sticky, salt sticky, sex sticky, too much sun sticky. Walking back to the parking lot, she steps in something hot and brown. She walks on, hoping it's tar, knowing it's shit, walks rubbing her foot in the sand, wanting it off before she gets to the car.

The day is turning sour; the heat, baking. In the drugstore, by the pharmacy counter, where a long line of people wait to pick up prescriptions for swimmer's ear, athlete's foot, Lyme Disease, someone pinches her elbow.

She turns. Still sun blind, she has the sensation of everything being down a dark tunnel, her eyes struggle to adjust.

"All better?" the woman asks.

She nods, still not sure who she's talking to—someone from before.

"You don't come to the club anymore?"

She catches the woman looking into her basket: sun block, bottled water, condoms, ovulation kits, plastic gloves, pregnancy tests, aspirin.

"Seeing somebody special?"

"Not really," she says.

"What's the saying—'Don't marry the ones you fuck? Don't fuck the ones you marry?' I can never remember how it goes."

She says nothing. She used to think she was on a par with the others, that for the most part she was ahead of the pack, and now it's as if she's fallen behind, out of the running. She feels the woman inspecting her, judging, looking through her basket, evaluating, as if about to issue her a summons, a reprimand for unconventional behavior.

At home, she showers, pours herself a glass of wine. If the accident threw her life off course, her grandmother's death made it clear that if this was something she wanted to do, she needed to do it soon, before it was too late. She pees on an ovulation stick, the stripe is positive—sometime within the next twenty-four hours the egg will be released. She pictures the egg in launch position, getting ready to burst out, she pictures it floating down her tubes, floating like slow-motion flying.

She slips back in time. A routine doctor's appointment, an annual occasion; naked in a paper robe, her feet in the stirrups.

"Come down a little closer," the doctor says. Using the speculum like pliers, he pries her open. He pulls the light closer and peers inside her.

"I've been wondering about timing—in terms of having a baby, how much longer do I have?"

"Have you ever been pregnant?"

"No," she says. "Never pregnant."

Everyone she knows has been pregnant, pregnant by boyfriends they hated, boyfriends who asked—Can't you get rid of it?—or worse yet, promised to marry them. Why has she never been pregnant? Was she too good, too boring, too responsible, or is there something else?

"Have you ever tried to get pregnant?"

"I haven't felt ready to start a family."

He continues to root around inside her. "You may feel a little scrape—that's the Pap test." She feels the scrape. "Try," he says. "That's the way to get pregnant, try and try again. It doesn't get any easier," he says, pulling the equipment out, snapping the gloves off.

Dressed, she sits in his office.

"I was thinking of freezing some eggs, saving them for later."

"Can't freeze eggs," he says. "Can freeze embryos. If you want to have a baby, have a baby, don't freeze one." He scribbles something in her chart and closes it. He stands. "Give my regards to your mother. I never see her anymore."

"She had a hysterectomy ten years ago."

Sperm banks. She looked them up online; one sent a list of possible candidates categorized by ethnic background, age, height and years of education, another sent a video with an infertile couple holding hands and talking about choosing donor insemination. She imagined what would happen later, when the child asked, Who is my father? She couldn't imagine saying R144 or telling the child that she'd chosen the father because he had neat handwriting, he liked the color green and was "good with people." She would rather tell her child the story of the guards, and that she was born of the sea.

Her preparations begin in earnest at dusk. As other people are shaking up the martinis, she puts on her costume: her sex pants with nothing underneath, a silk undershirt, and then the insulated top she wore when they went skiing. She rubs Avon Skin-So-Soft over her hands, feet, face. She puts on two pairs of high socks, in part for warmth, in part to protect against, sand fleas, ticks, mosquitoes. She pulls on a hooded sweat jacket, zips it and looks in the mirror—perfectly unremarkable. She looks like one of those women who walks a dog alone at night, a mildly melancholy soul.

She fills the pockets of her sweat jacket with condoms—Friday night, there'll be lots of activity.

She now thinks of herself as some sort of a sex expert, a not-for-profit hooker.

At dusk, she makes her rounds, visiting all the beaches, all the lifeguard stands. She distributes about thirty condoms. Regardless of what happens it is a good investment, a charitable contribution.

She cruises through town, stopping in at the local convenience store, ice-cream parlor, pizza place, the parking lot behind the A&P, getting a feel for the night to come.

There are families walking down Main Street, fathers pushing strollers, mothers holding their toddlers' hands.

She hears the sound of a baby crying and has the urge to run towards it, believing that she alone understands the depth of that cry, profound, existential. There is something unnameable about her desire, unknowable unless you have found yourself looking at children wondering how you can wrest them from their parents, unknowable unless you have that same need. She wants to watch someone grow, unfold—she likes the name mom.

She drives farther out of town, scouting. She goes to where they live—crash pads, shacks that would be uninhabitable if they weren't right by the beach. She knows where they live because one rainy afternoon she followed a truck-load of them home.

There are no cars, no signs of life. A picnic table outside one of the shacks has a couple of half-empty glasses on it. The door is open—it's actually off its hinges, so she doesn't feel so bad going in.

Stepping inside, she breathes deeply, sharp perfume. Dark, dank, brown shag carpeting, a musty smell, like old sneakers—hard to know if it's the house or the boys. Bags of chips, Coke cans, dirty socks, t-shirts, pizza cartons on the counter. It's an overnight version of the guard shack. Four bedrooms, none of the sheets match. In the bathroom a large tube of toothpaste, a dripping faucet, grime, toilet seat up, a single bar of soap, two combs and a brush—all of it like a stable stall you'd want to muck out.

She pokes around, taking a t-shirt she knows belongs to her best boy. She takes a pair of shorts from another one, a baseball hat from a third, socks from a fourth. It's not that she needs so much, but this way no one will think much of it, at most it will be a load of laundry gone missing.

As though the boys were still at summer camp, their names are written onto the backs of their clothes, each in his own handwriting—Charlie, Todd, Travis, Cliff.

She drives back to town, to a different beach, moodier, more desolate. Hunkering down in the dunes, she immediately spots two people in the water—male and female. She takes out her birding glasses, identifying the boy—one of the older ones, diving naked into the waves. He swims towards the woman and she swims away. Hide and go seek. The woman comes out of the water, revealing herself, long brown hair, her body rounded and ripe, a woman not a girl. He swims to shore, climbs out after her and pulls her down onto the sand. She frees herself and runs back into the water. He goes after her and, pretending to rescue her, carries her out of the sea to a towel spread over the sand. They are like animals, tearing at each other. He stops for a moment, rummages through his clothing, takes something out—she can't see what, but she's hopeful. Their mating is violent, desperate. The woman both fights him and asks for more. He is biting the woman, mounting her from the back, the woman is on her hands and knees like a dog, and she seems to like it.

Finished, they pack up. They walk past her, see her, nod hello as though nothing ever happened. The woman is older, wild looking, a kind of earthy goddess.

When they are gone she hurries across the sand. She finds the condom half covered in sand—limp debris. Something about the intensity of their coupling, so sexual, so graphic, leaves her not wanting to touch it. She unzips her fanny pack, pulls out a pair of latex examination gloves, pulls them on and then carefully rescues the sample—2.5 cc's, usable if a little sandy.

She goes back to the car, assumes the position and making an effort to be discrete, inseminates. She stays in position for half an hour and then continues her rounds.

The romance of the hunt. She walks up and down looking for her men. The beaches are crowded with bonfires, picnics, catered parties. The air is filled with the scent of starter fluid, meat cooking; barbecue embers pulse, radiant red like molten lava.

She puts on the night-vision glasses, the world glows the green of things otherworldly and outside of nature. Everything is dramatic, everything is inverted, every gesture is evidence, every motion has meaning. She is seeing in the dark, seeing what can't be seen. A cigarette sails through the night like a tracer. She has to maximize, it's not enough to try just once, she wants to fill herself, she wants many, multiple, may the best man win. She wants competition, she wants there to be a race, a blend, she wants it to mix and match.

It is still early—the girl doesn't get off until ten or possibly eleven. She lies back in the sand, rubbing the points on her head where the screws were, dreaming. She glances up at the bathhouse. On the roof is a weather vane—a whale, a mounted Moby spinning north, south, east, west, to tell which way the wind blows, its outline sharp against the sky. She dreams of old whalers, fishermen, dreams she is in a boat, far from shore, in the middle of the open sea. She thinks of her grandmother, freeing her. She thinks of how proud her grandmother would be that she's taken things in hand.

Finally they arrive. Creatures of habit they go back to the same spot where they were yesterday, this time moving with greater urgency. There is something genuine, heartfelt in the sex habits of the young— it is all new, thrilling, scary, a mutual adventure.

She retrieves and extracts her second sample. In the car, with her hips up high, she inseminates and she waits.

She imagines all of it mingling in her like sea foam. She imagines that with the sperm and the sand, she will make a baby born with pearl earrings in her ears.

In the local paper there is a notice for a childbirthing class. She goes, thinking she should be ready, she should know more. There are only two couples; a boy and girl still in high school and a local couple in their mid-thirties—the husband and wife both look pregnant, both sip enormous sodas throughout the class.

"When are you due?" the instructor asks each of them.

"In three weeks," the young woman says, rubbing her belly, polishing the baby to perfection. "We didn't plan for the pregnancy so we thought we better plan for the birth."

"Four weeks," the other woman says, sucking on her straw.

"And you?"

"I'm working on it," she says. And no one asks more.

On the table is an infant doll, a knitted uterus and a bony pelvis.

"Your baby wants you," the childbirth teacher says, picking up the doll and passing it around.

The doll ends up with her. She holds it, thinking it would be rude to put it back down on the table—she might seem like a bad mother. She holds it, patting the plastic diaper of the plastic infant, pretending to comfort it. She sits the doll on her lap and continues taking notes: gestational age, baby at three weeks, three months, six months, nine months, dilation of the cervix, the stages of labor.

"All pregnancies end in birth," the instructor says, holding up the knitted uterus.

Leaving the hospital, she runs into the cop coming out of the emergency room.

"You all right?" she asks.

"Stepped on a rusty nail and had to get a tetanus shot." He rubs his arm. "So, how about that coffee?"

"Absolutely, before the end of summer," she says getting into her car.

She is a woman waiting for her life to begin. She waits, counting the days. Her breasts are sore, full, like when they're were first budding. She waits, thinking something is happening and then it is not. There is a stain in her underwear, faint, light, like smoke, and overnight she begins to bleed. She bleeds thick, old blood, like rust. She bleeds bright red blood, like a gun-shot wound. She bleeds heavily. She feels herself, hollow, fallow, failed. And bleeding, she mourns all that has not happened, all that will never happen. She mourns the boys, the men, the fiancé, her grandmother, the failings of her family, and her own peculiar shortcomings that have put her in this position.

She becomes all the more determined to try again. She counts the days, keeps her temperature charts and watches her men.

She will try harder, making sure that on the two most viable days she gets at least two doses—no such thing as too much. She continues to prepare. August, high tide, peak of the season. The local newspapers are thick with record numbers of deer jumping in front of cars, a drowning on an unprotected beach, shark spottings. The back pages are filled with pictures of social events: the annual hospital gala, the museum gala, the celebrity tennis match, benefit polo, golf tournaments, the horse show. This summer's scandal involves a man who tried to get into "the" country club, was loudly rejected, and then showed up at the front door every day waiting for someone to sign him in as their guest.

She makes a coffee date with the cop. At the last minute he calls to cancel.

"They've got me on overtime. Can I get a rain check?"

"Yes," she says, "but it's not raining."

She goes on with her rounds, her anthropological education. She gets bolder. Out of curiosity she goes to the other beach, the one she has always heard about, notorious for late-night activity.

There are men in the dunes, men who tell their wives that they're running out for milk, or a pack of cigarettes, and find themselves prowling, looking for relief. With her night-vision glasses she can see it all quite clearly; rough, animalistic, horrifying and erotic—pure pornography.

A Planned Parenthood vigilante, throughout her cycle, she continues distributing the condom supply. She wants to keep them in the habit; she wants them to practice safe sex. She tracks her boys; she has to keep up, to know their rhythms and routines. She has to know where to find them when the moment is right. She adds a new one to her list, a sleeper who's come into his own over the course of the summer—Travis. An exceptional swimmer, it is Travis who goes into the undertow like a fish. He puts his fins on, walks backward into the water and takes off.

Every morning he is in the water, swimming miles of laps back and forth, up and down—the ocean is his Olympic-size pool. Sometimes she swims with him. She puts herself in the water where he is; she feels her body gliding near his. She swims a quarter mile, a half mile, moving with the current. She feels the sting of the salt in her eyes, strings of seaweed like fringe hanging off her ankles, the tug of the riptide. She swims not thinking she could be carried out to sea but that she is a mermaid and this is her habitat. She swims to the next lifeguard stand, gets out and walks back, having perfected walking on sand, keeping her feet light, barely making a mark.

It is nearly the end of summer. She has been taking her temperature, peeing on sticks, waiting for the surge that tells her she's ripe, ready.

Late afternoon at Main Beach, her boys assemble to be photographed for the town Christmas card. They pile onto the stand, wearing red Santa hats, sucking in their stomachs, flexing their muscles. On cue they smile. She stands behind the official photographer and with her own camera, clicks.

Does it matter to her which of them is the father of her child, whose sperm succeeds? She likes the unknowing, the possibility that it could be any one of a number of them, and then sometimes she thinks she wants it to be him, the boy with the hieroglyph, with the babysitter/waitress girlfriend—he strikes her as most stable, most sincere. Soon they will go back to school and the summer romance will end. They will leave and she will stay on.

The day the stick turns positive, she makes her rounds. Travis has a new girlfriend, a blonde who works at the snack bar. She finds them on the other side of town by the marina. They are new to each other and so it goes slowly: they make out for more than forty minutes before Travis leads her to a platform at the end of the dock. When they are done, they dive into the water for a quick swim and she finds herself checking her watch, worrying that the sperm is getting cold. When they leave she has trouble locating the condom, finally finding it, dangling from a nail on one of the pilings almost as though he knew and left it for her. 5cc's—a very good shot.

She inseminates herself, lying back in the car, knees hooked over the steering wheel, blanket over her for warmth. It is cooler in the evenings now; she has a layer of long underwear on under her sex outfit and a spare blanket in the car. The boys and girls all wear sweatshirts declaring their intentions, preferences, fantasies: Dartmouth, Tufts, SUNY, Princeton, Hobart, Columbia, NYU.

She lies back, looking up at the sky, there is full moon, a thousand stars, Orion, Taurus, the Big Dipper. She lies waiting and then moves on. The wind is starting to blow. At the end of every summer there is always a storm, a violent closing out the season, it charges through literally changing the air—the day it passes, fall begins.

Her favorite couple is hidden in a curve of dune. They are already at it when she arrives. Leaving the night-vision glasses in the car, she travels by moonlight with just her fanny pack. The wind is hurling sand across the dune; the surf crashes unrelentingly. They do it fast, now practiced, they do it seriously, knowing this will be one of the last times, they do it and then they run for cover.

The condom is still warm when she finds it. She holds it between her teeth and using both hands, scoops the sand, molding into a mound that will hold her hips up high. She inseminates herself lying in the spot where they had lain. She inseminates, listening to the pounding of the waves, the sea ahead of the storm, watching moonlight shimmering across the water.

A phosphorescent dream: she thinks she feels it, she thinks she knows the exact moment it happens; the sperm and the egg finding each other, penetrating, exploding, dividing, floating, implanting, multiplying. She imagines a seahorse, a small, curled thing, primitive, growing, buds of hands—fists clenched, a translucent head, eyes bulging. She feels it digging in, feeding, becoming human. She wakes up hungry, ready. In May she will meet her, a little girl, just in time for summer—Georgica.

A THREEFOLD CORD

by NATHANIEL MINTON

WHEN I LEFT my mother at the dead camel, she told me that the desert is no place for the ambidextrous. She may have been right, but it was her feet that were blistering like viral pustules and her ears sunburned to black flakes. I didn't see what my brain bilateralism had to do with the fact that we were probably going to die, especially considering the camel—perched atop a half-submerged and sandblasted Range Rover, legs folded up and body dried out—was not ambidextrous and did not have blisters and was uniquely suited to the environment and was dead. My mother decided to stay with the camel, claiming that if circumstances demanded she would cut it open and extract some greenish water from its bladders. "In fact," she said, "I might do that anyway."

The decision to abandon our own vehicle came after three days of trying to get it running again, neither of us having any mechanical aptitude, although I changed a tire once in Nyack, New York. After three days we had exhausted our limited water supply, and, being less than a hundred miles from what is locally called civilization, we decided to set out on foot. Two days later we'd drunk all the water we had carried, and twelve hours after that, from the top of a high dune that glowed brighter than the morning sky, we approached the deceased camel, and beneath it the Range Rover.

The radiator was dry but we found eight #10 cans of purified water buried in sand behind the passenger seat and thanked providence that tourists are weak, because we could live on that for a little while and maybe eat some camel, even though camel meat is bitter. We rationed one of the #10 cans and slept curled up inside the shade of the Range Rover. I took the camel as a sign of something good because in the desert, any sign of life is a good sign, even if it is dead.

When I woke up in the early evening, with temperatures in the low hundreds, I saw my mother through the windshield. She was leaning into the wind, faded linen billowing around her as she awkwardly shifted from foot to foot, balancing out the pain of well-sanded blisters. I crawled out, blowing sand from my nostrils, to stand next to her.

"I'm going to stay here," she said. "We'll use less water that way."

"I don't think we should split up," I said.

She shrugged. "It's what your father would do," she said. "Come on, I'll draw you a map. So you know where to find me."

She drew a length of string from her pack and carrying the empty #10 water can, dragged the string behind her and marked off its lengths, measuring out 198 feet, the sum of three Gunter's chains, because the family cares about tradition. She set the can down, marking the one baseline she needed, and did a quick angle sighting with her compass. Limping back, she laid out a clean 20x30 sheet of drafting paper on the hood of the vehicle. She unpacked the family's antique theodolite and sighted its spider-silk crosshairs on a distant dune, then on the empty can. She calculated angles, with compass and protractor, factored in the distance from us to the can, and triangulated our location in respect to our surroundings. When she finished, the map consisted of a dotted lump for the dune, a small outcropping of Precambrian-rock 7,293 feet away, for which she drew a small cluster of rough circles, and a clean little cylinder for the can.

"This is where we are," she said, pointing to a cartoony Range Rover with a camel on top. The camel was smiling. It was a splendid map.

"Okay," I said.

"So you can find me. With the water," she said. "With help."

"This is perfect," I said, rolling up the map and slipping it into my map tube among our completed maps. It was a good solid plan; I would walk out to the empty can, find its position in relation to different dunes, then pick one of those dunes and so on across the desert, leapfrogging within my own web of interconnected triangles, drafting a map that showed location only in terms of itself.

The project would be easier if I had a desert dweller's intimate knowledge of dunes. In the latter half of the nineteenth century, the French meharists navigated by the largest dunes, or oghurds, that rise from the desert floor in sharp triangular peaks and whose bodies operate on geologic time, unchanged in a lifetime, but whose sands, the particles of their form, are in constant transition, hopping along their slopes and ridges, creeping to the Mediterranean, but finally held in vast ergs by barriers of mountain. The finer of the sands, clay-like particulates, are swept in massive clouds across the Atlantic to the Americas where they burn in sensitive eyes from Venezuela to Myrtle Beach and prevent Florida from meeting national clean air standards.

The problem was not severe. I would have to learn the dunes.

"Just think of them as people," she advised me. "That one looks like your father," she said, pointing to a long incurving and subtle ridge that was nonetheless insurmountable in its sharp degrees.

I nodded. "I think I'll draw them."

"Okay," she said, "but doing both wouldn't hurt." Then she looked at me and, brushing a matted wad of hair from my eyes, said, "You'll make a good map."

The biggest setback, and real root of our problem, was the demise of our precious GPS locator, a mapping computer the size of a paperback, that triangulates position in relation to geosynchronous satellites, placing us, within a meter or two, at the bottom of a giant inverted three-sided pyramid whose invisible lines extend infinitely into a non-Euclidean space where nothing adds up to precisely 180 degrees. My father thought the GPS was cheating, so we had other tools, older tools, octants and sextants, plane tables and spirit levels, and he insisted that all his maps be made with them, for precision, for personality, and for the unmistakable character of human error. We were, however, allowed calculators, which saved us the weight of logarithm tables. The GPS was for emergencies and had, unbeknownst to us, expired at some point in the 27 hours between civilization and when our vehicle broke down and in that time we had not consulted a compass or a map or the stars.

The sun set in minutes, from day to night, skipping evening almost entirely. I packed all the water I could carry, and that's when my mother made the crack about ambidexterity. I didn't respond, knowing it was the envy of handedness, but kissed her cheek and told her I'd be back soon. As I set off into the night toward the empty water can, along the baseline she'd laid out, I heard her cheering, calling out "cartographer of Ch'ang-sha," whose maps grew vague with distance, and shouting "onward Ptolemy," who wrote the book, and singing "we are the Cassini family," who brought precision and politics to maps of France.

In the winter of 1615, Willebrord Snell created a network of 33 triangles across Holland in an effort to discover the actual distance of a latitudinal degree. He failed by only by three percent. But he had the advantages of working by day and measuring every baseline.

To a naked body, the desert wind is poisonous. Sweat glands become overwhelmed by increased evaporation and skin temperature rises above the air's. My mother and I knew this, so like the people who live here, we stayed clothed. To my father, life is a poison, naked or not. The minute we stepped off the plane in Chad, I knew why he had sent us alone, because even though this azoic environment would probably cure him quick from the litany of as-yet-undiagnosed microbial tropical infections that kept him bedridden, the place itself smelled like death. It was not the acrid stench of flesh consumed by bacteria and by itself. Nothing rots in a desert. Decay is eolian and death is slow, and its odor is the odor of air crackling apart from itself, of possibility... of waiting. Waiting for life to get lazy, to stop trying, to take a nap, and my father takes a lot of naps, even for someone with a chronic low-grade fever. The Tuareg say the winds have a depressive effect on man, and my father knew it. He didn't want the winds, he wanted the geometry. So we were alone, making his maps for him and sleeping for him in sands he couldn't bear. I didn't sleep that night but walked carefully with an eye for the next dune or rock that might serve as an angle in my triangles. At times throughout the night, surface winds drew undercurrents of sand that pulled at my feet and on the slight decline of dunes I could skate across the desert surface. Like early oceanic explorers, I could find my latitude by the stars, 17.4° 28N, but it meant nothing without longitude, not in these distances.

When my father had called, I was busy tracking Antarctic thaw. "The desert," he said, "the desert," like it was a rich chocolate brownie with candied walnuts. I declined politely. "You're a natural for those dunes," he said, "with that ambidextrous topography. Naturally those will be confident maps. Wish I could be there." Then he started coughing and put my mother on the phone. I changed my mind about the trip when she enthusiastically offered to go it alone.

She was alone.

I was alone.

Those were the least of the problems. Of primary concern on that night was the fact that solar calculators don't work in the dark and my flashlight barely coaxed a faint gray from the LCD making the trigonometry difficult. I longed for a logarithm book. These things happen. My father would say they are the stuff maps are made of.

At night the erg is brighter than the sky, and dawn comes when the stars fade. Time became short while I worked to complete my seventeenth triangle. The map was really shaping up. A spider would be proud of its precision. My father would be proud of its ingenious angles and intuitive topography, that I sketched with a pencil in each hand. I took pride in my brief descriptions of dunes; "Angry Stegosaurus," was written next to one corner of a triangle in perfect drafting letters. "Oghurd Bauble" read another. I sketched a small profile of each one next to the name.

I found the photographer while looking for something to sight as the final angle of the seventeenth triangle. A mile or so away, distances being difficult to guess on a barren landscape, I saw what appeared to be a thin stump protruding two feet above the sand. I sighted it, noted the angle, set off towards it. Temperatures rose quickly; the air already in the high nineties and the ground well into triple digits. Within half an hour, I was at the stump, which turned out to be a cardboard map tube, driven into a mound of sand with a red bandana held over its mouth with a rubber band. I approached cautiously, because who knows what people do out here, people like the Libyans who have strewn landmines and live shells throughout the sands. As I stepped onto the mound, the tube moved slightly, followed by a low guttural rumble that reminded me of the camel. I put my mouth to the bandana.

"Hello?" I said. Nothing. "Hello," once again and this time a little grumble replied. "Are you living?" I asked in the friendliest tone I could muster over growing unease.

"I'm sleeping," a voice echoed up through the tube, "come back later."

I wasn't sure but I could have sworn I detected a British lilt under the sand and beneath my feet, which were starting to melt. I needed to find shade and wait out the day trying not to sweat myself to death. I stepped off the mound and paced around looking for some rocks or something that could keep the sun off me. I had water, but without shade I would probably only make it through one more night.

"Are you still there?" the tube said.

"Yes," I said.

"I can't hear you," the tube shouted. "You'll have to come closer."

I walked right up to it and the tube grunted when I stepped on its mound. I had a quick fantasy of ripping off the protective bandana and scooping handfuls of sand into the tube but I just shouted back into it, "Yes. I'm still here. But I'm going to have to leave soon because there is no shade around here and I will probably die if I don't find some soon because as you know we are in the middle of a desert, but what I would really like to find even more than shade is a satellite phone or somebody with a vehicle so I can go back and get my mother, who I left at a dead camel last night, before she dies too."

There was a long pause and then the tube said, "Oh."

"You wouldn't happen to have any of those things would you?" I asked.

"Sorry," said the tube, offended perhaps that I asked at all, "You wouldn't happen to know where we are," it said. I told it that I knew exactly where we were and it jiggled a bit and the mound shifted under me.

"Are you standing on me?" it asked.

"Yes."

"Do you really know where we are? I feel like I'm lost."

"You are," I said, picking up a little sand and sprinkling it on the bandana. "I know where we are and I know where my mother is but I don't know much beyond that. My map lacks context." That context could take me a while. There is an awful lot of context in a place this size, but I didn't tell the tube that.

"You don't have any more idea where we are than I do," said the tube.

"Of course I do," I laughed, "I'm a cartographer."

"Can you read maps? I have some maps."

"Of course," I said, "Everyone can read maps—we make them that way."

The sun was above the horizon, and I was directly in it. At the tube's request, I removed the bandana, spilling a little sand into the tube, but other than a series of quick coughs I heard no complaints, and a moment later a roll of maps emerged from the tube like a paper piston. The paper was yellow and cracking. Unrolling them I saw why; the maps were drawn by Lenz and de Foucauld at the turn of the century, when their countries colonized this desert before losing it back to the Arabic people who had stolen it from Tibbu aborigines who were the true native peoples and are dead despite speculation of small tribes still scrabbling out lives in the Tibesti mountains that rise to ten-thousand feet in a small corner of the Libyan desert. The maps were useless. I had better maps in my roll, maps based on satellite imaging and precise measurement, and even mine were useless without knowing where I was within them.

"These are useless," I told the tube.

"What kind of bloody cartographer are you if you can't even read a map? At least as a photographer I have an excuse," the tube screamed back.

I crouched down on dried, cracking knees and started digging, burning my hands on hot silicate. In seconds I reached a sheet of yellow nylon. "What the hell are you doing?" this time the voice came from the nylon, not the tube. I didn't say anything. I kept digging, throwing handfuls of sand over my shoulders because it kept sliding back into the hole. It was a small one-person tent. It was ingenious really. A can of water buried in two feet of sand will freeze in a single desert night, and during the day temperatures can stay in the low seventies, because the air between grains of sand insulates it from heat. It was perfect shade.

With the Swiss Army knife my father gave me when I turned eighteen, I sliced open a nice section of the ripstop nylon that lay exposed at the bottom of my hole. It opened up and an angry bearded face popped out. The photographer emerged, stinking like gangrene and piss. I stumbled back and took a breath, deep, of sterile wind and sand.

"Damnit," he said, "Now we'll both die."

"I have some water," I said by way of apology.

"Oh, I have water," he huffed, scrambling out into the sun to sit next to me. "They left me with water at least."

When I asked who left him with water, he told me that he was out there taking pictures with some Nigerian salt merchants as guides and that after camping one day he woke up and they were gone. They'd left him with some camel meat and a fifty-five gallon drum of water. He didn't know how much water was left. He'd been there eleven days. He stopped taking pictures after the third day and decided to conserve water until they came back.

I told him I didn't think they were coming back, and he asked if he could take my picture. "Just in case we live," he said.

The photographer pulled a bulky large-format camera from his tent and started setting it up on a tripod. While I watched him struggle with the hot metal legs, I realized the salt merchants had sentenced the guy to death for being annoying, and he didn't even know it. Inshallah, they would say, that he lives, but knowing that he would self-desiccate in a self-desiccating place. But they left him water.

"They sent you out here alone?" I asked the photographer.

"Who?"

"I don't know. Whoever you work for."

"Oh," he said, "the magazine. No, there was a writer but he got heatstroke in Bilma so I went on without him, and if you try to kill me

and take my water I'll kill you first… I have a flare gun in my pocket."
He pointed to a bulge in the left cargo pocket of his British Army surplus pants that were predictably falling apart at the seams. Killing him
for the water wasn't part of my plan until he mentioned it, and even
then it didn't sound very productive.

I thought of my mother curled in the shade of the Range Rover
nursing her blisters that would heal quickly, would never become
infected, not here. I should have stayed. I imagined her smiling in her
sleep and dreaming of concentric amoebas of shifting topography and
somewhere among them, my father's hand, tracing every curve of
every elevation, of every angle of every mountain or river or canyon
that he could not map himself, that he could not physically witness.
But the maps moved him. He wept, running his fingers over my
mother's maps of Outer Mongolia. "Was it like this?" he had said, and
my mother nodded and blew him a kiss. Every time we returned home
with maps, he would make a recovery. Doctors marveled at his condi-
tion. "You're in good health for a man your age," they said, congratu-
lating themselves with handshakes and professional nods honoring
their brilliance and the efficiency of medicine. A few months later he
would relapse. "You pushed the envelope," the doctors said, but we
knew otherwise, and within weeks one or both of us were out charting
small plots of the globe.

"I don't want to kill you," I told the photographer. "I want my
mother." I screwed up my face. Click. He snapped my picture.

"Don't frown this time," he said. I crossed my arms and stared him
down while he took the next picture. "I got a great self portrait the
other day," he said and pointed to a dune that didn't have a single
angle on it. It was a perfect parabolic dome. "The light," he said. "The
sun was setting and it caressed that dune in shades of red and pink. I
sat on top and set the timer. It'll be beautiful. If you give me your
address I'll send you one, and also the one of you smiling. You can give
that to your mother."

I told him I didn't want to give him my address. I didn't tell him
that people who are about to die should concentrate on preserving dignity rather than the illusion of survival.

"The salt merchants don't use maps," the photographer said. "They
don't even have a compass."

"I know," I sighed. "They read the dunes. They live here, they don't need maps... Maps," I said, "are a way of communicating spatial relatedness. Space is the basis of all human understanding and is the foundation of...."

The photographer laughed. Loud. He doubled over clutching his sides and saying, "Oh, my sides." When he recovered he walked right over to me. Close. "There's maps of everything," he said. "Photographs from satellites," he pointed to the sky, then stuck his finger right between my eyes, "You're a stinking anachronism... Give it up."

I took a step back, caught my left heel on my right toe and stumbled back, snow-angeled in burning powder. I picked myself up and stood forty inches away from him. I knew it was forty inches because I have a thirty-nine inch reach and when I swung at his jaw I missed by one inch. He spat at me as I spiraled back onto the sand. This time I just lay there. I considered his suggestion. Give up. It wasn't a terrible idea. Lesser people had tried it with great success, like those honeymooning Swedes in a powder-blue Volvo who dried to death in the late eighties. I like to think that Bishop James Pike never gave up when he disappeared into the Jordanian desert with his wife and two bottles of Coca-Cola in search of the Holy Ghost, or maybe just God. I didn't want to give up. I had to finish a map. If I gave up, I would die. If I died, my mother would surely die. With both of us dead, no map would be made, and my father would very likely die also. That would leave the photographer, the snotty little Brit, alive and well with his buried drum of water.

I stood up, on the ground, my ground. "I'm leaving," I told the photographer. "I'm going back to my mother, and I'm not going to try to kill you but I want you to give me some water."

I retraced my map for the rest of the day, suffering out the sun, but I didn't care about the heat or my sunburn because I was among my own triangles now, laughing along a hypotenuse and adding up all angles of my seventeen triangles, isosceles and equilateral, exquisitely obtuse and acute.

I was on the baseline of the second triangle, climbing the side of "Delicious Windowshade" when I saw my mother. She stood atop the dead camel, unfolding herself in a Tai-Chi swan of eastern body geometry. Her arms rose and described arcs that pushed at invisible opponents. Approaching, I saw she was wrapped in gauze and white first-aid tape, every inch, from digit to digit, eyes and all. At the empty water can, I saw her pointing, first along the baseline then in a thirty-nine degree curve to implicate the dune she called my father. Standing on one foot then, she withdrew her forward hand and pushed, flat-palmed, the other toward the dune. She held the hand there, pushing along the adjacent side of triangle number one. Slowly she withered, her neck losing integrity, her spine condensing and her back arcing in almost heliotropic desire towards the dune as her legs lost definition and she melted bodily into the sanded fur of the dead camel. I was eighteen feet away from her when she spoke.

"I am the map," she said, "I am the goddamn map," and laughed. On the sand, I unrolled the map of my mother and the dead camel. I drew a square in the lower right corner. I wrote LEGEND across the top of the square. I copied my mother's drawing of the Range Rover mounted smiling camel, inside the box. Next to it I wrote: DEAD CAMEL. I drew a camera at the final corner of the final triangle and a corresponding camera in the legend: DEAD PHOTOGRAPHER.

"What are you doing?" my mother said, sliding down from the dead camel.

"Completing the map," I told my mother, whose face was obscured by gauze presumably scavenged from the dead camel's first aid kit. "I'm not going to just sit around waiting to dehydrate without at least knowing where it is that I die. I want to get away from the camel. The camel is creepy."

She turned her head toward the camel. She crawled into the Range Rover and emerged with Gunter's chain in one hand and an octant in the other. She tied the string around the camel's neck in a neat neck-tied little bow. "Let's lay a new baseline," she said and walked away from the dead camel, toward the southeast, away from the empty water can and the dead photographer. I wrote in big letters across the top of the map—CONTEXT—then I tied my shoes and hurried to catch up along the new baseline, 139 feet to my mother and 17 latitudinal degrees away from my father.

SAINT CHOLA

by K. KVASHAY-BOYLE

SKATER. HESHER. TAGGER. Lesbo-Slut. Wanna-be. Dweeb. Fag. Prep. What-up. Bad-ass. Gangster. Dork. Nerd. Trendy. Freaky. In a few weeks it'll be solid like cement, but right now nobody knows yet. You might be anything. And here's an example: meet Mohammadee Sawy. Hypercolor t-shirt, oversized overalls with just one hook fastened, the other tossed carefree over the shoulder like it's no big thing. In walks Mohammadee, short and plump and brown, done up for the first day with long fluffy hair and a new mood ring, but guess what, it's not *Mohammadee* anymore. Nope, because Dad's not signing you up today, you're all by yourself and when you get the form where it says Name, Grade, Homeroom, you look around and take the pen Ms. Yoshida hands you and you write it in big and permanent: Shala M. Sawy. And from now on that's who you are. Cool.

It's tough to do right but at least you learn what to want. You walk the halls and you see what's there. I want her jeans, I want her triple-pierce hoops, I want her strut, I want those boobs, I want that crowd, I want shoes like those, I want a wallet chain, I want a baby-doll dress, I want safety pins on my backpack, I want a necklace that says my name. Lipstick. I want lipstick. Jelly bracelets. Trainer bras from Target. It could be me. I could be anyone. KISS FM, POWER 106, Douche-bag, Horn-ball. Fanny packs! Biker shorts! And suddenly, wow, Shala realizes that she has a surge of power inside that she never knew was there. Shala realizes that she's walking around and she's thinking Yup, cool, or No way! Lame!

Shala? That sounds good. And that's just the way tiny Mrs. Furukawa says it in homeroom when she calls roll. She says *Shala*. And Shala Mohammadee Sawy? She smiles. (But not so much as to be uncool because she's totally cool.) And she checks out the scene. There's a powerhouse pack of scary Cholas conspiring in the back row, there's aisle after aisle of knobby, scrawny white-boy knees sprouting like weeds from marshmallow sneakers, and there are clumps of unlikely allies haphazardly united for the first time by the pride of patriotism: Serrania Avenue, row three, Walnut Elementary, row five, or MUS, first row. Forty faces. Shala knows some of them. Ido, Farah, Laura Leaper, Eden, Mori Leshum, oh great, and him: Taylor Bryans. Barf. But the rest? They're all new.

In Our World, fourth period, Shala learns current events. It's social studies. The book's heavy. But then there's a war. And then Shala's embarrassed to say Niger River out loud, and she learns to recognize Kuwait and a kid named Josh gets a part in a movie with Tom Hanks, but that's nothing she tells Lucy because she used to roller-skate at Skateland with the kid from *Terminator II*. And he's cuter. Way cuter.

It's L.A. Unified where there's every different kind of thing, but it's just junior high so you're just barely starting to get an idea of what it means to be some different kind of thing. There are piercings. There are cigarettes. Even drug dealers. And with all that, there's the aura of danger all around, and you realize, for the first time, that you could get your ass kicked. You could get pounded after school, you could get jumped in the bathroom, you could get jacked-up, beat-up, messed-up, it's true, and the omnipresent possibility swells every exchange.

Mrs. Furukawa's new husband is in the Army. She says so. She wears the highest heels you've ever seen a person wear. Her class reads *The Diary of Anne Frank* but you knows you're set, you already read it. Plus *A Wrinkle in Time*, and you read that one too. At home your mom says Get out the flag, we want them to know what side we're on.

On television every night Bush says Sad-dum instead of Suhdom and your dad says it's a slap in the face. Your dad, the Mohammad Sawy from which your Mohammadee came, says it's on purpose, just to drive that bastard nuts. You practice saying the name both ways, the real way and the slap-his-face way.

Gym class is the worst because you have to get naked and that is the worst. Gym is what your friends feared most in fifth grade when you thought about junior high and you tried so hard to imagine what it would be like to be with other people and take your clothes off (Take your clothes off? In front of people? Strangers-people? Oh yeah right. Get real. No way.) and you started trying to think up the lie you'd have to tell your parents because they just wouldn't get it. A big important thing is Modesty. You know that. It's your cultural heritage, and naked is certainly not Modesty. On the first day just to be sure, you raise your hand and ask If you were a non-strip every day would you fail? And Ms. DeLuca says Yes.

Some kids ditch but it's been three months. It's too late now. You're stuck with who you are by now and even though you're finally Shala you're still a goody-good brainy dweeb. And dweebs just don't ditch. Not like you want to anyway. Except in Gym. That's when you do want to. You sit on the black asphalt during roll call with your gym shirt stretched over your knees so that it's still all bagged out twenty minutes later when the volleyball crashes bang into your unprotected head for the fifteenth time like it's been launched from some mystery rocket launcher and it's got a homing device aimed straight for you.

At twelve, no one knows anything yet, so what kind of name is Shala? Who can tell? And, plus, who'd even consider the question if parents didn't ask it? Sometimes kids slip up to you in the crush of the lunch line and speak quick Spanish and expect you to answer. Sometimes kids crack jokes in Farsi and then shoot you a sly glance just before the punch line. Sometimes you laugh for them anyway. Sometimes you'll try and answer Sí, and disguise that Anglo accent the best you can. *Sí, claro.* But the best is when a sleep-over sucks and you wants to go home and you call up your mom and mumble Urdu into the telephone and no one knows when you tell your mom I hate these girls and I want to leave.

* * *

On Tuesday a kid wears a T-shirt to school and it says 'Nuke Em' and when Mrs. Furukawa sees it she's pissed and she makes him go to the office and when he comes back he's wearing it inside out. If you already saw it you can still kind of tell though. ME EKUN.

After school that day your cousin asks if you want to try Girl Scouts with her. Then she gets sick and makes you go alone. When you get there it's totally weird for two reasons. First, your cousin's older by one year and she already wears a hijab and when you went over to get her she dressed you up. So now you're wearing a hijab and lipstick and your cousin's shirt, which says 'Chill Out.' Uncool. But what could you say? She's all sick and she kept cracking up whenever you put something else of hers on and she's so bossy all the time and then before you knew it the carpool's honking outside and your aunt shouts that you have to go right now. So you do. Then, second of all, you don't know anybody here. They're all seventh graders. It sucks.

They're baking banana nut bread and the girl who gave you a ride says that you smell funny. What's worse than smelling funny? The first thing you do is you go to the bathroom and wash your hands. Then you rinse out your mouth. You try to keep the lipstick from smearing all over the place. You sniff your armpits. As far as you can tell, it seems normal. In the mirror you look so much older with Aslana's hijab pinned underneath your chin like that.

When you walk out of the bathroom you bump into the Girl Scout mom and almost immediately she starts to yell at you like you spilled something on the carpet.

Um, excuse me but this is a feminist household and hello? Honey, that's degrading, she says.

She must be confused. At first you wonder, is she really talking to me, and like in a television sitcom, you turn around to check if there's someone else standing behind you.

Don't you know this is America, sweetheart? I mean have you heard of this thing feminism?

Yeah I'm one too, you say, because you learned about it in school and it means equality between the sexes and that's a good idea.

That's sweet. She looks at you. But get that thing off your head first, she says. You know you don't have to wear it. Not here. No one's gonna arrest you. I didn't call the police or anything, honey—what's your name?

The Girl Scout mom shakes her Girl Scout head and she's wearing a giant Girl Scout outfit that fits her. She looks weird. Like an enormous kid, super-sized like French fries. You can just be yourself at our house, honey, she assures you. You can. What, your mom wears that? She's forced to? Right? Oh, Jesus Christ. Look at you. Well you don't have to, you hear me? Here, you want to take it off? Here, com'ere, honey.

And when you do she helps you and then after you're ashamed that you let her touch it. Then you mix the banana nut dough and you think it looks like throw-up and that same girl says that you still smell like a restaurant she doesn't like. You really, really want to leave. Maybe if you stand still, you think, no one will notice you. On the wall there's a picture of dogs playing cards. Your cousin's hijab is in your backpack and you hold your whole self still and imagine time flowing away like milk down your throat until it's gone and you can leave.

There are Scud missiles, yeah, but in sixth grade at LAUSD, there are more important things. Like French kisses. There's this girl who claims she did one. You just have to think What would that be? because no one would ever kiss you. At least until you're married. Lucy Chang says it's slutty anyway. Lucy Chang is your best friend. You tell her about Girl Scouts and she says Girl Scouts is lame.

On the way home from school you get knocked down by a car. With a group of kids. It's not that bad, kind of just a scary bump, from the guy doing a California-stop which means rolling through the stop sign. At first he says sorry and you say it's okay. But when you suck up all your might and ask to write down his license plate number he says no. Your dad must be a lawyer, he says, is that it? What, look, you're not even hurt, okay? Just go home.

You have some friends with you. You guys were talking about how you could totally be models for a United Benetton ad if someone just took a picture of you guys right now. You're on your way to Tommy's Snack Shack for curly fries and an Orange Julius. Uhh, I think we should probably just go, alright, Noel says, It's not that bad so we should just go.

Yeah, go, the man says. Don't be a brat, he says, Just go.

Okay fine, you say, fine I'll go, but FIRST I'm gonna write it down.

He's tall and he looks towards the ground to look at you. Just mind your own business, kid, she doesn't want you to. No one wants you to, he says.

Well I'm gonna, you say.

Look, you're not hurt, nobody's hurt, what do you need to for?

Just in case, you say. If it scares him you're happy. You're in junior high. You know what to do. Stand your ground. Make your face impassive. You are made of stone. You repeat it more slowly just to see if it freaks him out. *Just. In. Case*, you say and you're twelve and if you're a brat then wear it like a badge.

At mosque there's a broken window. It's a disgrace, your father says, Shala, I tell you it's a damn disgrace. The hole in the window looks jagged like a fragile star sprouting sharp new points. It lets all the outside noise in when everybody's trying to pray and cars rush past grinding their brakes.

There's a report in Language Skills, due Monday, and you have to have a thesis so on the way home from mosque your mom helps you think of one. Yours is that if you were living in Nazi times you would have saved Anne Frank. Your mom says that's not a thesis. Hers is that empathy and tolerance are essential teachings in every religion. You settle for a compromise: Because of Anne Frank's tolerance she should be a saint.

At home while your mom makes dinner she stands over the stove as you peel the mutant-looking ginger root and there are lots of phone calls from lots of relatives. What are we going to do, your mom keeps demanding each time she talks into the phone, What? Tell me. What are we going to do?

Saddam does something. You know it because there are television reports. Everyone's worried for your older brother. He's studying in Pakistan with some friends and if he leaves now then he'll be out one whole semester because his final tests aren't for two more months. He's big news at the mosque. Also people are talking about the price of gas and how much it costs just to drive downtown.

Then Bush does something back, and the phone cord stretches as your mom marches over and snaps the TV off like she's smashed a spider.

The ginger and the asafetida and the mustard seed sauté for a long time until they boil down and then it is the usual moment for adding in the spinach and the potato and the butter but instead the moment comes and goes and the saag aloo burns for the first time that you can remember and the delicate smell of scorched spice swirls up through the room as you watch your mom demand her quite angry Urdu into the receiver and you realize that she doesn't even notice.

You know why she's upset. It's because everyone can tell Ahmad's American and he can't disguise it. He smells American, he smiles American, and his t-shirts say *Just Do It* like a dare. And lots of people hate America. Plus, in that country, in general in that country, it's much more dangerous. Even just every time you visit, you swallow giant pills and still your weak sterile body gets every cold and all the diarrhea and all the fevers that India has to offer. It's because of the antiseptic lifestyle, your mother insists. Too clean.

In Science, fifth period, you learn that everything is made out of stardust from billions of years ago. Instead of it being as romantic as Mr. Kane seems to think it is, you think that pervasive dust feels sinister. You know what happened to Anne Frank, and you can't believe that when she died she turned back into people dust, all mixed up with every other kind of dust. Just piles and piles of dust. And all of it new.

There are plenty of other Muslim kids. Tons of them at school. Everyone's a little freaked out. In the hall, after science, you see an eighth grader get tripped on purpose and the kid who did it shouts, Send Saddam after me, MoFo, I'll kick his ass too!

After school that day at Mori Leshum's house everyone plays a game called Girl Talk, which is like Risk, except it takes place at the mall. It gets old fast. Next: crank calls! 1-800-SURVIVAL is 1, 8, 0, 0, 7, 8, 7, 8, 4, 8, 2, 5. Uh hi, I just got in a car accident and YOU SUCK A

DICK! You laugh and laugh but when it comes time for your turn to squeal breathy oinks into the phone the way you've heard in movies, you chicken out and everyone concludes that oh my god you're such a prude. Well at least I'm not a total perv, you say. Oi, oi, oh! Wooo! Ahh! moans Jackie and when Mori's shriveled grandma comes in the room to get you guys pizza, you all shut up fast for one quick second and then burst into hilarity. The grandma laughs right back at you and she has a dusty tattoo on her arm and it's not until years later that you realize what it is. Oh that, says Mori, It's just her boyfriend's phone number. She says she put it there so she won't get it lost.

Some things that you see you can't forget. On your dad's desk in his office where you're not supposed to touch anything, you see a book called Vietnam, and it's as thick as a dictionary and it has a glossy green cover. At random you open it up and flip. In the middle of a sentence is something about sex so you start to read quick. And then you wish you didn't. You slam it shut. You creep out of the office. You close your eyes and imagine anything else, and for a second the shattered starshape of your mosque window flashes to the rescue and you cling tight and you wish on it and you wish that you hadn't read anything at all. *Please*, you think, and you try to push the devastation shoved out through the sharp hole the same way you try to push out the sound of horns and shouts when you say prayer. *Please*, you think, but it doesn't work and nothing swoops in to rescue you.

Sex Ed is only one quarter so that for kids like you, whose parents won't sign the release form, you don't miss much. Instead of switching mid-semester, you take the biology unit twice and you become a bit of an expert on seed germination. Lucy tells you everything anyway. Boys get wet dreams and girls get cramps, what's that all about? she says. You look at her handouts of enormous outlined fallopian tubes and it just sort of looks like the snout of a cow's face and you don't see what the big deal is. You do ask, though, Is there a way to make your boobs grow? And Lucy says that Jackie already asked and No, there isn't. Too bad. Then Lucy says, I must, I must, I must increase my bust! And then you call her a Horndog and she calls you a Major Skank and then you both bust up laughing.

When it happens it happens in the stall at McDonald's. Paula Abdul is tinny on the loudspeaker. Lucy's mom asks what kind of hamburger you want and you say you don't eat meat, it has to be Fish Filet, please. With Sweet-and-Sour sauce, please. Then Lucy says Grody! and then you and Lucy go off to the bathroom together and while she's talking to you about the kinds of jeans that Bongo makes, and every different color that there is, and how if you got scrunchies to match, wouldn't that be cool? you're in the stall and you realize it like a loose tooth. Lucy, oh my god Lucy, check this out, wow! It happened!

Are you serious, she says, Are you serious? Oh my god, are you sure?

I'm sure, you say, and you breathe in big chalky breaths that stink of bathroom hand-soap, powdered pink. When you guys come back to the table and you eat your meal it seems like a whole different thing being in the world. And it is.

That night you ask your mom if you can stay home from school on account of the occasion. She doesn't let you. She does ask you if you want to try her hijab on, though, and you don't tell her about Aslana's. Shala, she says, Shala, I don't know about right now. This just may not be the time. But it has to be your choice. You don't have to if you don't want to, but you do have to ask yourself how do you represent yourself now as a Muslim Woman in this country where they think that Muslims are not like you, Shala, and when you choose this, Shala, you are showing them that they know you and that you are nice and that you are no crazy, no religious nut. You are only you, and that is a very brave thing to show the world.

Now when you guys walk home, you're way more careful about not trusting any cars to do anything you expect them to. When you get to the 7-11, you try different ways of scamming a five-finger-discount on the Slurpees. The woman behind the counter hates kids. Timing is everything. Here's how it goes: one person buys and you mix every color all together and try to pass from mouth to mouth and suck it gone before it melts. It's hard because of brain freeze. You try to re-fill and pass off, which the woman says counts as stealing and is not allowed, but that's only when she catches you. Trick is, you have to look like you're alone when you buy the cup or she'll be on to you and then she'll turn around and watch the machine. So everyone else has to stand outside with the bum named Larry and then go in one by one and sit on the floor reading trashy magazines about eyeshadow while the buyer waits in line. Today that's you. You wait in line. You've got the collective seventy-nine cents in your hand. You freeze your face still into a mask of passivity and innocence.

As the trapped hotdogs roll over sweating on their metal coils, you hear the two men in front of you discussing politics and waiting with their own single flavor Slurpees already filled to the brim and ready to be paid for in full.

Same goddamn ground war we had in 'Nam, and hell knows nobody wants to see their baby come home in a body bag. Hey.

The way I see it is, you got two choices, right? Nuke the towel-heads, use your small bombs, ask your questions later, or what you do is convert.

With you on the first one, buddy.

No, no listen: *convert*. Hell yeah, whole country. To Islam. To mighty Allah.

Shit, man, you and the rag-heads?

But I got a point, right? Right? 'Cause what'd you think these fuckers want? Right? Oh yeah, hey uh, pack of Lucky Strikes, huh? And how 'bout Superlotto? Yeah, one of those, thanks.

Next: you. You try to gauge how much this straggly woman sees. Can she tell? Muslim? Mexican? Does she know that your clothes are Trendy, that your grades are Dweeby, that your heart is Goodygoodie? Your face: unreadable, innocent, frozen. One Slurpee. Please.

You walk around the counter and towards the magazines and when your friends see you, you try to look triumphant and cool and with it. But you feel like a cheat. Like maybe if it is stealing, you might not be such a good Muslim, you might be letting your kind of people look bad.

Not *stealing,* says Lucy. Sharing. It's just sharing.

So you share. You slurp cherry-cola-blueberry-cherry layers until your forehead aches. Then Jackie opens up her mouth and throws her head back and gets down on her knees and another girl pulls the knob and you all stop to watch the Slurpee slurped straight from the machine. Gross, someone says, but you're all impressed with the inventiveness and Jackie's daredevil status is elevated in everyone's eyes.

Oh, for Christssake! Give me a break! You goddamn good-for-nothing kids, get out of here! Get! Never again! You're banned, you hear me? Banned! Out! Get out!

Scatter giggling and shrieking across the parking lot, and the very next day dare each other to go back like nothing happened and you know you can because you know she can't tell the difference between any of you anyway. You could be anyone for all she knows.

The day you try it out as a test, someone yanks hard from behind and when it gets ripped off your head, a lot of hair does too. You think about how when hard-ass what-up girls fight they both stop first and take out all their earrings. It hurts enough to make you cry but you try hard not to. *Please don't let me cry, please, please don't let me cry.* First period, and Taylor Bryans sees your chubby lower lip tremble and he remembers the time you corrected his wrong answer in front of the whole class (Not pods! *Seeds*! Duh!) and he starts up a tough game of Shala-Snot-Germs and the cooties spread from hand to hand all around the room as your face gets hotter and hotter and your eyeballs sting and your nose drips in sorrow. Your dignity gathers and mounts as you readjust the scarf and re-pin the pin. You can't see anyone pass Germs, you can't hear anyone say your name. You are stone. You are cool. You will not cry. Those are not tears. The bell rings.

Then the bell rings six more times at the end of six periods and when you get home that day you have had the hijab yanked on seven occasions, four times in first period, and you've had your feet stomped twice by Taylor Bryans in the lunch line, and after school a group of eighth graders, all of them past puberty and huge with breasts in bras, surrounded you to gawk and tug in unison. And you've made up your mind about the hijab. It stays. No matter what. The fury coils in your veins like rattlesnake lava, the chin pushes out to be held high, the face is composed and impervious and a new dignity is born outraged where there used to be just Shala's self-doubt. It stays, you think, No matter what.

Still, at home you cry into your mom's sari and you shout at her like she's one of the merciless, I'm just regular, you wail. I'm the same as I ever was!

Oh baby, come on, shhh, it's going to be okay, she says. And then your mom suggests that maybe right now might not be the right time to start wearing this. She assures you that you are okay either way, that you can just take it off and forget about it. She says all this, sure, but she wears hers knotted firmly underneath her own chin as she strokes your back with reassurance.

That night, before you get into bed, you think about your brother and what it must be like for him. You look in the bathroom mirror and you slip the hijab on over your young hair and you watch like magic as you're transformed into a woman right before your very eyes. You watch like magic as all of the responsibilities and roles shift and focus.

You get it both ways. In your own country you have to worry, you have to get you hair pulled. And in India there you are: the open target, so obvious with your smooth American feet and your mini Nike backpack, the most hated. With anger and envy and danger all around you. The most hated. The most spoiled. An easy mark. A tiny girl. With every thing in the world, and all of it at your disposal.

You think about your brother and you wonder if he's scared.

As you get dressed for bed you check things out with a hand mirror. You poke at the new places you hadn't looked at before. You look at the shape in the hand mirror and you think *Hello me*. It's embarrassing even though it's only you. You feel a whole new feeling. You think about how much you hate Taylor Bryans. Indignation rises up like steam. You stand there in the bathroom with blood on your hands and you know it. *I am Muslim,* you think, *I am Muslim, hear me roar.*

In third period PE the waves of hot Valley sun bake off the blacktop asphalt and from a distance you see squiggly lines of air bent into mirage and your head is cooking underneath the scarf and your ears feel like they're burning in the places where they touch the cloth and your hair is plastered to the back of your neck with sticky salty sweat and when you group up for teams, someone yanks hard. You topple right over. You scrape your knees and through the blood they're smudged sooty black. Everyone turns around to look, and a bunch of girls laugh quietly behind hands. The hijab is torn from where the pin broke loose and your dad is right, it's way better that it isn't a knot or you might choke. Your neck is wet with a hair-strand of blood from where the popped-open pin tip slipped along skin. And you figure, That's it. Forget it. I quit. I'm ditching. I hate you.

Someone says, Aw shit, girl, you okay?

You scramble up and walk tall and leave the girls in their bagged out PE uniforms and you go back into the cool dank locker room where you can get naked all by yourself for once. As you wash the gravel out of your hands you stare at yourself in the mirror. You think *Bloody Mary* and squeeze your eyes shut tight, but when you open them it's still just your face all alone with rows and rows of lockers. No demon to slice you down.

Now when you walk in late you're not Nobody anymore, you're not Anyone At All. Instead, now, when you walk in you have to brace yourself in advance, and you have to summon up a courage and a dignity that grows strong when your eyes go dull and you stare into unfocused space inches away while Taylor Bryans and Fernando Cruz snicker and snicker until no one's looking and then they run up and shout in your face: Arab! Lardass! Damn, you so ugly you ooogly!

Your inner reserves fill to full when Fernando stomps on your feet and your white Reeboks get all smeared up and your face doesn't even move no matter how much it hurts.

The bell rings. Lunch. You push and shove your way into the cluster of the Girls' Room, and there's no privacy and you try to peer into the tagged-up piece of dull-shine metal that's bolted to the wall where everyone wants a mirror, but there are girls applying mascara and girls with lip-liner and the only air is a fine wet mist of aerosol Aqua-net and it's too hard to breathe and you can't see if it's still pinned straight, because that last snatch was like an afterthought and it didn't even tug all the way off. But you can't make your way up to the reflection and you can't see for sure. So here it comes, and then you're standing there in the ebb and flow of shoulders and sneakers and all of a sudden here it comes and you're sobbing like you can't stop.

Hey girl, why you crying? You want me to kick some mother-fucker's ass for you, girl? 'Cause I'll do it, bitch, I'm crazy like that. You just show me who, right, I'll do it, homegirl.

And through your tears you want to throw your arms around the giant mountainous chola and her big-hearted kindness and you want to kiss her Adidas and you want to say Taylor Bryans' name and you want to point him out and you want his ass kicked hard, but you stop your-self. You picture the outcome, you picture the humiliation he'd feel, a skinny sixth grader, a scrub, the black eye, the devastation of public boy-tears, the horror of having someone who means it hit you like an avalanche. You look over your back and past all the girl-heads, the stiff blondes and permed browns and braided weaves, the dye jobs, the split ends, all of them elbowing and pushing in to catch a dull distorted glimpse in graffitied monochrome, and you smooth over the folds of your safe solid black hijab and you snuffle up teary dripping snot and you picture what it would be.

You picture her rush him: Hey BITCH, yeah I'm talking to you, *pendejo*, that's right you better run outta my way whiteboy, cuz I'm going to whup your ass, punkass motherfucker! You picture her and she's like a truck. Taylor Bryans stops cold and then he startles and turns to flee but she's already overcome him like a landslide, and she pounds him like muddy debris crushing someone's million-dollar home. You picture the defeat, the crowd of jeering kids, Fight! Fight! Fight! The tight circle of locked arms, elbow in elbow so the teachers can't break it up, the squawk of adult walkie-talkies and then the secu-rity guards, the assistant principal, and all the teachers on yard duty, all of them as one, all charging over to haul kids out of the fray and into detention, and all the while you can picture him like he's a photo-graph in your hand: the tears, the scrapes, the bruises, the giant shame in his guilty nasty eyes and you know that it wouldn't solve a thing and you suspect that it probably wouldn't even stop him from pulling your hair out and stomping on your feet and you picture it and you open up your heart and you forgive him.

Then you gather up all that new dignity, and then you look up at her, stick your covered head out of the girls' bathroom, and point.

NOTES FROM A BUNKER ALONG HIGHWAY 8

by GABE HUDSON

I KNOW THIS is going to sound corny, at least to all the angry, cynical people in the world, but they can go to hell, because in the midst of everything that's happened with this screwy-ass war, yoga, and the deep concentration that I attain through yoga, has pretty much saved my life. I am probably a little addicted to it, but Dithers says that I am a complete fruitcake, and that yoga isn't going to save my butt from getting caught and thrown in the brig. Dithers says it's my queer dad that's the reason I like yoga so much. Just recently Dithers shouted, "G.D., you know they're going to find us. You know Captain has men on us right now. It's just a matter of time. And when they find us, I'm going to be laughing my ass off at you."

I was crouched in the Wide Galaxy pose with my eyes closed, and pretended not to hear him.

"I know you hear me, G.D."

The Wide Galaxy is my favorite pose. It is the pose I like to finish with at the end of a sequence. I raise my palms to the sky, which is really just the concrete ceiling of this bunker, allowing "my hands to become my eyes," and victoriously breathe in 1-2-3-hold, and exhale 1-2-3-4-hold, and after fifteen minutes in the Wide Galaxy, my mind is right up into the void, and I feel truly shocked with bliss, grateful for the existence of every single atom in the universe.

"Hey, G.D. Hey, Zen Master. If you're looking for love, I'm your man. Come and get me."

I opened my eyes, blinked, and strolled over to the far end of the bunker, and, with my e-tool, banged on the wood slats of Dithers's cage very hard. The chimps erupted into a chorus of screeches and started shaking the slats of their cages, which pretty much sealed the deal for me: getting my head up into the void was obviously out of the question now. So, choosing to ignore Dithers's laughter, I ambled down the hall and flung back the hatch and hoisted myself out of the bunker. I went for a walk in the cool desert night, where I mentally reprimanded myself for letting Dithers get the best of me.

But I should explain: I am not by nature a violent man, not anymore anyway. I believe in the sanctity of all people. And now my only allegiance is to Life, that Golden Kaleidoscope which turns always in circles, riddled as it is with its patchworked bits of magic and beauty. Here in my underground bunker, which is where I'm writing this from, and which was abandoned by Iraqi soldiers well before I ever arrived on the scene, I salute Life every day to the fullest, and beyond the steel hatch of the bunker, and moving thirty yards south, lies Highway 8, which is the main road that runs from Basra to Baghdad. And it's on this highway that the starving, the depraved, the war-weary Iraqi civilians, mothers carrying their dead babies, one-legged orphans, whole caravans of families with shattered faces from witnessing the catastrophic demolition of their homes and villages, the fleeing Iraqi soldiers, not the demonic Republican Guard, but the scared boys and old men forced into service by their vicious dictator, where hundreds of charred tanks and scorched cars line the highway and the ditches alongside the highway, still even tongues of flame reach out to lick the sky, and the noxious odor of burning human flesh chokes the air—like some kind of permanent backyard barbecue smell—this apocalyptic highway, are making their pilgrimage on foot to the supposed safety of Baghdad, where they will probably be blocked from the city's gates anyway.

Now some people might call me a criminal, a traitor, or worse even, because I deserted my Green Beret brothers and my country, but they are fools, because I know now that the heart is the highest law there is. And I find that if I turn an ear inward and pay very close attention, then my heart speaks to me louder and louder each day.

So there I was, strolling along that night and chewing myself out for the Dithers thing, when I stumbled upon a kindly old Iraqi woman crawling in the ditch along the highway. This was my first patient of the night and my heart quickened. I slid my ruck off and dug out my medical kit. I got down on my knees and set this woman's mangled leg in a splint. She started to speak, but I gestured shhhh. I cleaned the infected area on her calf, and picked maggots out with tweezers. I rubbed the wound down with salve, which I knew must have burned. And it was then, as I was cleaning her leg and I saw the hot tears of gratitude in her eyes, it was then that I found the peace of mind that had eluded me back in the bunker.

HUNTING FOR SCUDS, AND HOW I HELPED PREVENT A NUCLEAR WAR

It doesn't matter who you are, at some point something will happen to you out of the blue and your life will instantly be changed dramatically and forever. There's the crackle of lightning, the clouds part, and you see a muscular arm reach down and the Big Guy in the Sky deals you The Card. Well, I got The Joker. And it's funny, because once you realize the joke's on you, the last thing you want to do is laugh. And so it was for me, though even looking back on it all now there still doesn't seem to have been any sign of what that night had in store. This is how it started: Our team was on patrol up near Al Haqlaniya, right along the banks of the Euphrates River. I was behind the wheel of the Land Rover and Marty was scoping the landscape with his thermal sight. Our mission was to hunt and destroy Scuds deep inside Iraq, and a Scud is almost as dangerous as a beebee gun, and definitely less accurate. They have no guidance system, and so the Iraqis just point them in a general direction and presto: off goes a deadly Scud. Of course, our gazillion-dollar Patriots, courtesy of that genius Reagan, are just as ridiculous, because when a Scud starts to drop it shatters into a thousand little parts of scrap metal, and when we fire a Patriot it just locks in on one of those little pieces, and those jerkoffs claim they shot down a Scud. CNN runs the story, then everyone back home waves their flag, and the whole thing starts to remind you of a professional wrestling match.

"Hey," said Marty, "what's up with this shit detail?"

"You're stopping a nuclear war," said Dithers, "so quit your bitching. You're going to be able to tell your grandchildren about this."

That was our little joke. The thing about the nuclear war. On January 14, some dozen Scuds smashed into Tel Aviv and Haifa. Next thing you knew Israeli prime minister Shamir aims mobile missiles armed with nuclear warheads at Iraq. The Saudis stated in no uncertain terms that if Israel got involved in Desert Storm, then they'd yank their ally status. Bush convinced Shamir to hold off starting a nuclear war by sending his best men, Green Beret, behind Iraqi lines for the sole purpose of Scud busting.

"Yo," said Marty, "what's that?" pointing. "I think those might be Scuds."

We turned and saw a stoic shepherd surrounded by teeming sheep. The shepherd angrily waved his cane at us. He was Bedouin, and these guys hated us. They were the black magic gypsies of the desert.

Everyone started whooping back at the shepherd. "Yeah," said Dithers, "those are some deadly looking Scuds. We'd better call it in."

Cynicism was at an all-time high. We'd been inserted by Pave Lows three weeks ago and other than a couple skirmishes with some weak-ass Iraqi soldiers, there'd been no real action to speak of. And no Scuds. Every couple days an MH-60 Blackhawk would shoot out to deliver fuel supplies and drop off our mail. It was freezing up there, with these wicked sandstorms, shamals, I think they're called, and we'd cruise all night in our Rover, and then hide out and catch some Z's during the day.

I jerked the wheel and said, "Hold on, gents." I started cutting sharp circles around the sheep. They panicked, bleating, scrambling every which way, some tumbling on their faces and others trampling them. The next thing I knew, I heard the crack of a rifle shot, and Marty says, "Damn." I glanced over and there's blotch of blood on Marty's shoulder. But there was no time, another shot, and our right front tire exploded, and in a blur I wrestled with the wheel as the Rover swerved and rolled up on its side. I tumbled out and aimed my Beretta at the Shepherd, who was sighting in on us with a rifle. Then, and this is like nothing I'd ever seen, seven or eight of the sheep stood up on their hind legs and cast off their wool coats, and I saw that underneath were Iraqi soldiers brandishing AK-47s. A volley of machine-gun fire cut the dirt around our position, tink-tink-tink in the Rover, and I lunged and radioed our SAS counterparts for backup.

Some of us scurried through the smoke and dove and set in on the backside of a little dune. Diaz was calling in our coordinates to air support. I heard a buzzing sound and saw a team of SAS on motorcycles burning up in the rear. I was lying on heavy fire with my Heckler, and next to me Dithers was blasting rapid-fire bursts with his SAW. A feather of smoke curled up off the tip of Dithers's SAW. "Your barrel!" I shouted. "You're melting." And that's when I saw the moonlit shadow fall in the sand in front of me, and that's when Dithers let out an earsplitting scream. I rolled over just in time to see the Iraqi soldier lunging at me, driving his WWII-style bayonet glittering with Dithers's blood right at my chest. Dithers's arm had been sliced off, and was lying in the sand off by itself, and the hand of the arm was still clutching the barrel he'd been trying to change out.

There was a chainsaw buzz and an SAS dude in a black jumpsuit plowed into the Iraqi with his motorcycle, planting him in the sand next to me. The Iraqi was doing the funky chicken, flopping around like something neural had been severely damaged. I looked at Dithers and a red flower of blood had begun to bloom at his armless shoulder socket. "Oh Jesus! Oh Jesus!" he cried out. "I can't feel my legs! Oh Jesus! I'm so cold! I'm so cold!" Now there was blood everywhere. Blood on Dithers, blood in the sand.

"Hang in there, buddy! You're okay! Just relax, Dithers!"

MY VISION OF GEORGE WASHINGTON, AND THE ENSUING EPIPHANY

Then, and I don't know why I did this, I glanced up for a split second, and I saw George Washington right out there in the middle of all the smoke and chaos. He was shirtless, sitting in a wooden hot tub with his arms draped around two blonde Bud Girls in bikinis. There was a patch of fuzzy, white pubic hair on his chest. I saw a half-eaten burrito perched on the edge of the tub. George had his head tilted back in open-mouth laughter, with the moon light winking in his giant ivory teeth, but suddenly he stopped and looked at me and his face lit up, and he said, "*There* you are. I've been looking all over for you, G.D." He smiled. "Come," he said, and lifted one hand and nonchalantly waved me over, mafioso style. "You must be tired. Come reap some of the rewards of all your toil on the battlefield, son. This is Carrie and Belinda." The girls giggled. Washington held up an apple. " We're going to bob for apples. How does that sound? You want to bob for apples? I sure could use your help, son, because I don't think I can handle it alone, if you know what I mean?" he said with a wink, and gestured expansively, spreading his arms wide behind the girls' shoulders. Just then a young African American man strolled up behind George carrying a tray on which were three silver goblets, and said, "Yous ready fo ya'lls drinks, mastah?"

Dithers yelled. I glanced down at Dithers, and when I looked back up George Washington was gone. And that's when the weight of it all: the senselessness of war, the absurdity of America and ideals, its bloody history of oppression, its macho Christian religious certainty, finally came flooding into my mind like a great white ray of liquid light. What the hell am I doing here? I asked myself. How can you defend a country that slaughtered the entire Native American race, a majestic civilization which patented the mocassin and controlled the weather through a primitive, wireless form of breakdancing? Why should We The People be exhalted for having obliterated the peace pipe in favor of irony and the crack pipe? A country whose publicity-starved flag is a prophylactic against compassion, and is synonymous with a heat-seeking penis (God), waving its ignorant seed of disregard and enititlement in every beleagured face it can find. A country whose secret service conspired to shoot its premiere motivational speaker, Martin Luther King. A country which steamrolls across the planet like an obese golf ball, contaminating innocent indigenous peoples with its tech-based White Virus, while knighting murderous dictators as CEO's in the so-called new global economy. A country where women are deported to a cell (kitchen) and held captive in the shackles of an apron, handcuffed with spatulas and cake-making devices, and where in the currency of human dignity a vagina relegates its owner to the status of a green-stamp. Why doesn't America's Power Elite recognize that a person who can issue milk from their nipples is clearly superior to a person who can not. A woman president would be able to feed America's hungry babies with her nipples. And where does the word love fit into all this? Then I gave myself the answer: You are a goddamn fool.

So right then and there, with the unshakeable resolve of a man who has had the blinders ripped from his eyes after wandering for so long in complete darkness, I scooped up Dithers, who'd passed out by then, and started to walk off. Marty, firing his pistol desperately, glanced at me and shouted, "G.D. what're you doing?!" There were maybe twenty Iraqis now, firing and advancing on our position, rushing up and hitting the sand on the fly. Dead sheep littered the landscape like fallen clouds. I could hear screams, weapons cooking off, motorcycles, sheep bleating, but in a sense, it already seemed far away. I kept walking, picking up my pace, and glanced over my shoulder. Marty shouted again. "Hey, G.D., get your ass over here, motherfucker. What're you doing?" Marty was on his feet now, still firing his pistol. I slung Dithers over my shoulder and started to jog, looking back at Marty. As Marty was glaring at me, a flying Iraqi bum-rushed him and they were instantly grappling in a sandy commotion till death did they part. And then, with Dithers slung across my shoulders in the fireman's carry, I fled for my life, south, my heart in my throat, away from the fighting and chaos, leaving Dithers's arm and Green Beret behind me forever.

MY DAD THE VIETNAM HERO, WHO NOW READS CHOMSKY, PLUS DAD'S VIGILANT ANTI-WAR PROTEST

Everybody in Green Beret knows about my dad. He's a distinguished Green Beret alum, with a Medal of Honor from Vietnam, and you can find his name on the Wall of Fame at the Special Forces Training Center in Fayetteville. Like a lot of veterans, Dad never talked about The Nam. Whenever I asked him about it he'd tell me to shut up. And when Desert Storm started and we were called up, my dad wrote a letter to my commanding officer, Captain Larthrop, telling him that as a former Green Beret he vehemently opposed America's participation in Desert Storm. He quoted Noam Chomsky's famous essay, "The Invisible Flag," which apparently states among other things that the Invisible Flag "waves for all of humanity." My dad wrote Larthrop that he couldn't sit by and watch American boys get bogged down in another Vietnam quagmire, another "intervention," and so as an act of protest—he has a twisted sense of humor—he was coming out of the closet, was turning gay. He wrote me a letter explaining the whole thing. He informed me that he'd taken a lover, a forty-six year old criminal lawyer named Rob who he'd met at his yoga class at the Y. The same Y we used to do yoga together at when I was growing up. I felt betrayed. He said Rob had been openly gay for his entire life and that Rob was being a great support during the transition period. The whole letter was Rob this and Rob that, like I was supposed to be grateful or something.

I wrote my dad back. Lots of times. I begged him to reconsider his position. I used whatever logic suited my argument. I told him first and foremost that what he was doing was an affront to the gay community, and that he should be careful about what his method of protest inferred. I sent him articles clipped from Science magazine explaining how gay people had no more choice over their sexual preference than heterosexual people did, that it was all genetics. He wrote me back to inform me that he'd just sent a letter to Jesse Helms's office, suggesting that North Carolina make a motion to legalize gay marriages. He said, maybe I'm jumping the gun here, but this is the happiest I've been in years. I sent him a Times article about the vicious underground militia of the gay organization B.P.C., Better Population Control, and that he should watch out because they'd be pissed if they heard about the mockery he was making of their sexual orientation. He sent me back a full-color photograph of a naked blue-eyed man siting on a porous rock on a beach in Jamaica that had been clipped from a magazine called Out, and scrawled at the bottom of it in my dad's handwriting was: "This is still a free country, right?" And he'd drawn a little smiley face.

That last letter took the wind out of my sails, and I didn't write him back. I guess I thought it would blow over, but my dad called the Raleigh News and Observer and they broke the story. The story spun, and it suddenly got a ton of media play. A highly decorated Vietnam soldier, former Special Forces with a Medal of Honor, as an act of protest, announces that he will be gay until every single American boy is home safely. My dad was a guest on all the TV and talk-radio shows, liberal, right wing, it didn't matter to him, he was just looking to get his message out. Rush Limbaugh had a field day with it, brought him and Rob on his TV show for an interview. I didn't watch it, but Dithers did. Dithers said the title of the show was American Hero Bends Over for Peace.

My dad's got a pretty good sense of humor, so he wore a wry grin the whole time and busted jokes and kept the aggressive audience in stitches, is what Dithers said. When it comes to being a wise-ass, you really cannot mess with my dad.

DITHERS'S DANGEROUS COMA, AND THE INADVERTANT DISCOVERY OF BUNKER

With Dithers slung across my back in a fireman's carry, I fled south along the foamy bank of the Euphrates. I ran for hours and hours, not stopping to think about the magnitude of what I'd just done, afraid that if I did I might lose my nerve and turn back around. The cold night wind bounced off the water and blew through my bones, and in the chaos of my mind I hoped maybe it would sweep me up like a kite and carry me to a land far, far away from there. Dithers had slipped into a dangerous coma, and I kept stopping to douse his wound with water, and then patched it up as best I could with a T-shirt. Then it was more shuffling, guided by the North Star. I recall a rock I camped under at the bank of the river, and I remember Dithers, coming to at one point and shouting, "Help," and then passing back out. It was well into the second night that I saw from a distance the great paved highway with the fires blazing alongside it. I was gasping for air as I came up to the edge of the highway. I heard someone shout something in Arabic, and the flash of a muzzle lit up next to the skeleton of a bombed out car. "Stop," I shouted. "Salam alaikum!" Which is the only Arabic I know, and it means peace be with you. A whole slew of orange flashes erupted, and the sand around my feet was jumping in the air, making it difficult to see. I didn't have any fight left in me, and I resigned myself to whatever happened, and in a way, that desperation was what gave me courage, I knew nothing could hurt me now, as I scrambled to the other side of the six-lane highway in a flurry of enemy fire, nothing, that is, except for an errant round that shaved off a quarter inch of my knee cap. The pain exploded up my spine, and my brain went wet with shock and fear. Even now I've got a slight limp. I collapsed face first into the sand, using Dithers to break my fall. I got to one knee and dragged Dithers behind the cover of two huge boulders, and that's when I spotted the steel in the sand. One of the Iraqis was blowing a whistle, and there were shouts, and I heard a pack of men scrambling in my direction. I yanked back the steel hatch, and threw Dithers in first, and then I jumped down in, pulling the hatch to. The fall was about ten feet, and Dithers and I landed in a heap on the ground. It would only be later that I found the steel ladder fastened to the wall. I heard the soldiers shouting in Arabic up above. I held my breath in fear and my heart knocked on the door of my rib cage. I saw the milk white of my kneecap where the bullet had shaved off the skin and felt woozy. Finally the soldiers up above us moved on. It was only then that I noticed the horrible stench of the place. Screeching sounds erupted from what sounded like the center of the earth. With Dithers in my arms like a newlywed, I ventured cautiously down the hall, casting the beam of my flashlight over the concrete walls.

THE CHIMPANZEES WHO WERE HERE BEFORE US

Something furry crashed on my head as I crossed the threshold, and a cacophony of screeches erupted, reverberating off the inside of my skull, threatening to split it down the middle. I envisioned the dust that my brain had become spilling out. Dithers fumbled out of my arms and I felt leather hands pounding and tugging at me. In the commotion I managed to light a flare from my cargo pocket and then I sprang to my feet and shrugged off my attackers, and in the fiery shadows I saw several chimpanzees screeching at me and waving their fists over their heads. Their yellow eyes were filled with hate. Like everyone else I'd seen the psyops pamphlets Iraq had dropped with a picture of King Kong eating the heads of terrified American soldiers, but I never thought there was anything to it. I spotted Dithers motionless on the floor in a heap. His forehead was pale and slick with sweat. His shoulder was a gory red flesh mess, and I realized he could be dead for all I knew. I shouted, "Getoutahere!" and waved the flare around in my hand like a sparkler and then franticly chased the chimpanzees into the back of the bunker with it.

The bunker looked like it had been abandoned in a hurry. Later, once I'd found the light switch, I also discovered the pinewood cages and figured out that the chimps must have escaped from them after the Iraqis deserted the bunker. There was a giant metal table against the south wall, which was strewn with papers and booklets I couldn't read, but, judging by the pictures and illustrations, I guessed they were booklets describing how to make chemical weapons. Then there's the hand-to-hand combat stuff, and an English dictionary from 1964. In the closet I found a big box of MREs. There was also a giant cache of weapons, but with no ammo. RPG's, AK-47s, M-16s, the works. On the north wall was a little bathroom area complete with toilet and sink. And a couple lightbulbs dangled from the ceiling. And like I said, the wooden cages, eight total, stacked up on one another, pushed up against the east wall.

HOW I CAME TO BE KNOWN AS G.D.

This was at Fort Bragg, North Carolina. We were rehearsing hostage rescue. My team crashed through the third-story window, and I hit the deck, lying on cover fire with my 9mm, while Dithers scurried forward with Marty to search the bedrooms and bathroom and laundry room. A robot, The Dad, came rushing in from the kitchen, crying out, "Help help, they've got my son." A three-dimensional hologram of a German shepherd appeared on the wall. The dog started barking at me and baring its teeth, threatening to compromise our mission, so I blew its head off with my 9mm, and synthetic blood splattered everywhere. The graphics were amazing. I leapt up and moved swiftly to The Dad, reciting my lines, "We're here to help, sir. Please lie down on the floor under a table until further instructed. You are safe now." I was in mid-speech, on the word table, when Dithers dove back into the room, squeaking, "Hit the deck, hit the deck!" as he sprayed The Dad with his Koch MP-5 series machine gun, so that the robot's chest ripped open and a fuse shorted and blazed momentarily, and then the machine's lights went out. I turned to Dithers, and shouted, "What the hell?" But he was already beside The Dad, and he yanked off The Dad's face, revealing the grinning, pockmarked mannequin face of the Middle Eastern Terrorist (MET) we'd been instructed to terminate. A baby in diapers waddled out from the kitchen, and I said, "Here's number one. Got'em," and scooped him up, then sprinted into the kitchen, where the baby's dad was lying, apparently blud-geoned by the MET with a toaster. The father gasped, "You took too long, and now I will die because of you. If I were a real person you would now have to live with the burden of my death for the rest of your life, soldier." Marty came bursting through the kitchen door and I jumped and the baby dropped from my arms, landing on its head. "You moron," he said. The baby started howling like a fire engine, and Captain Larthrop's voice crackled on the intercom. "Christ Almighty, son, where the fuck is your head? Good job, Dithers, but it looks like the real terrorist here is you-know-who." You-know-who was me. "Grab your gear and get in the frigging Debriefing Room, you knuckleheads."

On the way to the Debriefing Room, Marty turned to me and spit, "Nice job, Mr. Gay Dad. Next time why don't you just hug the MET to death." Dithers started laughing, and said, "Yeah, G.D. Why don't you give him a big kiss next time," and it was with that laughter that my new name was born.

DITHERS'S NEAR-DEATH EXPERIENCE, AND MY SPIRITUAL CONVERSION TO THE ART OF HEALING, NOT HURTING

It was touch and go for a week or so there, but then I finally got Dithers to regain consciousness. Snatched him right out of the jaws of death. Those first couple days I tended to him around the clock. He was shaking and his teeth were chattering and not once did he open his eyes. I gingerly pulled back his eyelids with my thumbs and saw noth-ing but white. I thought maybe hypothermia and shock. I squeezed perfect droplets of water into his mouth with a wet rag. Endlessly wiped his damp forehead with leaves. Changed his soiled skivvies. He'd lost a ton of blood. I patched up his shoulder with gauze dressing from my medical kit. When the gauze was saturated red I would change it out. I changed and I changed and I changed. On the third day the bleeding stopped. Just like that. And throughout all this I would talk to Dithers in his fevered state, words of consolation.

"Hang in there," I'd whisper into his ear. "You're in for a little shock, buddy. You've lost your right arm. But you shouldn't worry about it, even though some people are going to think you're a one-armed freak, screw them. Do you know why, my friend? Because that missing arm is a symbol of something very important. It's a symbol of the sickness you left behind when you quit the war." Then I would pause to let all this sink in, before going on. "You don't know yet that you've quit the war. But Dithers, you can rest easy now, buddy. Because all that stuff is behind us now."

When Dithers finally came to, his eyes fluttered, and then they opened very wide as if for good. He smiled. "Hey," he said. "It's good to see you." He reached for my hand and squeezed it. "God, it's good to see you, G.D." Then he asked me where the rest of the team was. "Where are we? Hey," he said, looking around. "You're not going to try and make a move on me now, are you G.D.? G.D.? Hey, what's wrong?" he said with a cocksure grin.

MY DAD'S PROPAGANDA CAMPAIGN, IN THE FORM OF LETTERS SENT TO ME SINCE I'VE BEEN IN THE MIDDLE EAST

Dear Son,
You amuse me. When you say I have dishonored my country, and the uniform I served in, and the proud Tradition of American Warfare, just because I prefer to make love to men rather than women, you drive home my point even further, that the biggest mistake I ever made was putting my dick inside your mother. That was truly a "dishonorable discharge." You are emblematic of everything that is wrong with your pansy, self-conscious, haven't-worked-for-anything and have-no-sense-of-history generation. Let me tell you something about honor. I fought the mighty Vietcong, and here you are in the Persian Gulf war, sitting in the desert, making sand castles. I piss on your war, and it has no more bearing on history than an ant's testicle. I can't wait to see the great stories your generation writes about their war. Oh boy. That's going to be fascinating. What do you know of honor, of sacrifice, of death anyway? And what are you fighting for? Oil. How dignified, how noble, how principled. What is the battle cry over there, "Filler up?"

So I could care less if your team is making fun of you for having a gay dad. I broke dink necks with my bare hands because I could, danced with a dead gook in my arms for an entire night while smashed out on opium. I saw a boy from Georgia keep himself alive by holding his guts in his hands. You tell Marty or Dithers or anyone else from your team that if they were here with me right now, I would bend them over and "break them off something."

Now listen, son, let me give you a piece of advice. It sounds like you are all wound up over there, and that you are focused on all the wrong things. What I recommend is the next time you find yourself in a foxhole with Dithers, you get him to give you a blowjob. I cannot recommend this highly enough, and I think you will instantly recognize the sagacity of my advice. Who else would know best how to give a blowjob but a man? That is my one real regret. When I think back to The Nam, and consider how many lonely nights I spent, I feel the bitter taste in my mouth of lost opportunity. Of dark regret.

As ever,
Dad

ESTABLISHING ALLIANCES, THE FIRST STEP TOWARD THE PROJECTED COALITION

It has not been easy getting used to these chimpanzees. What kind of disgusting creature has a carpet of pubic hair all over its body? A chimpanzee. They are dirty and they stink. I can smell them right now, which is why I tend to stay on this side of the bunker. But they are my friends, or at least they will be soon. I am training them to be my friends.

After setting up shop here, I went ahead and named the chimpanzees, respectively: Ingrid, Ronald, Beverly, Lorraine, and Dennis. Ingrid is gentle, and the first thing she tried to do after that first bit of unpleasantness was pet my cheek. Her favorite song is "Happy Birthday." When you sing "Happy Birthday" she tries to bounce up and down on her head. Ronald likes to make kissing noises and then look around as if he didn't know where they were coming from. Beverly is deaf. It took me a while to figure out she was deaf until finally I snuck up behind her and clapped my hands. Lorraine. Well, Lorraine is the brooding poet type, she just sits around and stares with a superior look on her face. And Dennis is a gigantic male with big biceps. I've seen Dennis amble up and mount each of the other chimps at will, girls and boys. I keep a close eye on him. So you might wonder how I could be sure which are the girl chimps and which are the boys. Well this would tell me that you've never seen a chimpanzee in person before, because a chimp's penis is something that can't be ignored.

It wasn't until later that I put them back in their cages. Of course there wasn't any way for me to know if I was putting them back in their original cages, but I didn't care. A cage is a cage is a cage. And at first the chimps didn't take to the idea, and Dennis and Lorraine tried to gallop down the hall to the bunker hatch, but I've always had a quick first step and even with this bum knee I was able to get the jump on them. In fact, and I don't want to step on anyone's toes here and presume to speak on behalf of the chimps, but I'd be willing to bet that if these chimps could speak English they'd say they prefer this arrangement to the one that they had before. If for no other reason at least they're safe from Dennis now.

I MAKE MY CASE TO DITHERS,
WHO HAS SOME TROUBLE SEEING THE LIGHT,
BUT EVENTUALLY COMES AROUND

The penalty for desertion is the brig. Pure and simple. The Brig's where they can, because it's Military Law, strip you naked and throw you in solitary "think tanks" all in the name of Justice. If you make too much noise they'll break your jaw and then wire it shut. Standard cuisine is bread and water. I met a blind Marine once at the V.A. hospital, a young private who'd spent three months in the brig, he had a white bandage over the top of his head, and apparently a guard had conked him in the nose with a club and those things that hold your eyeballs in place had come detached. "They float every which way now," he said. "Every which way but loose," and then started cracking up. "Because check it out. They're sending me home with a medical discharge as long as I don't make a stink about it. Full benefits."

And because my heart tells me that I don't deserve to spend the rest of my life in the brig, I have now, metaphorically speaking, changed my identity, and so I've renamed myself Help People. Help People's my name because help people is what I do. Every night, following a long yoga session, after getting my mind up into the void, running through the routine of Peaceful Rainbow, Fierce Cricket, Sun Salutation, and then finishing off with Wide Galaxy, I slip out into the night with my medical kit and tend to the wounded Iraqi pilgrims littered along the sides of the highway.

I'm a quick study. And I've learned the Ways of the Desert, so fueled on by the victorious breathing that I feel all the way down to the soles of my feet, when I go out on my nightly forays for the Good of Mankind I'm basically an untouchable phantom. The secret is to move with the land not against it. One night I might filter myself out amongst the stars, and on another I might blend into the billions of grains of sand that line the desert floor. I become and do whatever's needed when I let my heart steer me through the madness. I always wear my NVGs, night vision goggles. I've still got all my gear: rifle, rucksack, e-tool, flak jacket, Gore-Tex, helmet, gasmask, poncho, poncho liner, maps, and of course the most important item of all, my medical kit.

So, when Dithers came out of his coma, lying there holding my hand, and started hammering me with all those questions, I told him the truth. "G.D. is dead," I said. "My name's Help People now, Dithers."

One of his eyebrows arched.

"Help People?!" he said with a half grin, his voice raised.

I tried to figure out what else he needed to know. Then I spoke. "Yes. Help People. And I move with the Ways of the Desert."

His smile grew wider. "Come on man. What are you up to? We've got to get back and blast those Scuds, right? What about the nuclear war?" he said, smiling.

I told him about seeing George Washington. I told him how America had no real culture of its own and how that burrito was a symbol for what we'd done to our downtrodden neighbor, Mexico, how America raped other countries of their cultural artifacts and then filtered them through its sadistic and glamorous lens of ultra-consumerism. "We put everything in neon letters," I said. I told him how America was the home of the gun-toting white supremacists, and that Charlton Heston was really the Grand Wizard of the KKK. The more I talked the more pissed I got. I told him that the Native Americans were living works of art and we'd murdered them, that even the term Native American was an oxymoron. I said, how can we fight for a country where only forty years ago it was no big deal to lynch an African American. My mouth ran on and on. I redressed his shoulder with gauze bandages as I talked, and I watched as the smile slid right off Dithers's face. I could see the wheels churning in his head as I talked. Finally, breathless, I stopped, and the second I stopped talking he spoke right up. What he said popped right out of his mouth as if it had been on the tip of his tongue the entire time.

"So when do we leave here, G.D., and get back to the guys?"

"We're not leaving," I said. "That's the whole point. Haven't you been listening to a word I've said?"

"I could be ready in a couple days," he said, and tentatively stretched one of his legs out. "Of course it's gonna be difficult with this," he said, and nodded to his bandaged shoulder. "But I'm willing to give it a shot." And as he said this his head slowly turned and his eyes met mine and held them.

I think the look on my face said it all. My eyes were stone that burned fire in the middle. I waited for the idiocy of what he'd just said to sink into his head. Finally he turned away and stared at the table with all the papers and books spread over it. I watched his brow furrow. His brain appeared to be chewing something over.

Then his face broke into a smile and he turned to me and said, "Well, it seems like you've been doing a lot of thinking. And I'm glad you're doing what you're doing. Help People, huh? I like that." He glanced at his armless shoulder. "Because let's face it. If it weren't for you I probably wouldn't be alive right now." Then he looked back up at me, the smile widening. "So how about that, Help People? Say. You got any chow around here? What do we eat anyway? I'm starving."

PROPAGANDA LETTER #2

Dear Son,

Everyone's saying Desert Storm looks like a video game on the TV, but from where I'm sitting you couldn't get me to pay a quarter to play it. Hell, I'd rather play Pong—remember how I used to kick your butt at Pong—or pinball. I have one question for you. Is that war as boring to fight as it is to watch on TV? I sure hope not, for your sake. Because too bad for you, you can't just click the remote and flip to another channel. Rob said he wondered if the ratings sink low enough on Desert Storm, they'll yank your prime-time spot and put it on late night with all the infomercials. Have you even got to fire your weapon yet? I heard on NPR where American soldiers in Saudi Arabia had to conserve ammunition over there, so when they practiced drills they had to make sounds that approximated the sounds of rounds being fired. I heard one grunt going, "Bata-tat-tat-tat." What kind of war is that, where you have to pretend to fire your weapon? Shit. There's more killing in the American inner cities everyday then there is in your entire Desert Storm so far. Compton, California, is more dangerous than Kuwait! Maybe if you want to prove your manhood by shooting people, Mr. Bigshot, you should start dealing crack over there, then you might see some action.

Get your head out of your ass and come home, son. Have you ever thought about why you're over there in the first place? Did you know that the American government used to consider Saddam an ally in the fight against the Russians and Iran, and that we funded him and gave him weapons? That we supported him when he pulled a Hitler and gassed the Kurdish town of Halabja in 1988? America beds down with any country that will do its dirty work. American foreign policy amounts to being a slut. Can't you see how the government is playing you for a fool? They're setting you up, son, you've inherited that myth. So don't believe it for a second.

But listen, if you do insist on fighting over there, let me give you another lesson in history. Did you know that almost all the men in Rome were gay, and did you know that the Romans were some of the mightiest warriors who ever walked the face of the earth? The reason for this is the young gay couples in love would be sent out together into the battlefield. This way, when a man took up arms, he wasn't just merely fighting for his empire, or even for his own survival, he was fighting to protect his gay lover, who was right next to him in bat-tle—now that's what I call esprit de corps. And this ingenious mixture of love on the battlefield elicited a fierceness and aggression in the Roman soldier that could not be matched by his enemies. So, if you're still not sure, consider this: Wouldn't you be more inclined to fight to the death if Dithers were by your side, he being the man whom you had made passionate love to the night before? Just wanted to plant that thought in your head.

As Ever,
Dad

DITHERS'S GRATITUDE, AND HIS SENSE OF WONDER AND NAIVETÉ, WHICH SEEMED TO MASK ULTERIOR MOTIVES

At first Dithers was grateful as hell to me for saving his life. And I have to admit it felt nice to be appreciated like that. Of course hiding out in this bunker took some getting used to, for both of us. But we stuck it out together, making do with what we had. It was difficult for both of us, scary even, but we toughed it out together. It's a pretty gruesome scene up there on the highway. Packs of roving dingoes that feed off the dead. Sometimes a car will pass through, weaving around the demolished cars spilled in the lanes, rubbernecking to stop and stare at the accident. And buzzards wheeling in the sky. And that stench is sometimes too much. I have no idea what battle took place up there, but it was definitely huge. Yesterday I stumbled across a busload of civilians, lying on its side, just fully charred, and when I opened the door, I couldn't help it: I puked. I hadn't said anything to Dithers yet, but I was hoping eventually, when he was well enough, that we could start going out on these missions together. Of course that was a ways off.

We had some good talks during that first week or so. I told Dithers more about my recent revelation, and he seemed to listen to me with much interest. I really couldn't have asked for a more attentive audience. Sometimes I'd talk to him as I cleaned the chimp's cages, making sure he watched closely, so that when he was well enough he'd know how to do it. He'd say, "Roger that, Help People," and, "I couldn't have said it any better myself," as he munched on a chicken a la king MRE. Dithers sure had worked up a huge appetite during his time in never-never land. I didn't care though, we had more than enough chow.

But at some point I sensed Dithers wanting to get back to the killing, to the mayhem. I also got the feeling he wanted to go back and see if he could find his other arm. This was just a hunch on my part, and there was no concrete evidence that that's what was on his mind. "You know they can sew these things back on," he'd say, holding his right arm out in front of him. "I'm not complaining or anything. So don't take this the wrong way. But it sure would've been nice if you'd grabbed my arm when you split like that." And then after some really loud bang, one of those explosions that comes every few days where the bunker rattles and little pieces of plaster flake from the ceiling and twirl to the ground, Dithers would raise up off the sleeping mat I'd set up for him and say, "What the heck do you think's going on out there? Huh? What do you think that was, Help People?"

His curiosity seemed to have an ulterior motive. In the mornings when I came back I'd climb down the ladder, flushed from the night's rescues, and almost land on Dithers. He'd be standing right at the base of the steel ladder, staring, I guess, up at the hatch. I knew he couldn't get out. Because whenever I left, I shoved a big boulder on top of the hatch so it couldn't swing open. I also did this to ensure that nobody on the outside would discover the bunker if they happened to be wandering around. It was a perfect, simple system. Then one morning I came back and found that Dithers had rooted through my stuff and found the maps. "Look what I found," he said. I didn't say anything. I figured he was just bored and that he'd lose interest. But then he started spending all his time looking at the maps. Too much time, as far as I was concerned. I'd come in and he'd have the maps spread out on the table, and he'd be making notations on them with his one arm. He'd look up from a map and say, "Now where exactly are we? What are the coordinates, Help People?" I hoped I wasn't being paranoid.

Eventually I had to take the maps away from him. "We're here to celebrate Life," I said, folding up the maps and putting them in my cargo pocket. Then I made a tube with my fingers and held it up to my right eye to indicate the Kaleidoscope of Life. "Who cares where we are."

His eyes glazed over, and he said, "Life, right. Sure. Definitely Life." But I could tell I was losing Dithers. And I knew I was going to have to do something to help him see things my way. I had to make him love his newfound life here, as I did. I knew we needed to get closer, to become friends. That this was going to take some personal investment on my part. You can't just expect someone to care about what matters to you, if he doesn't see that you care about him too.

PROPAGANDA LETTER #3

Dear Son,

I mean what business does America have in the Kuwait? If it's really defending certain ideals, then why don't they go to all the other places in the world where there's oppression? I'll tell you why. Because they don't have oil. The US government is no better and no worse than any other government. The only difference is we've currently got the most original and innovative story in the world to guide our ship by—the Constitution. Throughout history the most successful populations have always been the best storytellers, because they know how to redress reality with a great story that justifies their cruel instincts and desire to survive. Our forefathers, those liars, those storytellers, have given America a way to feel morally justified when we do the same thing as every other country: murder, conquer, breed our population, and generate income and luxury. America the so-called big kingpin for freedom came to this land and murdered the Native Americans who were here before us. America the so-called big kingpin for freedom bought Africans from the Dutch and then kept them in chains. Don't even get me started, the contradictions are too numerous for me to note. But we're not alone in our hypocritical ways, every government is just as guilty, and so it seems like man is doomed the instant he starts to live in organized groups, but in this late stage of history, with overpopulation, man is doomed if he doesn't. That's why I've got Rob. At night, the soft moon outside the window, and with Rob's hard dick in my hand, all the worries of the world just seem to melt away.

As ever,
Dad

MY CAMPAIGN TO RESTORE HONOR
AND HETEROSEXUALITY TO MY DAD

I was subjected to all kinds of humiliation because of my dad. The guys would be like, "Hey, G.D., were you scared when your dad tucked you into bed at night? If he read you a story at night, what was that, like foreplay?" I was deeply ashamed, so much so that I didn't even point out that they were buying into the stupid myths that surrounded gay people, that they were more inclined to be promiscuous, that they were somehow a greater sexual threat to children. It was idiotic, but then so was my dad. Gay people were fine, in theory. But not so fine in reality, if they were your dad, who was your absolute hero. My Dad had dishonored not only his service to our country but mine too. He'd made us a laughingstock. You always assume your dad won't do something to make you the butt of every joke you hear. And I didn't have the will to fight back when the guys ganged up on me, because in a sense, I knew they were right. I wanted to kill my dad for this.

Of course I'd known for a while that after Vietnam my dad had flirted with communism. I'd seen the red flags up in the attic. I knew my dad went though the disillusionment that many Vietnam soldiers felt. Plus my dad had been through some hard stuff. Enter my mom. He'd met my mom in China Beach and he'd fallen in love with her, and brought her back to the States. But things went awry after that, my mom embraced Americana one hundred percent, and starting spending her days in the mall and at beauty salons, much to my dad's distress. They drifted apart and when I look at the pictures of her in Vietnam standing next to a moped in a mini-skirt with no makeup I can't believe it's the same person. And then the day my mom came home from the salon with three inch tape-on leopard-striped fingernails, my dad went through the roof, and started shouting that's why he fell in love with her because she wasn't like the women over here, but she didn't understand. Mom didn't speak English. Finally she took it one step too far and tried to get breast implants on the sly from a doctor she'd seen on a late night paid advertisement on TV, but there was a complication (the doctor claimed afterward that he'd warned her that 36Ds were too much for her little body frame, and then showed us the release forms she'd signed absolving him of any responsibility—the signature was the familiar X), and her heart stopped forever under the weight of all that silicone. I was devastated but because of the language thing we weren't super close. And plus I was only eight when all this happened. I do remember some things though, like how at night she'd hum pretty Vietnamese songs to me in bed and stroke my hair. So yes, my dad had definitely gone through some hard times, but that didn't do squat for my shame.

A couple days before we shipped out for Saudi, I hopped on my motorcycle, a Kawasaki Ninja, and shot up to Raleigh, North

Carolina, to put an end to all this. On the way, my hopeful thoughts muffled inside my helmet, I envisioned myself sitting down at the table and hashing everything out reasonably. I thought maybe if I let my dad know how important he was to me that would help. Maybe the whole gay thing was from low self-esteem, I thought. So I roared into the driveway and barged through the back door and spotted a man with a brown mustache seated at the dining room table, and my dad swept into the room wearing an apron and his customary rope sandals and said, "Son, what a nice surprise. I had no idea. Hey," and he opened his palms toward the mustache man, "ta-da! Here's Rob. You two have heard a lot about each other. Wow. This is a special moment." This was even worse than I thought, my dad was the femme of the relationship.

I've never liked men who wear mustaches. All my life this is something I've felt deeply. It's a gut instinct and you've got to trust those. My fourth-grade gym teacher Mr. Jenkins, who used to come in the locker room and watch us boys change had a mustache. My dad's brother, Uncle Ray, who was always borrowing money for his get-rich-quick schemes had a mustache. Hitler had a mustache. In my experience a man with a mustache is someone who doesn't play fair. And this Rob character was no exception.

Rob stood up and put his arm around my father's waist, drawing him in close, and said, "Nice to meet you. We were just about to have some pancakes. Would you care for some? They're blueberry."

"In your dreams!" I shouted. "Pancakes?! Are you fucking crazy?!" I knew my face was bright red.

"Listen, you," I said, and I took a menacing step toward Rob. Then I told Rob in no uncertain terms that I'd be back tomorrow and that if I found him in my house I'd kick his ass from here to kingdom come. I told him that he was sick, ruining my family like this and that I'd cut off his head and stick it up his ass.

Rob sneered. "Which one is it? Are you going to kick my ass? Or are you going to stick my head up my ass? Because I don't know how my head would fit up my ass if you're busy kicking it."

My dad laughed. "Ha!" I noticed a red barn stitched on the apron he was wearing. There was a girl skipping rope in front of the barn. A friendly cow smiled from behind a wood fence. Then my dad put his hand over Rob's hand, and said, "Take it easy, Robby. I told you he'd be like that. Don't pay attention to him. He's a good boy with a good heart, just a little misdirected." I knew why my dad was laughing, and he knew I knew why he was laughing. My dad was all fun and games until he got mad, and then he was the scariest thing I'd ever seen and there's no question that he could kick the living crap out of me if he wanted to. I couldn't believe it. My dad was taking sides. So I did the most hurtful thing I could do: I announced to my dad that from this day on, I had no dad. I said, "You're dead to me, Mr. Fag-man. I sure hope he's worth it. Because from now on you don't have a son." I instantly saw the hurt in his blue eyes, and even though part of me wanted to run to him and say, "I'm sorry," my principles wouldn't allow it. I stood my ground. He'd always been my hero, and now what he was doing was sick.

That was 107 days ago, and we haven't talked since.

THE CAGES, AND WHY THEY ARE NECESSARY TO INSURE PERSONAL SAFETY AND TO MAINTAIN ORDER

How I got the idea for using the cages was from Dithers. It wasn't Dithers's idea, it was my idea, but it came about because of Dithers. Because when I had to leave him to go out on my nightly missions, I realized he was still too weak to fend off the chimps. After one of my first missions for the Good of Mankind I came back and the chimps had dragged Dithers to the rear of the bunker. They were punching him and jumping up and down on him. He was shouting, "Help People! Help People! Help People!" When I came bounding back there, the first thing I saw was that Ingrid had Dithers's big toe in her mouth. So I put Dithers in one of the cages in the back of the main room. And it worked. I'd return in the mornings and the chimps would be screeching and banging on Dithers's cage with the empty ammo cans that were strewn around on the ground, but they couldn't get in. Then when I appeared at the base of the ladder, the chimps would scatter to the very back of the bunker. Especially since I always came in with a handful of rocks. No chimp likes to be pelted with a rock.

Eventually I just stopped letting Dithers out of the cage. It seemed like I was always coming and going, and it became too much of a hassle to be putting him in there and taking him out again and putting him in there and taking him out again. At first Dithers didn't even seem to mind, he even claimed to see the logic in it, but when his stump was almost fully healed, he started begging me to let him out.

"Look, Help People, I want to stretch my legs. I can keep things clean around here, straighten up. I'll clean the cages. I'm strong again. I can hold down the fort while you're out running your missions for the Good of Mankind. It'll make things easier on you."

"Dithers. To be perfectly honest with you. I've just grown accustomed to you being in there. I mean what if I came back and accidentally mistook you for a chimp and pelted you in the head with a rock?"

"That won't happen. How could that happen. The chimps are in their cages now. So why would you be throwing rocks?"

"Good point," I said.

Finally I relented. I didn't know for sure if I trusted Dithers. He was still acting funny, but my heart told me I had to be big and give him the benefit of the doubt. I truly believe that if you want to make progress, you have to learn to trust people. To take risks and put your faith in them. Plus Dithers did make a lot of sense. He was a lot more useful to me free than he was stuck in that cage. I was sick to death of cleaning those foul cages. And I was rewarded for my trust. Because even though Dithers only had his one arm, it turned out that he was a really good worker. It was like he used his missing arm to his advantage, as an inspiration. He got to where he could do one-armed push-ups. It was pretty damn impressive. It was like he would do something just because he knew technically he wasn't supposed to be able to, with his disability. I respected this quality in him. Dithers even fashioned this little broom out of a board and a stick. He hummed while he swept. One time I heard him humming "Amazing Grace," which is my favorite song now, because of the lyrics. "I once was lost but now I'm found." So I started humming along with Dithers. And he looked up at me and we grinned together.

It warmed my heart. I could feel what I considered to be a real bond beginning to form between the two of us.

*   *   *

A BRIEF SUMMARY OF MY MISSIONS
FOR THE GOOD OF MANKIND SO FAR

I don't mean to pat myself on the back here, but this is what it's all about. Straight up. This is the justification for my very existence. And so I think it's important to keep track of all that I've done for other people. All total, I've administered medical aide to twenty-seven Iraqis, and most of them have been civilians. I put little notches into the wall of the bunker for each person I've helped.

It can be heartbreaking work, and you never know what you're going to find. A little over a week ago I came up over a dune and found a young Iraqi man gasping for air by the side of the highway. He had a nasty sucking chest wound. He had a bushy head of hair and a big nose and a mustache. He had sensitive eyes, and they were bulging, as his head rocked back and forth. When I knelt down over him, I saw all the pores in his face.

He was ugly.

His chest rattled each time he gasped for air and it sounded like somebody shaking a tin can with a rock in it. The lung had already collapsed, so there wasn't much I could do. It was pretty clear he was about to make the journey to the Great Beyond. Through the gaping hole in his chest, you could see his insides. His liver was a shiny white in the moonlight. It didn't seem like he even knew I was there. But I never give up hope, so I pushed down on him, getting him to exhale, and then stretched a piece of plastic over the chest. Then I slicked on the first aid dressing over the plastic. His breathing smoothed out a little, but he also closed his eyes, which wasn't a good sign. Then I held his hand for a moment and whispered, "Go ahead, friend. There's another world out there somewhere. A world where there's no pain. A world where you can be young forever. Hurry, my brother." I shed a quick tear, which twinkled on my cheek in the moonlight, and then let go of his hand and took his rifle and went further on into the darkness.

DITHERS'S REHABILITATION

I knew I had to go out of my way to make sure Dithers enjoyed his life here. And I knew I'd made real progress over the past couple weeks. It got to where we were talking all the time. He'd tell me about his dreams, and I'd tell him what I'd done the night before on my mission. He still wasn't, in my opinion, well enough to leave the bunker, and so of course he was really curious about what it was like up there. I'd tell him about the carnage. The innocent civilians. And he'd say, "That is seriously screwed up. I wonder if those people have any idea how lucky they are that you're around to tend to them." It was a question I'd asked myself plenty of times. I knew we were making real progress if Dithers could see things like that. I thought the day was fast approaching when we could go out together. I looked forward to it, because sometimes those nights got lonely. The fires by the highway burned constantly, and the sight of it all could definitely get a person down.

So I did what I could to speed up Dithers's recovery. And once while Dithers was sweeping up, I said, "Hey Dithers, have you ever tried yoga?" The chimps were fast asleep, and the peaceful atmosphere made me feel generous. Having personally benefited from the extreme results of regular yoga, I was anxious for him to reap the rewards too.

Dithers rolled his eyes. "You mean that stuff that you're always doing. The bending down and the breathing. Tying yourself up in knots stuff."

I chuckled. I hadn't thought to consider what my yoga looked like on the outside. Since for me it was such a spiritual thing. The whole point was to burrow so deep down into my body that I'd forget I even had a body. I know a lot of people say it's about self-realization, connecting the mind, body, and soul, but that's not my take on it. "Yeah," I laughed. "The knot stuff."

Then Dithers nodded his head and stated unequivocally that he hadn't ever done yoga, and that yoga was for fags. I opted to ignore the dig, because I knew he didn't mean it like that, that he wasn't thinking of my dad when he said it, and I asked him if he'd like me to show him some moves.

"Thanks but no thanks. Maybe in my next lifetime, Help People," said Dithers. "You just do your thing. I'll keep cleaning," and he moved into the corner, away from me, energetically whisking the broom around.

I took his response as a yes. "Here," I said, taking the broom from his hand and setting it against the wall, "this'll take just a couple of minutes. You'll thank me for it later, I promise. If you don't like it, you'll never have to do it again."

Dithers got this numb look in his eye, his arm slumped by his side, and he said, "Okay."

I moved in close and put my hand on his hip. I was suddenly conscious that this was the first time we'd touched since I nursed his wound. "Let's try this first," I said. I showed him how to get into position for the Downward Facing Tree pose. "Now envision the roots of your feet slowly growing down into the ground, anchoring you to this spot," I said. I reached down and adjusted the back of his leg, and he laughed. A short, quick, "Ha!"

I looked at him like what the hell was that.

"Sorry," he said. "That just felt kind of funny."

We spent the rest of that afternoon going from pose to pose. I showed him how to flow from one to the next. We got all sweaty. There were some obviously embarrassing moments, like when I told him to raise his hands to the sky, but the mood was light, and he forgave my blunders. It was suddenly late. We were having so much fun I decided to skip my Mission for the Good of Mankind that night, and instead we just hung out in between the yoga stuff, and rapped about things. Dithers told me that his dad was an albino. And an alcoholic. He said, "It was kind of sad. But I think my dad used to drink to try and forget." Then he told me that when his dad started getting rough with his mother, shoving her around and yelling at her, he'd always step in the way and let his dad beat him instead of his mom. I said that I'd always known he had a good heart, and that story was proof positive. There was a moment of silence.

"I've never told anyone that," said Dithers, looking over at me. I turned and saw the steam coming up off him from all the sweat.

"You're all steamy," I said. I looked over at the chimps in their cages. They were staring back at me, patiently, expectantly. Dennis cooed, "Hoo-hoo-ha." I realized I hadn't fed them dinner yet.

"Hey, Help People." Dithers slid over a little closer. "I'm sorry, man."

Everything was very quiet. I was getting this weird vibe I couldn't explain.

"For what?"

"For calling you Gay Dad. That G.D. stuff. Back at the base. For giving you such a hard time about all that. That wasn't cool." He said it was probably his insecurity, because of who his own dad was. I tried to envision Dithers as an albino.

Then I told him, don't worry about it, that my dad was a fucking queer, and that I hated his guts for it. "So don't sweat it," I said. "No biggie. Trust me." Then I rolled away from Dithers and grabbed some MREs and started to feed the chimps their dinner.

PROPAGANDA LETTER #4

Dear Son,

War sure has changed, and frankly I think whatever dignity used to be in it has been bled out of it by the stupid technology. Last night on Nightline they were showing how a little remote-control airplane with a live video feed, an Unmanned Vehicle or something like that, was flying over Saudi Arabia and a bunch of Iraqi soldiers ran up to it waving white flags. The Nightline guy kept saying it was a historic moment in warfare, the first time humans surrendered to a machine. And I was thinking, wow, this is the fourth most powerful army in the world? How do they grade these things, on a bell curve, because I'd sure hate to see the fifth most powerful army in the world. Do you realize that the citizens of Iraq don't even want to be in a war, and that Saddam has forced them into military service, so that when you are killing Iraqi soldiers you are killing innocent people who don't want to be there anyway. I've read in the news that most of the Iraqi soldiers are little boys and old men, what does that tell you? And why is it that our government won't let any journalists in the war theater? Why the censorship? They're denying us the liberty that they claim you're over there defending.

Rob's been asking me a bunch of question about my time in Vietnam, and recently I haven't been able to sleep because all these memories keep flooding back. Sometimes I feel like I'm back in the shit all over again, and I can smell the rice paddies and the water buffalo in the bedroom with me. Rob suggested maybe I was being too hard on you. He said how do you expect your son to understand where you're coming from when you've never even talked about your own war experiences. When Rob said this he was holding my Medal of Honor because he'd asked to see it. I know you think I'm a hero but I want you to know that I'm not. There was nothing heroic about what we did over there. I was a sick young man back then. Sometime I think Nam is the hangover that Bush is trying to cure by a silly victory over there in Iraq. Because you know in the big picture we got our asses kicked over there, right? Don't let anyone tell you different, the NVA and the Vietcong were the toughest and mightiest warriors that America has ever seen. The government tricked us into fighting that war with all their bullshit about the heroics of WWII. They used words like evil and honor and dangled our fathers in front of us so that we wanted to go over there and be heroes too. We walked into a war that had been going on for twenty years before us and got our asses trounced.

And the things I saw. You'd be out on patrol and come up on a mine site, where some gooks had been blown apart. There'd be pieces of bodies strewn everywhere, arms, legs, half a skull, a torso with the ribs poking out, a kneecap, and the thing is I stopped looking, I didn't even care. What happens to a person when he stops caring? You forgot that the Vietnamese were even people. One time I was crawling though this underground tunnel, because we'd been told there was some NVA officers in there. I heard these voices, all this chattering, and I was thinking, hot damn. So I crawled up to the opening where the voices were coming from and chucked a grenade in there and then bam. When I went to inspect the damage you know what it was, it was a room full of women. They had on some kind of religious costumes. They were all dead. I've got a hundred more stories like that. The things you do in war you have to live with for the rest of your life. How am I supposed to live with something like that? You tell me. How am I?
Dad

FINALLY THE DAY CAME FOR DITHERS
TO LEAVE THE BUNKER

Finally the day came for Dithers to leave the bunker. We'd been getting along great for the past couple weeks, and I knew he needed to get his endurance up, if he was going to accompany me on my missions. So

I suggested we go out and play some catch. To help that arm of his get stronger. We exited the bunker and went about thirty clicks off the highway so that we were out of sight.

"Oh my God," said Dithers when he saw the highway from a distance. Plumes of smoke were trailing up off the smoldering cars.

"See," I said. "Can you smell it?" The barbecue smell was especially strong that day. And then we threw a detonated grenade back and forth. It made me feel like a kid again, and we both laughed, especially because Dithers was having to learn how to throw with his left arm. He looked positively goofy.

"Try to get your hips into it," I shouted at Dithers, after retrieving yet another dud throw from the sand. I looked at Dithers and he was grinning. The sunlight was catching in his hair. I decided right then and there that we'd make an effort to get out more. I reared back, signaling to Dithers that I was going to really hum this one.

I played all the sports as a kid, but baseball was my favorite. In Little League I played third base for the FANCY DEATH LIFE INSURANCE BOMBERS. My dad never missed a practice. He'd stand out there in his rope sandals with a couple of the other die-hard parents. And my whole thing was I would pretend as if I didn't know dad was there. I'd make a flying leap to stop the ball and whip it to first like a cannon. I'd skin my hip to a pulp sliding into home. Then when I stepped up to the plate I would blow my arms out trying to knock the ball out of the park. I knew a lot of the kids thought I was jerk. For trying so hard. But I didn't care. This didn't have anything to do with them.

I threw the ball and Dithers dove to catch it, and ended up doing a face plant in the sand. He came up laughing. "Hoo! I don't think I'm going to the big leagues any time soon," he shouted. A breeze picked up and the barbecue smell came up off the highway. I tried not to think about all the rotting corpses out there.

"Here," I said. "Throw me a fly ball. Make me work."

Dithers got to his feet, and then did this little hop-skip, and chucked the grenade way, way up in the air, so that I thought it was going to knock the sun out of the sky.

I remember one game we were getting routed by the fourth inning. Coach moved me from third base to pitcher because he'd used up the other pitchers' eligibility the week before, and because I guess he figured he had nothing to lose. Dad and I always secretly suspected that I'd make a great pitcher, I had a strong arm, and this was my big chance to save the day and show the coach what Dad and I secretly knew: that I should be the starting pitcher. I could almost hear Dad tighten up in the bleachers with excitement as I trotted out to the mound and threw some warm-up pitches. I was really humming them, and I could feel the world smiling at me, claiming me for one of its marvelous creatures. I touched the bill of my cap. I wet the tip of my fingers with my tongue. I blazed a couple more fastballs across the plate for good measure. Then the umpire shouted, "Play ball." And for the rest of that inning, until we had to forfeit, I've never felt more shame in my life. I threw wild ball after wild ball. I walked six batters straight. And when I wasn't throwing wild, the other team was connecting with everything I threw. Even their benchwarmers were getting a piece of me.

I sprinted after Dithers's fly ball and leapt and stretched out, my body soaring parallel to the ground, and there was the smack of the grenade as it landed in my palm. I crashed into the sand, victorious.

"Damn," shouted Dithers. "Awesome."

I stood up and waved the grenade like a trophy. I took a bow.

"I'd give you a standing ovation but," and he nodded at his shoulder, "you know the whole sound-of-one-hand-clapping thing."

My face was flushed, and I felt the thrill of the catch rush through my body. I felt like running into the highway and picking up a tank and throwing it.

"Hey," said Dithers, trotting up to me. "That was really fucking amazing. Did you used to play ball or what?!"

All the blood rushed out of my face. I felt the crushing reality of our situation set back in. I wanted to puke because of that smoky smell. All those dead people. If I ran out into the highway, I'd probably just get run over. I thought about my dad, who was dead to me now. I thought about how it was probably his fault that I was stuck in this mess. Suddenly Rob's mustached face was hovering there in front of me. "Which one is it? Are you going to kick my ass? Or are you going to stick my head up my ass? Because I don't know how my head would fit up my ass if you are busy kicking it." Then I heard my faggot dad's laugh.

"Naw," I said, to Dithers, turning to head back to the bunker. That life was buried and gone. "I never did get to play. I always wanted to, though."

After my humiliating pitching experience, I couldn't stop crying on the drive home. There was a purple can of grape pop in my lap that I hadn't even bothered to open. I was crying because I was so embarrassed that I was crying. Dad had this tight look on his face and he didn't say a word the whole time. I could tell he wasn't upset, he just felt my pain and knew there was nothing he could say to make it better. When we pulled into the driveway and the car came to a stop, he squeezed me on the shoulder and said, "We don't have to try and explain this to your mom. You go in and get washed up. But I don't care what happened out there. I'm proud of you. Do you hear me? You are my son. Don't ever forget that."

THE DAYS BEGAN TO BLUR

The days began to blur, and it got so I couldn't remember life any other way. There were more and more Iraqis on the highway at night, trying to make it back to Baghdad. Some nights I'd tend to as many as three people. My only concern was the MREs. We still had plenty, but between me and Dithers, and the chimps, we'd already run through half the box. Dithers and I fell into a routine of doing yoga together in the evening, right before I'd head out for the night. He was a natural. Sometimes I'd inadvertently come out of the void because I lost my concentration, and I'd look over and Dithers would be crouched down, holding the Half Moon pose, with this very serene look on his face. I have to admit I was a little jealous.

But one time I opened my eyes, and Dithers was standing right in front of me with a big smile on his face. I tried to hide my surprise.

"Dithers," I said. I didn't know what else to say. "Hi."

"Hey," he said. "I want you to show me that one pose you do."

I said I didn't know what he was talking about. He was right up in my face.

"You know the one. Where you lay down like this." He got down on the ground face first. He looked idiotic.

"You mean the Half Locust?" I lay down in the Half Locust.

"Yeah," he said, smiling even wider. So I showed him. I put my arms around him, guiding his limbs into the correct posture. I knelt beside him as he lay there.

"But what about this part here?" He said. "This doesn't feel right," pointing to his hip.

"Looks right to me," I said. I reached down under him and before I knew what was happening, Dithers had adjusted himself so that my hand was cupping his groin area. I got a very strange feeling in my stomach. An odd sensation. His hand came up around my neck and pulled me to him, very hard. It felt aggressive. "Help me, Help People," he murmured, but there was some menace in his voice and my hand was pinned between his groin and the ground. I felt things spinning out of control, and that weird feeling had bloomed so that it was running through my entire body. The closest I could describe it is electricity.

"Help me, Help People," only this time louder, meaner. Like a growl.

I swung my elbow around and clipped his jaw and then leapt to my feet.

"What the fuck," I shouted. The chimps joined in, barring their teeth and hooting.

Dithers looked genuinely surprised to see me on my feet. He was rolling his jaw around. I noticed he had an ammo can in his hand, which he tossed away.

"I'm sorry," he said, getting to his feet. "I don't know what that was. I think it's the stress. Maybe being cooped up down here is starting to get to me. My bad. Okay. I'm sorry. No problema, right?"

I was confused. I didn't want to know what any of this meant. I couldn't quite get my mind around what had just happened, and the confusion turned to anger. I looked at the chimps and wanted to chop their heads off. They started hooting and screeching, as if they could read my thoughts.

I threw the broom at Dithers and said, "Here. This place is a fucking mess."

* * *

A QUICK CLARIFICATION,
BEFORE WE GO ANY FURTHER

No matter what I may be accused of, I am definitely not gay. I want to put that right out there. The closest I have ever come to being gay was in the fourth grade, and that was a long time ago. I mean, to be perfectly honest with you, my fourth grade year was probably the gayest year of my life. That was the year that I spent each recess out on the corner of the playground playing Truth or Dare. And on that fateful day in late spring, Freddie Slacknit produced a carrot he'd smuggled from the cafeteria, and double-dog dared me to stick it up his "pooper." At first I didn't know what to do. The other kids looked at me expectantly, and Freddie already had his pants down around his ankles. I almost walked away. But in the end Freddie had to go to the school nurse to get the carrot out, and by the next day word of what had happened spread through the Parent Majority Coalition. And somehow I was being pegged as "the ringleader." The kids at school started calling me Rabbit Butt. They'd spank themselves and start howling when I walked by. Secret PMC meetings were held. Teenagers from the high school drove by and hummed carrots and lettuce heads at our house. Four months later it was so bad we had to move to a house on the other side of Raleigh, and I transferred schools. That was a long time ago. So obviously I didn't feel compelled to mention any of this to my recruiter when he asked me if I was gay.

PROPAGANDA LETTER #5

Dear Son,
This is going to be hard for me to talk about, but I am doing it for you, so that you recognize how empty the pursuit of killing other human beings is. I hope that by the time you're done reading this you will realize what a hollow word bravery is in the context of war. I wore the craziness of the war like a cheap suit and sealed the lock from the inside so I couldn't get out even when I wanted to. One day we were on patrol, near the town Dak Tho in the province of Quang Mgai. We'd gotten word there might be some NVA in the area, and so we were roving through the banyan trees and bamboo thickets. Suddenly

Charlie caught us in an ambush. My buddy Kitrick falls into a tiger pit. He yelled, "Fuck," and then the light went out of his eyes. We're suddenly taking a lot of fire, and I'm scared and confused. We scrambled for cover, and Gordon got his leg shot to shit. I bent over to check the wound, and Gordon moved and something blew up in my face and I was blind. I hear screams and I know the VC are moving in on us. I wiped my eyes and there was blood on my hands but I could see, and then I ran out into this little clearing and started blasting with my pistol. There were five dinks total, and there was a split second where we all looked at one another and the colors were ultra-vivid and it was if we were on stage and this was the scene we'd all been waiting for, and then the pistol is guiding my hand, jerking it around dropping them out. When I was done I started calling out for our guys to come up but it's quiet. The wind was coming through the banyan trees and it was almost pretty. Everyone dead except for me.

That's how I got my "Medal of Honor." Two more tours and my mind just shut off and I didn't even think about the killing and I wondered about that later. My mind was a blank slate. When I rotated back to the world, I had to pick up a piece of chalk and start writing my new life story on it. I'm sorry to be having to tell you this and for you to know it about me.

I'm not the same person I was back then, son. Read Chomsky.

As ever,
Dad

HOW OUR COVER WAS ALMOST BLOWN

A couple days after that strange yoga incident, I was returning to the bunker when I spotted a lone figure in the distance. A human dot on the landscape. There'd been a lot of Republican Guards in the area recently, making my night missions more difficult. The sun was just starting to dawn, a blood-red symphony of light, playing its chorus of hope over the horizon. I was worried this figure was some Iraqi soldier snooping around the hatch to my bunker. Maybe he'd sat on the boulder and saw the shine of the metal underneath. I didn't know what I'd do if that were the case. Should I sneak up behind the Iraqi and club him with a rock? What would I do with him then, drag him down into the bunker for questioning? But I wouldn't be able to question him because I don't speak Arabic, so then what? Just keep him in the extra cage? What would Dithers think. Plus surely he'd be missed. How long would I keep him in the cage, because it's not as if we had all the food in the world? We were already starting to run out of MREs. And it didn't seem right for me to hurt someone who was sneaking around. But then again, it didn't seem right for me to be discovered and captured. Because who would care for the wounded pilgrims then? So I got down in the sand and speed-crawled up very quietly on the Iraqi in a roundabout fashion, until he was about thirty yards away.

I raised my binoculars to my eyes and I was relieved to see that it was only Dithers. In the binoculars he was suddenly close, and I could see a drop of sweat dangling from the tip of his nose. By now he was walking very fast alongside the highway and kept checking over his shoulder. He was headed north. I wondered if maybe one of the chimps had escaped and he was trying to catch it. I knew Dennis had been acting funny recently. Then a very strange thought came into my mind. I realized that Dithers was not in the underground bunker, which is where he said he would stay, and I realized that if Dithers were in the underground bunker, there was no way Dennis could get out.

I stood up. "Dithers," I called. "What are you doing?"

I guess he couldn't hear me because he didn't turn around. So I called out again.

"Dithers!"

He turned and saw me.

I waved.

Now this is the part that left me stunned and heartbroken. When Dithers saw me he started running in the opposite direction from where I was. I realized right then and there that if Dithers made it back he'd rat me out. All of his previous questions suddenly came flooding back. "What exactly are our coordinates? Is there a landmark you use to know where the underground bunker is? Do you ever get lost?" And there was no way I was going to the brig. My only crime was my compassion. It was easy to catch him. Even with my limp. I tackled him.

PROPAGANDA LETTER #6

Dear Son,

I have a confession to make. I didn't want to tell you this, but Rob encouraged me to come completely clean with you. He said if I was being all high and mighty with you, then I had to lead by example, so I am going to come clean. I want you to know the truth about your mom. Now I know you were never close to your mom, because of the language thing, and because she tragically passed away when you were eight and it's true I often expressed my disappointment in her to you. I shouldn't have done that. And sometimes you may wonder why I stayed with her all that time? Especially if I was so unhappy. The answer is because of the guilt. When I met your mom she was a green-eyed ten-dollar whore in China Beach. My team was on a twenty-four hour R&R. We didn't have any language to share, your mother and I, so we communicated through clumsy, passionate hand signals, under the sheets. And when the weekend was over, your mom stood at the edge of town in a red white and blue straw shawl and waved goodbye to me as our Jeep pulled out, her head full of my empty promises that I passed on to her through a translator. That I would return soon in a giant yacht named O Powerful One to marry her and bring her back with me to America, where we would live in a gold mansion. But as you well know, I did come back for her. And though her life was sad and strange, I am always grateful to her for having given me you. I didn't mean what I said earlier, about you being the worst mistake I ever made. Sometimes I get angry and loose my cool.

As you can probably tell, Rob's a pretty good influence on me and keeps me walking a straight line, and what once started as an ironic gesture, with this protest, which I still stand by, has become very serious and sincere. I think I am in love. Did I mention that Rob isn't circumcised? I'll admit that that freaked me out at first. It looked so silly to me, but now I've grown used to it and sometimes when I look down at my own unit I wish it wasn't circumcised, because Rob says he gets more pleasure that way, and based on the noises he makes I believe him. But all that aside, I'm ashamed of the way you acted when you came over here and started yelling right before you shipped out. Now I realize this can't be easy for you, but you're going to have to trust me on this one. Homophobia is one of the ugliest things on earth, and it stems from ignorance and fear. All I am trying to say is I hope you will give Rob another chance. He's a really good man. And he's got an interesting past, can you believe he grew up in London? And he said he has forgiven you for your rudeness and looks forward to really getting to know you. I know if you would just give him a chance the two of you could maybe become friends. I hope you will consider this while you are over there, and realize that I am finally happy after all these years and that should stand for something. Happiness is not easily come by in this world.

Love,
Dad

DITHERS WAS BACK IN THE CAGE FULL-TIME NOW

Dithers was back in the cage full-time now. And I began to see him for what he truly was, a liar, a conniver, a coward. He started having these mood swings and shouting a lot. "Let me out of here. I won't tell anyone you're here. I promise. I just have to get back to the guys. My mom will be worried about me. Can't you understand what that's like? Please." Then he'd start crying. Other times he'd turn angry and violent. "Help People, I'm going to kill you. Your days are numbered, Help People. See this bare hand?" And here he held up his one arm. "I'm going to kill you with my bare hand."

WRESTLING AS A FORM OF CONNECTION,
AND AS A PREVENTATIVE MEASURE AGAINST
POSSIBLE FUTURE ATTACKS

The only time I let the chimps out of their cages is when we wrestle. This was my idea too. Not Dithers's. I thought it was good for the chimps to have physical contact. Dithers didn't seem to care for the chimps one way or another. He wouldn't even acknowledge they were there. Like he was better than them or something. Lots of times I'd see that they were lonely and go over and talk to the chimps and make funny faces. But not Dithers. And beating a chimpanzee in a wrestling match gave me confidence, and I knew if I could take a chimp then

Dithers wouldn't have a chance against me if he ever did try anything. Dithers's one arm was a trunk, and I'd seen him doing all those push-ups. But you go five rounds with Dennis and a little guy like Dithers becomes a joke. Even with the trunk. That's why I always wrestled the chimps right in front of Dithers's cage, where he couldn't miss any of the action. Every fight is 80 percent intimidation. So I made it my business to psyche Dithers out before he made his move.

A couple days ago, while wrestling with Ronald, I got myself in a pinch. I was crouched down low, circling around with my arms spread kung-fu style, when suddenly I slipped on an ammo can and fell over backward. The bunker has gotten real messy with Dithers in the cage all the time. Ronald leapt on me and started punching me everywhere at once. I was surprised. There'd always been a playful undertone about the wrestling matches but Ronald wasn't holding back. He knocked the wind out of me. He stomped on my bad knee, and I saw a hairy fist in front of my face. Blood came spurting out of my nose. I heard, as if from very far away, the chimpanzees start screeching. Then there was the unmistakable sound of Dithers's cackling. My vision went foggy under Ronald's little concrete fists. Boom boom boom boom boom. I decided I needed to do something fast because this situation was about to turn very bad for me, and then I blacked out.

When I came to I saw Ronald poised with an empty ammo can raised over my head. I quickly slid out from under him and flipped Ronald over on his back and then pinned his shoulders to the ground with my knees. I punched Ronald hard in the face and he went limp. Then I looked up at Dithers and shouted, "You want some of this?! You want some of this?! Come on then! Come and get some, Dithers moth-erfucker!" But as soon as I said it I knew I'd crossed a line and I felt pretty bad about the whole thing, and I tried to apologize to him later.

Beverly's the best wrestler. She's got a headlock that could crush a shark. Chimpanzees are five times stronger than human beings. So when I beat one of the chimpanzees like that, I have to wonder if I'm something better than a human being. Some sort of super human being.

* * *

THE DEBILITATING CONUNDRUM OF FOOD
AS AN ENERGY SOURCE

Despite my impressive defeat over Ronald, this situation with Dithers only got worse over the next couple days. It was highly unpleasant. And it worried me too. Because when I left the underground bunker at night I wondered if Dithers would be able to get out. I always checked the lock on his cage before I left, but you never knew. I wasn't free to be my new self anymore. My identity as Help People was being compromised by Dithers. I didn't understand how he could do this to me considering how I'd saved his life and helped him rehabilitate his arm. And how could I devote myself to giving medical attention to the innocent victims of war when I was worried that this maniac Dithers was going to be there waiting to crush my skull when I came back to the bunker in the morning?

To make matters worse, it was about this time that our food rations started to run out. Even though I'd carefully rationed out our MREs they were dwindling fast, and then one day they were gone. There were no more. I felt bad about this, because I knew how hungry the chimpanzees and Dithers were getting. And that didn't seem fair. But I've always been resourceful, and soon after that I started catching lizards for food. There are these little pink lizards that skate around on the concrete walls of the bunker and disappear in the cracks. The lizards are translucent, and you can see their tiny skeletons under their skin. Their eyes are almost half as big as their bodies and look like Tic-Tacs. About the only thing you can't see is their thoughts.

MY EFFORT TO ELIMINATE ANYTHING
THAT POSED A THREAT TO MY NEWFOUND MISSION

Catching enough lizards to feed two men and five chimpanzees takes a lot of time, and I found that I was sleeping less and less. I tried to catch catnaps here and there. But I was starting to see lizards in my dreams. Then I started to dream that I was a lizard. I would scurry around on all four legs and people would laugh at me because they could see my insides. Until finally I just quit sleeping altogether. I found that I didn't need to sleep. Now I haven't slept in weeks, and it seems strange to me that this was something that I ever did.

INCARCERATION AS A FORM OF REHABILITATION, BECAUSE I REMAINED HOPEFUL AND OPTIMISTIC

And I still didn't know what to do about Dithers, but I hadn't given up hope on him yet. I was confused but optimistic. Sometimes it's hard to make someone see the light. I was crushed because I felt like all my hard work was down the tubes. I tried my best to come up with ways for him to like our new life here. I told him to look inside his heart. I told him I wanted him to be able to come out with me at night on the missions. I was getting tired of witnessing all the atrocities of war alone. I begged and pleaded with him to consider my position in all this. He'd yell at me. But still I didn't give up. I even offered to let him do some yoga with me. I told him I'd let him out of the cage if he wanted to do some yoga. He kept yelling. I told him how he was becoming just like his alcoholic dad. I told him, Don't be that way.

"You're not an albino. You're not an albino," I said.

But Dithers began to show the true darkness in his heart. He was talking all the time. Nonstop. Every time I tried to do some yoga. Shouting at me. Yoga was out of the question, and I started to lose my internal balance. It was a racket. I couldn't think straight. The void was slipping further and further away. It was like garbage can lids banging in my head. Taunting me. Heckling me. Calling me Gay Dad. Gay Dad. I'd come back to the bunker and lie down with my hands over my ears. Gay Dad. Gay Dad. Gay Dad. Gay Dad.

WHAT HAPPENED WHEN THE LIZARDS RAN OUT, AND THE PURSUIT OF ALTERNATIVE ENERGY SOURCES

The lizards ran out. At some point I realized there weren't any lizards left. Dithers saw me scrabbling around for lizards and realized what had happened and started laughing. "Great, what are you going to do now, Gay Dad? I'm hungry!" he shouted. But then Dithers said a curious thing.

He whispered ever so softly, "Eat me."

I turned on him. "What did you just say?"

"Eat me. I'm delicious. I taste good."

That time I knew exactly what I'd heard. I said, "Why did you just tell me to eat you, Dithers?"

He got this funny look on his face.

"Shut the hell up. I didn't say anything. I haven't said a word since you got back. I'm being good for once. What the hell are you talking about?"

But then he followed that up with his whisper again, "Eat me. Eat me. Eat me. I'm yummy. Look at this arm of mine. This arm looks delicious."

I turned and looked at his arm.

"What the hell are you looking at," he said.

"Don't worry yourself about it. No need to play games. I heard you the first time, Dithers."

I went back to scrounging around in my rucksack, but then in an instant I knew exactly what I was going to do. I went to the back of the bunker. The chimps were hissing and screeching. Dithers was shouting. Then I picked up an empty ammo can and started for Dithers's cage.

MY DAD'S FINAL PROPAGANDA LETTER, WHCH I RECEIVED THE DAY BEFORE I SCOOPED UP DITHERS AND QUIT THE WAR

Dear Son,

The idea that I have fathered a son who wants to kill other human beings in the name of his country breaks my heart. I am begging you, please don't do the things I did you will regret them for the rest of your life, I promise you. Man is not made to relish pain in others and it is the sickness of war that propagates this belief, and we have to hold on to what makes us human, and not revert back to the life of animals. I butchered human beings and killing became a pleasure I do not want for you to suffer the black scars on your soul that I have on my mine because of Vietnam please listen to me I am not joking anymore this is the most serious thing I have ever said to you you are my son and don't forget that.

Dad

THE INEVITABLE LIBERATION OF DITHERS

I flung open Dithers's cage and swung the ammo can at his head and missed. The chimps were banging on the slats of their cage and screeching, and in the chaos I closed my eyes and focused and swung again, this time it was different though, this time I swung with the confidence and ease of a man who knows it's going to be a homerun. I opened my eyes. Dithers's cage was empty. In that split second I was shoved from behind and heard the ominous click of the lock as the cage door slammed to. I whirled and crashed into the slats and fell over. Dithers was beaming. For the next half hour as I calmly stared out through the slats while seething with outrage, Dithers went around the bunker packing my ruck with stuff for his journey, informing me as to how he was going to grab Marty and the guys and that they'd be back to beat the living shit out me and then flexcuff me and ship my ass to the brig. "The game's up, Mr. Fucking Asshole Freak. I sure hope you like those bars, cuz you're gonna be seeing a lot more of them from here on out," said Dithers, and then he breezed out of sight, and I heard the hatch swing open and then slam to. A half-hour later I finally jimmied open the lock with a paper clip from my pocket, and sprinted out of the bunker and out into the night, scanning the horizon desperately for Dithers. I searched all up and down the highway for the next several hours until the sun came up, ignoring the wounded Iraqi boy who called out to me as I raced past. But Dithers was gone.

And then today I came back and paced around the bunker, consumed with bitterness and rage and a deep sense of betrayal, but I finally caught my snap and moved past that, realizing that these emotions were of no use to me. I found forgiveness in my heart. I realized that Dithers did what he did not because he's a hateful person, but because he's simply misguided. And, most importantly, I found confirmation that I was a good person. And then tonight, exhausted but with a renewed sense of resolve, I started to go out on my mission for the Good of Mankind, with hardly any of my stuff because Dithers had stolen it all, and I reached for the handle on the hatch but it was stuck. I shook it harder, but it wouldn't budge. Then I heard Marty's snickering voice call out, "Hey, what's going on down there, Help People." A chorus of laughter erupted, and I could tell there was a bunch of them up there. I heard Dithers's distinctive cackle, "Hoo! What's amatter, can't get outta there! Hey, whadya know, there's a boulder up here! Ha-ha!" Then Diaz called out in a low voice that rose as he went on, "Hey, help help. Help me, Help People! Help Help!," and then they all chimed in and were roaring it together, over and over, "Hey, help help. Help me, Help People! Help! Help!"

And it hurts, because they don't know this but I really would, I'd rescue each and every one of them if they needed it. There's no ocean or stretch of land I would not cross to save their lives, and here they are, just fifteen feet away, doing everything they can to keep me from it.

SOUL OF A WHORE

by DENIS JOHNSON

*Act One of a three-act play, written for Campo Santo Theater Company
and Intersection for the Arts as the third part of a trilogy, preceded by*
Hellhound On My Trail *and* Shoppers Carried by Escalators
into the Flames. Soul of a Whore *will receive its world premiere at
Intersection for the Arts in San Francisco in February, 2003.*

Dark stage.

HT's voice [*sings*]: Let the Midnight Special
    Shine a light on you

PINPOINT SPOT lights a sign, overhead left: "SURPLUS STORE."

WOMAN [*O.S.*]: Guys, I need your papers of parole
    And state ID to cash that check, OK?

MAN [*O.S.*]: Dump your whites up there on the second level.
    The second level is where you dump your whites.
    Use the changing room, sir, will you please?

WOMAN [*O.S.*]: Your middle name is printed on that check,
    Then go ahead and spell your whole name out.
    Sign the *back* side: first name, middle name
    If middle name is printed on your check,

And then your last name; *and* I want your writ
Of discharge *or* parole certificate
And your official Texas state ID;
Or else your check will *not* be honored here.

HT's voice [*sings*]: Let the Midnight Special
    Shine a ever-lovin' light on you

LIGHTS UP: Greyhound station in Huntsville, Texas. Plastic pews; standing ashtrays;
    Coke machine; door to Surplus Store; ticket counter; payphone.

CLERK *behind the counter, silent. On the counter a hand-bell. He bangs it when the mood*
    strikes. Sometimes furtively he nips clear liquid from a screw-top canning jar. He's got
    a little radio.

MASHA *talks on the phone. Very brief shiny blue sleeveless dress and big blue platform san*
    dals with white straps. White sunglasses; great big blue-and-white purse.

HT, *a black man: wants the phone; needs change.*

HT [*sings*]: Shine a mothaluving light on you…

MASHA [*on phone*]: I *won't* come *back* till *you* stop *mak*ing me—
    OK! Come on!—you just come zooming up
    To Huntsville like some crazed, spawning salmon:
    I'm on my bus before you hit the highway.
    … I just don't *want* to. Things like that, they aren't—
    Huh-uh, not de*mean*ing, just, it's more—
    Unnatural. I mean, for me. Or, well,
    For anyone. And I'm not even sure
    I really do it, even when it happens,
    I mean in any verifiable… "Uh!"
    "Uh uh uh uh uh uh!"
    Can't you get that worked on, ugly man?
    Can't they drill your head and fix that stutter?
    … Your bank account is real. I realize that.
    I just don't really have the *gift*. I don't.
    There's such a thing as *luck*, you know—like isn't
    Luck what everybody's betting on?
    Wait a minute, got to feed the baby,
    Baby's hungry—[*to HT:*] Sir, it's gonna be
    A little while—OK?—'cause I'm addressing

Certain urgent business—so, could you—?

HT: Man get crazy when his bus don't come.

MASHA [*on phone*]: If you can hear me, I'm depositing—

HT: I just live in Willard, but the bus
  Won't go there. Got to go see Houston first.

MASHA: "You ever get to Houston,
  Boy, you better walk right."

HT: I will. I do. I got no sheet in Houston.

MASHA: It's just a song.

HT: I never been arrested
  Any way or shape or form in Houston.

MASHA: It's just a song. It's just a song.

HT: Lead Belly.
  Sure. I know the song. But I'm just saying.
  —The guys get outa prison yet today?

CLERK: At noon, like always. Bus already left.

HT: Uh-oh. The Houston bus?

CLERK: The Dallas bus.

MASHA [*on phone*]:—No, no! I didn't say the Greyhound station!
  My *cous*in—good ole Cousin *Gus* is coming,
  Not the *bus*. I wouldn't go by Greyhound
  Ever except in abject desperation!

Meanwhile an old woman in black enters from street door.

GRANNY BLACK: Hot! Hot! And while I fry in my own fat
  I hear my dead relations singing in Heaven.
  I ain't a-gonna drive on that highway!
  You don't get *me* behind no chariot wheel!

Ninety miles of carburetors steaming
Like cauldrons in a line from here to Dallas.
Is it carburetors, now? Or radios?
Or what's the things that steams, where you put water?

CLERK: That'd be the radiator.

GRANNY BLACK: Radiator!
Well!—unless you like that funny music,
I guess you'd best not wet your radio.
This is eighteen twenty-five for one
To Dallas. I won't give a penny more.
They like to raise the rates with every breath
They drag, and someone's got to hold the line.

MASHA: ... No! It ain't the money! Money stinks!
I haven't got the gift! I haven't got the power!
Just a minute, let me feed this thing—
{Deals with coins, etc.}
Hello? Hello? Hello? *Hello?* HELLO!
My call is what? Well! You sound sweet as pie!
You sound just like my mother, operator—
I want my dollar ten, or you can kiss
My Rebel ass.—Hung up on by a robot!
... *This* is how the vandalism starts!

CLERK: Now, honey, don't molest my telephone...
[*To HT:*] No. Don't ring the bell. The bell's for me.

HT: Lemme have it all in quarters, please.

CLERK: Try the change machine.

HT: It doesn't work.

MASHA [*offering coins*]: Two bucks for a fistful. Gamble.

HT: Thanks.
You didn't see a guy...

CLERK: A dozen guys.
A couple dozen. Three. The usual—

You know. The Dallas took the most of 'em.
The usual recidivists in transit.

HT: You see a guy, a white guy, maybe looked
A little not so much a criminal?

CLERK: All human beings look like criminals.

HT goes to the phone.

GRANNY BLACK: Hot! Hot! Hear how this poor old woman sizzles!
I pity the crappies and crawdads on account
I feel now what it hurts like to be cooked.

CLERK: It's twenty dollars fifty cents to Dallas.

GRANNY BLACK: Eighteen twenty-five. No more, no less.

CLERK: It doesn't work that way.

GRANNY BLACK: It used to do!
It used to was a twenty-dollar bill
Counted!—once upon a memory.
I'll sit down here and let you ponder that…
I'll let you ponder where the whole world went…

MASHA: I'm not worried if he's after me.
By now he's probly halfway out of Texas,
Blazing a trail for Huntsville, Alabama.

CLERK: Huntsville was named after Huntsville. You knew that.

MASHA: Uh—no. I didn't. But it stands to reason.

CLERK: After the one in Alabama. That's
The explanation for all the confusion, see?

HT [*on phone*]: Hello? It's all—It's jammed. Hello? Completely.
Fine. You busted it. Are you content?

MASHA: I'm just as happy as a clam in shit.

HT: Oh yeah? I think you got that saying wrong.

MASHA: I think you never saw a clam in shit.

HT: When's the Houston come?

CLERK: It comes as scheduled.

HT: Scheduled when?

CLERK: It's not that type of schedule.
It's theoretical. Four a day.

HT: In theory.

CLERK: No, the vehicles themselves are real,
But all the rest is veiled in mystery
Because from here to goodness idiots
Are tearing up the road and moving it
West eleven inches. Traffic's stuck
For hours at a time in all directions:
Miles and miles of stationary drivers
Contemplating this minute adjustment.

HT: Sound like the joint.

CLERK: It kinda does, at that.

HT: You been inside?...

[*HT gets himself a Coke.*]

MASHA: ... He'll hop the barricades.
He'll ride the back roads and the shoulder, then
He'll drive on top of all the other cars.
He will. He's on his way. I get no rest.

HT: Gah-dam, gah-dam, gah-*dam!*

CLERK: Excuse me, sir.

HT: I think it might be eating me *alive*.

CLERK: Crazy folks are not allowed in here.

HT : Crazy folks are *too* allowed in here.
　　　Is this the Greyhound stop in Huntsville, Texas?—
　　　Crazy folks get born and *die* in here.

CLERK: I know you, sir. They call you Hostage-Taker.

HT: Yeah, yeah, it's good to see you, good to see you.
　　　Man, the bus don't come and the bus don't *come*.
　　　Man, I got to get on down the *road*.
　　　Man, this whole block used to jump with gypsy
　　　Hot-shot cabs'll take you there right *now*—
　　　For twenty bucks they're gonna fly to Houston,
　　　Dallas, anyplace on earth—and they
　　　Got *reefer*, they got *beer*, they got te*qui*la—

CLERK: I thought they sprung you couple months ago.

HT : Sooner or later all god's chillun be free.
[*Raises his Coke:*]
　　　"Wardens, jailers, presidents and kings—
　　　They all must bow to calendars and clocks."

CLERK: Then what puts you in Huntsville not a block
　　　From where you did hard time? Guilt? Or nostalgia.
　　　Or some concoction of the two.

HT:　　　　　　　　　　　　　　　　Touché!

CLERK: Touché?

HT:　　　　　　　　Touché! That's what you say! You say
　　　Touché! when someone jabs you with a word.

CLERK: I jabbed you what? I jabbed—

HT:　　　　　　　　　　　　　　　　You see…
　　　You dig… You don't begin your day with things
　　　Like taking hostages on the agenda.
　　　"Things To Do: Do NOT take hostages."
　　　Supposed to be a simple robbery.

You march inside, extend your weapon towards
The frightened people, and receive the money.
PO-lice Do not Come sah-ROUND-ing you!
Megaphones and telephones and shit!
And no one's hurt! And NO ONE GOES TO PRISON...
I'm waiting on a guy. But I can't wait.

CLERK: If you can't wait, I guess you're better off
To don't. So see you later, Hostage-Taker.

MASHA: I thought you said the bus—you live in—where?

HT: I never tell the truth. It's too confusing.
You wanna get a drink? Or take a walk?
Something? Maybe feel the feelings of
The outside world? Fresh air?

MASHA: No thanks, I'm good.

HT: I didn't mean—

MASHA: I know.

HT: I didn't mean—

MASHA: But I'm just comfortable. I'm good right here.

HT exits through Surplus Store.

CLERK: Now, there's a guy got bubbles in his brain...
Well, looky here: The show's not over, folks.

BILL JENKS enters from the Street Door.

MASHA: You are *sucking* on me with your *eyes*...
You're staring like a laser beam.

BILL JENKS: My wife was here
She'd read my mind and kill me on the spot.
... Did I hear someone singing, while ago?

CLERK: Just some bubble-brain with vocal chords.

BJ offers Masha a smoke. She ignores it; finds her own.

BILL JENKS: You hang around the Greyhound all the time?

MASHA: Don't mistake me, hon.

BILL JENKS: For what?

MASHA: For what you think.

BILL JENKS: And what am I thinking?

MASHA: That's for me to know.

She lights his smoke.

BILL JENKS [*smoking*]: I'm ready to believe in God again!

MASHA: Could you, like, hold the revival over there?

BILL JENKS: The gods combust our dreams for sport and suck
    The fumes. Our spirits serve as censers.

MASHA: Shit.
    You dudes are never right when you come out.
    [*Smoking:*] What's a censer?

BILL JENKS: It's the—hell, you know—
    Those things they burn the incense in at Mass?
    Come on, don't kid around—a name like Masha—

MASHA: From where do you know my name?

BILL JENKS: From here.
    I overheard. Your lovely back was turned.
    You breathed your name into the telephone.

MASHA: That was my boss! I didn't breathe a-tall!

BILL JENKS: Masha's Russian. You could be Orthodox:
    They're always swinging censers during Mass.
    I bet you're fond of onions. Overly fond...

I bet your legs get thick when you hit forty.
Your lovely back will get all hunched. You'll get
These cheeks like two crabapples and a nose
Could find employment with the KGB
All by itself.

MASHA: Well ain't you Mr. Stooge,
      'Cause I ain't Russian! I'm from Texas, son.

BILL JENKS: So where'd you get the Masha from? Odessa?

MASHA: Hell if I know. It's my name, is all…
      How long were you in prison for? This time?

BILL JENKS: What makes you think I've been incarcerated?

MASHA: The checkered pants, the Ban-lon shirt, those big
      Enormous shoes, no belt, that stubbly head—
      The outa prison used-up fashion show.

BILL JENKS: They don't have threads like these in prison, doll.
      Except the shoes. And shoes like these are common.

MASHA: You cashed your fifty at the Surplus Store
      And dumped your whites and bought the nearest thing.
      Last week the streets were full of guys with boot-camp
      Hair-cuts sporting stripéd polo shirts
      And almost iridescent green bell-bottoms.
      Pouring rain outside, and here they come,
      This mob of palpitating free men kind of
      Trailing a verdant dribble off their cuffs…
      Their T-shirts shrank right on them while you watched.

BILL JENKS: "Palpitating?" "Verdant?" What a smarty.
      "What's a censer?" What a smarty pants.
      Ain't you a genius. Where'd you go to school?

MASHA: I didn't go. I didn't need to go.

BILL JENKS: You knew it all.

MASHA: Enough to not get busted.

BILL JENKS: But not to not divide infinitives.

MASHA: Fucked-up grammar is not a crime in Texas.

He smokes. Offers one. She ignores it.

BILL JENKS: They cost a buck a piece inside... How much are
  you?

MASHA: I dance. I'm not for sale. I dance.

BILL JENKS: You strip.

MASHA: I'm not exactly a ballerina, no.

BILL JENKS: But you done quit the life. Or so I heard.

MASHA: Heard when? When I was on the telephone?

BILL JENKS: Yeah, and I could smell the putrid karma
  Percolating in the interaction,
  And I say this: Whatever's going on
  With you and him can only improve with distance.

MASHA: I didn't see you around. Just prisoners.

BILL JENKS: One was me. And then I bought the outfit...
  Pack of smokes... and we're not prisoners.
  We're out—How do!—We move among you now.

MASHA: What were you in for? Dealer? Killer?—Rapist.

BILL JENKS: Victim of religious persecution.

MASHA: Jewish, huh?

BILL JENKS: I was irregular.

MASHA: And went to prison for it?—What'd you do,
  Diahrrea all over somebody?

BILL JENKS: My *conduct* was irregular. That is,

With money.

MASHA: Sure. You stuck somebody up.

BILL JENKS: I was convicted of co-mingling funds…
    It means a stick-up with a fountain pen.

MASHA: Do tell. Co-mingling funds. Is that Chinese?

BILL JENKS: Lady, is that the way you play your game?
    Hang around the Greyhound lookin' down,
    Makin' fun of other folks's clothes—
    And Masha is a Russian nickname, Sis.

MASHA: No, it's not. "Sis" is a nickname. Masha's
    What I got at birth. My name is Masha.

BILL JENKS: … *Mar* - sha—!

MASHA: Yeah…

BILL JENKS: Well, I like Masha better.

MASHA: You're not from Texas.

BILL JENKS: No, ma'am. Mississippi.
    But I was mostly raised in California.
    Don't get me wrong, I love you Texas women.

MASHA: When I dance I'm Fey or I'm Yvette
    Or I'm Nicole and then I'm naked.

BILL JENKS: Naked!

MASHA: I start out topless and proceed from there,
    And logic does the rest.

BILL JENKS: I'll bet it does.
    I'll bet it ends up running down the road
    Yodelling and firing off both guns.

MASHA: You're pretty slick with words.

BILL JENKS :   Ain't but a tic.

MASHA: I'll bet your mouth gets you in trouble. Lots.

BILL JENKS : And where would someone fresh from prison go
    To watch you executing logic so
    Ruthlessly and gracefully? To Heaven?
    Or someplace even higher?

MASHA: Try the Texas.

BILL JENKS: The Texas Bar?

MASHA: The Big-As-Texas.

BILL JENKS: … Oh!—
    Sylvester's Big-As-Texas Topless Lounge!
    I guess I wasn't off by very much:
    "Just 50 miles from Houston and right next
    To Paradise on Highway 35."
    How do you get to and from? You got a car?

MASHA: No, but I can always catch a ride.

BILL JENKS: I do believe you can. I guarantee it.
    And what's your next stop? Dallas?

MASHA: I'm not sure.

BILL JENKS: Not sure?

MASHA: I need to pick the proper move.
    It's heads or tails, and devil take the hindmost.

BILL JENKS: Sounds like you better grab the first thang smokin'.

MASHA: The *tips* were big as Texas—then the road
    Got all torn up, and now it's like a tomb,
    And I got Peter Lorre for a boss, who just
    Keeps jacking up the price of doing business.

BILL JENKS: I guess that happens all the time.

MASHA: Huh-uh,
It ain't what you imagine. It's much weirder,
Wilder—*unnatural*—and no, no, no,
It still ain't what you're thinking. It's not sex.
… You mentioned a wife.

BILL JENKS: Oh! yeah. I probly did.
And did I mention that her lawyers mentioned
A divorce?

MASHA: It wasn't really necessary.

BILL JENKS: You turn me on. I think you make me wild.
Smart women get me going. Thus my downfall.

MASHA: Step right up and blame it on a woman…
How long did Texas guard your purity?

BILL JENKS: One and one-sixth years. That's fourteen months.
— And I went in there in a monastic spirit:
I've been voluntarily celibate,
And celibate, God willing, I'll remain.

MASHA: Well, you've been talking like your holy vow
Escaped your mind and pulled your trousers down.

BILL JENKS: Matter of fact it did. Wow. Fourteen months.
… I like the way your heel's a little dirty.
I like the way you point your toes. I like
That silvery sort of robot-colored sort of
Sequined toenail polish.

MASHA: You are sick!

BILL JENKS : Wow. Just the sight of your foot makes me drool.
Your human foot. Wow. Fourteen months locked up.

MASHA: Aren't there any humans with feet in there?

BILL JENKS: Humans? Yeah. Humans too goddamn human:
Misused and violent Negroes, and abused
And violent Texas crackers, and confused

> Bilingual Meskin desperados—also
> Violent—and sweet, retarded boys
> Who can't recall the violence they've done…
> Deranged mulattos, and mestizos scrambled
> In their natural brains…
> Saints and suckers stirring in a stew
> Of HIV and hepatitis-C and walls
> And years. And, yes: I guess they've all got feet.
> But none of them ever dreamed of a foot like yours.

MASHA: You're not a lover, are you… You're a preacher…

BILL JENKS: Fourteen months exactly to the minute,
> The same as Elvis did in *Jailhouse Rock*.
> [*He goes to the counter.*]
> Got me a voucher for the Dallas bus.

CLERK: Dallas'll be along behind the Houston.

BILL JENKS: The Houston bus came not an hour ago.

CLERK: The Dallas end of things is crumbling.
> While Texas undertakes repairs, there's just
> This formless ooze of throbbing vehicles
> From here to there and back that never moves…
> I would love to strafe those motherfuckers…

BILL JENKS: That lady got a pulse?

CLERK: That's Granny Black,
> Mourning her man who died in the electric chair.
> Yeah, she was young and wild. And he was wilder.
> Crazy little gambler with a temper.
> Shot four niggers in a poker game,
> Killed 'em all though he held the winning hand.
> Well, you could get away with shooting one
> Or two along back then around these parts,
> But even colored you can't slaughter by
> The dozens and not expect to meet Joe Byrd.

MASHA: Joe Byrd?

CLERK: The man with the electric chair.

BILL JENKS: The executioner for fifty years
Or something like that.

CLERK: Captain Joseph Byrd—
The guy they named the cemetery after,
    The resting place for prisoners, I mean.
    He executed seven hundred men.

BILL JENKS: Well—not quite seven hundred.

CLERK: It was plenty—
    You want facts and figures, read a book.
    She walks among the graves up there all night.
    Yeah. She's a cheerful, harmless thing in daylight.
    Always dickering on the price to Dallas.
    Never has the price. Just comes to talk
    And settle down and sleep all afternoon.
    Nights you'll spy her drooling on his grave,
    Wailing for the Resurrection, weeping.
    But ain't she sweet and harmless in the daylight?

BILL JENKS: Do you know what? If something moved you to,
    If curiosity prompted you, or pity,
    You could take three hundred steps from your
    Pink chair in those pretty blue shoes and stand
    Exactly in the holy chamber where
    Tonight they'll execute a human being.

MASHA: I read about it. Hey. If guys like you
    Weren't punished, where'd we be? All you
    Deranged and violent mulattos and
    Your numerous other friends. If you
    Were just forgiven, where would we be then?

BILL JENKS: In Heaven. Watching Masha shake her thang...
    Look. In the joint the cereal don't go
    Snap crackle pop. It pewls and moans.
    The dogs don't go bow wow. They say, Achtung!
    They say Jawohl! Sig Heil! et cetera.
    The whistle doesn't blow. It reams your brains.

MASHA: They have a whistle?

CLERK: Lady, they sure do.

BILL JENKS: Every morning, middle of your dreams.
    You maybe did a little stretch?

CLERK: Why, no…

MASHA: I never got your name.

BILL JENKS: Name's Bill. Bill Jenks.

MASHA: You realize your initials are "BJ."

BILL JENKS: It hadn't escaped my attention entirely, no.

MASHA: … So you're a preacher. Or you used to be.

BILL JENKS: I don't look familiar? Not at all?
    Really?

MASHA: I very seldom cruise the links.

BILL JENKS: Don't you watch the TV?

MASHA   I'm the show.

BILL JENKS: It happens I was poorly represented.

MASHA: Legally or journalistically?

BILL JENKS: Both ways. And up and down and back and forth.
    When schism racks a flock, some sheep are torn.
    The shepherd too sometimes. That's show biz, folks.

MASHA: Shepherd or showman?

BILL JENKS: Shaman,
    Shaman of the Children of Jehovah.
    My scheme went wrong. My streetcar hopped the track.
    A woman was the ripple in the rail.

MASHA: Were you a preacher, or an engine driver?

BILL JENKS: I was a shaman, babe, a shaman with a scheme.

MASHA: Shepherd, shaman, engine driver—hey,
    All I know—you just got outa prison.

BILL JENKS: ... *Crimes*... No... *Love*... *Love*... Let me
        make my case...

MASHA: Oh, Jesus Christ!—Love! That's a crazy word.
    Ain't no bigger than a postage stamp,
    But go to pry the corner up, you're peeking
    Upon a continent.

BILL JENKS: OK, OK,
    I rest my case.

MASHA: What case?

BILL JENKS: Hell, *I* don't know.
    If I had courtroom skills, I'd be a judge.
    I wouldn't be no puppy-blind parolee
    Strolling around in pegged and checkered pants.
    At least they fit.

MASHA: At least you think they do.

BILL JENKS: Come on now, Masha, honey, have a heart.

MASHA: Look, I've got a heart, and I've got feeling
      For the luckless, and I've even got two cousins
      Locked up—or one; they let the other loose.
      But I've got troubles too, that's all. Okay?

BILL JENKS: You think I didn't know that? It's the Greyhound.
    This train don't carry no senators' sons.
    ... God. Is it possible... on this day of days?
    ... Okay. It is. I'm sitting here... I'm drowning.
    To think the dropdown blues could ambush you
    The day they pour you from a prison cell,
    First day in years you own your own footsteps,

First day the breezes carry a whiff of choice—
Fifty bucks, your hair growing back,
Your feet up, waiting for the two pm
To Dallas, and drowning. A guy should be ashamed,
You know? Humanity should be ashamed.

MASHA: Because you didn't want to leave them there.

BJ purchases a Coke and sadly raises a toast:

BILL JENKS: Negroes, Meskins, Crackers, and Mulattos—
    "Wardens, jailers, presidents and kings—
    All must bow to calendars and clocks."
    I raise to you one ice-cold Coca-cola...
    Shoot, I drank this stuff inside. Somebody
    Bring me something civilized!—a pale
    Green olive sharing a freezing bath
    Of Gordon's with a solitary molecule
    Of sweet vermouth. I mean I like 'em dry.
    Can I get a Hell Yes?

CLERK: *Hell* yes!

MASHA: *Hell*...

BILL JENKS: Good... Low-erd...

*Meanwhile, JOHN CASSANDRA enters: large, rounded, slouching; somewhat the Biker, but
    shaved and shorn and wearing prison-issue whites and work shoes.*

*He totes a wooden cross taller than himself, his shoulder in the crotch of the crossbeam. This
    burden rolls along on casters fixed to its base.*

MASHA: What—a—blowjob!

JOHN makes his way slowly toward the ticket counter.

BILL JENKS: I think my order has been misconveyed.
    I asked for liquor. Not the crucifixion.
    I seek libation. Not religion. Well,
    Howdoo, Christian?—Or do I assume too much?

MASHA takes a seat and stares in shiny-eyed silence at JOHN.

JOHN [*to CLERK*]: This here's a Dallas voucher, from the Walls.

BILL JENKS: You bought that thing!

JOHN: Bought it or stole it, one.
    ... Keep yours sights!
    In the heights!
    Keep your eyes!
    On the prize!

BILL JENKS: ... I saw that gizmo leaning in a houseyard.
    I didn't inquire was it available—
    Not to imply I'd have availed myself.

JOHN: The sign said For Sale. The man named his price. I paid it.

BILL JENKS: You blew your fifty bucks on Jesus.

JOHN: Yep.

BILL JENKS: On Jesus Christ, the famous savior guy.

JOHN: I didn't blow it on checkered pants and cancer.

BILL JENKS: Now, here's a man resists the cigarettes,
    A man with strength to stand against such things
    As checkered pants and, he'd have us assume,
    The random crimson Ban-lon shirt. But, now:
    While golfing, aren't you known to make a wager?

John: I don't gamble, no. But I'd play golf
    If someone ever thought to ask me to.
    They'd have to show me how it works—you know—
    They'd have to point me down the fairlane.

BILL JENKS: O Holy One: You ever take a drink?

JOHN: Not the alcoholic kind.

BILL JENKS: OK.

JOHN: Or not no more, at least.

BILL JENKS: Uh-oh.
        That Not No More can get to be Right Now
        Right quick the day the let you out of jail.

JOHN: I know. I gotta keep my eyes on Heaven.
        Keep your sights!
        On the heights!
        Keep your eyes!
        On the prize!—

BILL JENKS:—Hey. Martin Luther. What about tattoos?
        What kind you got? Describe us your tattoos.

JOHN: There's not a one. I wouldn't mark my body.

BILL JENKS: Come on. You've gotta have one swastika.
        One Born To Raise Hell. And at least one silly
        Very Dixie-sounding woman's name
        In a vague and fading heart—like Sally,
        Sally June. Or Junie May. Come on,
        What's the name inside your heart?

JOHN: It's Jesus.
        Jesus Christ.

BILL JENKS: O-K.—You want a coke
        Before your bus? Before we nail you up?

JOHN: No, thanks.

MASHA: No, thanks, "BJ."—Now, there's
        A nickname you don't want to take to prison.

CLERK *hands* JOHN *a ticket.*

CLERK: One to Dallas. Be about an hour.

BILL JENKS: Give or take.

JOHN: I see your radio.

Your radio?

CLERK: Well, I'm not hiding it.

JOHN: I was gonna ask to have it on.

CLERK: No sir. Nope. We've got *way* too much static
     Cluttering up the air in here already.
     I'm gonna have to make it policy.

JOHN: Just at the hour? Just to catch the news.
     You could listen—look, I hate to ask—
     And you could tell me what the news is saying.
     They're ruling on my Mom today... My mother.
     Today's her last appeal. She's on Death Row.
     I hate to ask.

CLERK: Also I hate to say:
     We execute great swarms of people here.
     No, we don't fool around down here in Huntsville.
     Try 'em and fry 'em.

BILL JENKS: Boys, don't mess with Texas.

CLERK: This is an appeal.

JOHN: Appeal, that's right.

CLERK: She's already on Death Row.

JOHN: Correct. She is.

CLERK: So she'd be—well, you've got two females
     Waiting on the reaper up in Gatesville,
     And Alice Allenberry's way too young
     To be your mom—so she'd be Bess Cassandra.

JOHN: Correct. That's her.

BILL JENKS: Cassandra! *There's* a name.

CLERK: The one who killed Jane Doe. Known as

"The Jane Doe Killer."

JOHN: Now you're *not* correct.
     You're absolutely *wrong*. That's *false*.
     She's innocent.

CLERK: Like you. Like Mom like son.

JOHN: In one quick life I couldn't do the time
     For even half my sins, for just a small-
     Size portion of the ones that I forget.
     But I've been baptized and, you know—new-minted,
     Thanks to prison preaching. Not my Mom.
     My Mom's not baptized. She's just innocent.
     Her hands are clean. She didn't kill that girl.

CLERK: I'm really not the one to tell. Greyhound
     Doesn't hire clerks to sit in judgment.

JOHN: You think they care who killed that girl?
     She was in for worse stuff than my Mom.
     They needed to close the book on it, they needed
     To stamp it with their imprint, needed to make
     A simple picture for the media,
     And so they put my mother in a frame.

CLERK: Hey, I don't sit here judging. All I know
     Is what the TV wants for me to know,
     Like all Americans everywhere. That girl
     Was sort of innocent, too—I mean, the years
     Of booze and dope had bleached her brain to white,
     To where she couldn't even tell her name.
     She'd woken up in bed with some deceased
     Farmer with the handle of a dagger
     Jutting from his neck—or, I don't know,
     A belly full of buckshot—anyhow,
     The whole bed squishy with his murdered gore
     And this amnesiac harlot rolling in it
     Like a log in a flood. So, you say the crimes
     You can't remember? Well, she did her time
     Without a memory of *anything*. All right,
     There's some folks think she lied, but I'm not one.

She went along through prison never knowing
Did I or didn't I? What's my name? And ever
Will I find the people to call me family,
Will I find the answers to the simplest things?—
And then somebody killed her with a broomstick.
These are the details of a blameless life.
If your mother's blameless, too, another
Innocent heading for the axe—all right:
Now you know what universe you're in.
But I will listen to the radio.

BILL JENKS: For I've been purged with tears! baptized by water!
    Washed in saving blood! and turned out blank
    And white as platinum on a sunny morning—
[*As FIRST BUS DRIVER enters:*]
    Which bus is this?

CLERK: The Magic Bus, I guess,
    Materializing most miraculously.
    Have I got everybody's vouchers here?
    Has everybody got their tickets? Ma'am?
    He's gonna want a ticket. Ma'am?

DRIVER 1:   OK,
    I'm hardly pausing to relieve myself.
    Line 'em up and march 'em on, let's roll.
    Folks, come on, I haven't got till Xmas.
    You wanna get your big old cross aboard?

JOHN: I didn't think you'd take it.

DRIVER 1:   Crosses, stars,
    Hearts-and-arrows, circles, figure 8's—
    It pays, it rides. This ain't no limousine.

BILL JENKS: This ain't no paradise.

MASHA::   This ain't no blowjob!

DRIVER 1: Hey, Patoot. You better curb the lingo.
    'Board for Houston, Texas! Rock and roll!

JOHN: But I don't go to Houston, Mr. Driver.

DRIVER 1: Today you do. The northbound lanes have had it.
    You want the Dallas bus, then be prepared
    To languish. This day, everybody's Houston.
    Yeah—sooner or later, everybody's Houston.
    Git it while you can! Last call for Houston!

He exits.

BILL JENKS: Sooner or later Houston gets us all.

CLERK: Well, sorry—I can't rewrite all y'all:
                Your vouchers say to Dallas And, now, Ma'am.
                I'd like to write you up for Dallas, since
                The fact is otherwise you're loitering.

MASHA: Fact is I know a blowjob when I see one.
    Fact is I'm here to use the phone.

SOUND of bus leaving.

CLERK: There he goes... He didn't waste no time.
    Folks, we're on the bus schedule from Hell.

BJ extends his hand to JOHN.

BILL JENKS: William Jennings Bryant Jenks. The first.

JOHN: That's funny. 'Cause my Dad is named like that.
    Oliver Wendell Homes Cassandra... Yeah.

BILL JENKS: Cassandra. There's a name I've always hated.

JOHN: Also the first. His folks mispelled it, though.

BILL JENKS: Mispelled "the first?"

JOHN: No. "Holmes."

BILL JENKS: Don't call me Holmes.
    This ain't the 'hood.

JOHN: No—They forgot the "L".
          H-O-L-M-E-S. Get it? "Holmes."

BILL JENKS: Don't call me Holmes. I ain't your homey, John.

JOHN: Don't call me John. Aah—

BILL JENKS: Well, then, what's your name?

JOHN: —Shit. It's John. But not like *that*, I mean.
          Just call me John like *John*. Like it's my *name*.

BILL JENKS: I see. And—missing any letters, John?

JOHN: My dad is missing the L in his, is all.

BILL JENKS: "Oliver Wendell Homes Cassandra." Wow.
          I think your family may be known to me.
          You wouldn't have a brother?

JOHN: I'd have two.

BILL JENKS: Would one be Mark?

JOHN: We call him Cass.

BILL JENKS: I had some dealings with a Mark Cassandra
          From California. Actually, I shot him.
          Actually, more than once. I shot him twice.
          Not twice on one occasion—once
          On each of two quite separate occasions.
          Once by mistake—the second time, on purpose.
          Popped him like a Coney Island Clown.

JOHN: I know all about it. He's my brother.

BILL JENKS: Mark Cassandra.

JOHN: Yes, sir. Mark Cassandra.

BILL JENKS: I don't think we're going to be friends.

A SECOND BUS DRIVER enters.

DRIVER 2: Folks, I got as many seats as you got butts
　　　To fill 'em up, but what I lack is time
　　　To mess around and all, so git along,
　　　And all aboard, and off we go, and so on.

JOHN: Sir, can you point me where to put this cross?

DRIVER 2: I don't believe I will. That's not allowed.
　　　The glory train don't carry no religious
　　　Signifying statues of any type,
　　　No banners, emblems, images, or icons,
　　　No crosses, crescents, Hebrew hexagrams,
　　　No Guadalupey Ladies, no Buddhistic
　　　Eight-armed elephants from Hindustan;
　　　None but the uncreated, changeless, true,
　　　Eternal, kind of gray and kind of blue
　　　Dog in flight. I guess you could say pewter.
　　　Pewter is the color of the greyhound…
　　　Houston! Austin! San Antonio!

JOHN: You're going to *Houston*, is it, sir?

BILL JENKS:　　　　　　　　　　　　Far—out.

JOHN: But—what about the bus to Dallas?

DRIVER 2:　　　　　　　　　　　Houston,
　　　Houston Texas! San Antonio!

JOHN: But we just had a man in here announced
　　　That *he* was the Houston bus.

DRIVER 2:　　　　　　　　　Nope. He was Dallas.
　　　A Dallas driver will generally lie.
　　　That's why I stay the heck away from Dallas.
　　　Heck, they killed the President in Dallas.
　　　Houston's the place you need to be.

BILL JENKS: But then, of course, *you* could be lying, too…

DRIVER 2: That's absolutely the case. You're catching on.
　　　Yes. I could be a lying Dallas driver...
　　　Aboard for Houston! If thou dost believe! ...

[*Exits; fading O.S.*]

Ten nine eight seven six five four three two...

SOUND *of bus leaving.*

JOHN: This is total bullshit. Nothing less.

BILL JENKS: If they can mess with you, they mess with you.
　　　That's a fact of nature here in Texas —
　　　I'm speaking as a Mississipian —
　　　But, also: Don't you ask for disrespect
　　　By travelling your way in prison whites?
　　　I speak now as a Mississipian
　　　With nothing but the highest, deepest, fullest
　　　Regard for the West Coast Cassandra clan,
　　　Excluding, naturally, that full-on, rank,
　　　Hellborn, Hellbound slut-soul, your brother Mark,
　　　Who spawned his own self fucking his own mother.

JOHN: That's some rowdy talk! You better hope
　　　The prison preaching holds, and I stay Christian!

BILL JENKS: I'd never've done my time without that kid
　　　Making himself such goshdarn fun to shoot.

JOHN: He dropped the charges.

BILL JENKS:　　　　　　　　　That was good of him —

JOHN: He'd never send a guy to jail. He's just
　　　A crook himself. But, now, revenge —
　　　Revenge is something I'd be counting on.
　　　It's truly amazing he passed up on that;
　　　It's basically miraculous he failed
　　　To hunt you down and gut you like a frog.

BILL JENKS: He did run me to ground—the second time.

That's partly why I let him have another.
The first time was by accident, and then
Instead of letting bygones just be bygones,
Here he comes *again* —

JOHN: To make *amends*.
... That's right. My brother's sober now
About a year and seven months: I'm proud.

BILL JENKS: Amends? Amends?

JOHN: Like in the 12-step Program.
Number Nine, you go and make amends.

BILL JENKS: Alcoholics Anonymous, you mean?
He never said.

JOHN: You didn't let him say.

BILL JENKS: Then let *me* say the little lunatic
Stole near a pound of my cocaine, then *flushed* it.
How was he going to make amends for that?
Hell, it was just a .22. A Derringer.
Shot him in the hand, just like a western.
Just like a good ole T-X Ranger, boy.

They're squaring off—CLERK intervenes —

CLERK: John Cassandra!—well, they cut your hair
And shaved your beard, but I think you're the man
Stood on the roof of a parking ramp in Dallas
Shooting folks and threatening suicide.

JOHN: I didn't shoot nobody.

CLERK: Shooting *at*.

JOHN: In the *direction* where they *were*, let's say —

BILL JENKS: I guess it's fortunate no Kennedies
Happened to be strolling by that day.

CLERK: Just settle down. Just settle down. RIGHT NOW.

JOHN: I'm willing to. I didn't come for this.

CLERK: I can get you back in prison quick!

JOHN: He's the one who's escalating from
    A simple conversation to a riot!
    — Why? Because you want to stop your ears.

BILL JENKS: I what? I what?

JOHN: You want to stop your ears
    And hide your heart from the Holy Spirit's prompting.

BILL JENKS: Come again? Sorry—my ears are stopped —

JOHN: Peruse the facts: You shoot my brother twice,
    He lets you skate, but you get busted later,
    Exactly at the proper time and place
    To land you in the Walls the same as me,
    And get you *out* the same as me, and put you *here*—
    The same as me. Is this coincidence?
    You and I are strangled up together.
    We've got our fates in a knot. And here we stand.
    Guided by the Holy Spirit, here we stand.

BILL JENKS: I ain't the quickest rabbit in the pack,
    I guess the record proves that much, but, God,
    I hope to Christ by now I've learned enough
    To leave that Holy Spirit shit alone.

JOHN: Look. I recognized you. You knew that.
    I recognized your face a year ago,
    My first day on the yard. I watched you stand
    Exactly still, more left-out and alone
    Than any creature there, not halfway in
    Your own skin, more the newcomer
    Than me—but you'd been there two months.
    Never saw a prisoner looked so much
    Like somebody in prison. Every inch
    And ounce of you in bondage. Sure, they had

The background on you, all the Christian bunch,
But nobody could figure out your story —
The famous shaman, healer of multitudes,
Standing in the yard with this, like, music
Coming down around your head, this
Jazz falling apart around you, man…
Look, my mother, I… my mother, sir…

BILL JENKS: There's nothing I can do to help your mother.

MASHA bangs the reciever against the pay-phone unit repeatedly.

MASHA: WHAT! A BUNCH! A MOTHAH! FUCKIN! COCK-
            SUCK!
        GAAAAAAAAH!
{MASHA strikes the machine harder and harder. She doesn't stop.}
        WAAAAAAAAH!! !
[Keeps beating the machine. Sings like Bessie Smith:]
        GIMME A REEFAH
        AND A GANG A GIN
        SLAY ME 'CAUSE I'M IN MY SIN!
[She's berserk, assaulting the phone.]
        YAAAAAAAAAAAAAAH!!

Simultaneously, the CLERK erupts.

CLERK: I have HAD IT HAD IT HAD IT HAD IT, BOY.
        Do you think I'm more than human?
        I've only got two hands!
        I can't take care of everything at once!
        I don't have super strength and X-ray eyes
        To deal with you-all! I'm not Superman!
        I'm not Captain Marvel! I'm not the Hulk!
        To drag myself each morning from sweet dreams
        Into your sleazy Greyhound station nightmare
        Of God-forsaken apparitions with
        Madness and sadness congealing in their eyes
        And sell them TICKETS TICKETS TICKETS TICKETS!
        Look at this!—look at this woman doing
        All a human can to destroy that thing!
        Nothing stands between the realm of sanity
        And total chaos but myself alone!

I'm all alone at the bulwarks of the world!

MASHA: HAAAAAAAH!! GAAAAAAAHHHHHH!!!

MASHA lifts the nearest standing ashtray. She slings it mightily at the payphone.

CLERK stops open-mouthed in mid-tirade. MASHA repeats the action, going at it full tilt.

She busts the device clean off the wall and attacks it on the floor. Her fit worsens. She col lapses, jerking, growling.

OTHERS: Get her off the floor. Put her on a bench.
    Get her lying down.
    Get her sitting up!
    Get something in between her jaws!
    Don't let her bite!

SYLVESTER enters from Street Door…

SYLVESTER [*aside*]: There you are, you little magic thing! …
    STAND ASIDE, PLEASE, DOCTOR COMING THROUGH.
    GIVE WAY, THE DOCTOR'S IN THE HOUSE.
    UH UH UH UH DOCTOR COMING THROUGH.

OTHERS: Thank goodness, Doctor. Hold her! Hold her!
    She is strong!
    Her spit is foaming like a case of rabies!

SYLVESTER: Nothing to alarm ourselves about.

CLERK: It's typical! It's standard stuff! It happens
    All day long in here! It's par for the course!

SYLVESTER: Loosen her uh loosen her uh… clothing.
    I deal with this stuff daily, too—the human
    Body, human physique, the human form…
    Did the patient make any predictions?
    Often this variety of seizure
    Takes them in a way they make predictions —
    No? Perhaps you didn't recognize —
    Uh sometimes they uh sometimes—Have a look
    Now, at the racing form. Anything sound familiar?

Any of those names of horses there?

OTHERS: Missy, can you hear?
Somebody get some water —

SYLVESTER: I don't like uh I don't like to seem
Presumptuous, but I'm in charge here now.
Stand back and let me practice medicine!

BILL JENKS: Where's your bag?

SYLVESTER: My bag?

BILL JENKS: Your bag of tools.

SYLVESTER: My bag? Where am I, eighteen eighty-two?
I'm not a country doctor. I don't drive
A buggy through the daisies. That's a 'Vette
You'll see out there, you care to look, the blue
Corvette, the '98. And I paid cash.
And anyway we don't need implements.
We're not on the brink of surgery here.
A little air, a couple minutes' rest is all.
But I, myself, could use a little shot.
What're we sippin' behind the desk today?
Spare us an ounce or two, my boy, come on,
Don't balk—we understand, and we approve:
Only a natural monstrosity
Uh uh uh uh uh
Or penitential masochist endures
Eight hours in the Greyhound totally sober.

CLERK: I'm in agreement with you there! I quite
Agree!

SYLVESTER: Well—save a drop for company!
Can't have the citizens dispatched along
The routes by a comptroller in a state
A state of uh uh giddy inebri*ation*—
Who knows uh uh *how* things would end up?

CLERK: They'd end up just exactly like they are,

With no one getting anywhere. Go on,
Kill it, sir, it's Everclear—they sell it
Under the counter over in the smoke
Emporium-cum-tattoo parlor. Cheers.
They say it won't betray you with an odor,
But what they don't say is it sets your breath
More or less on fire, also your mind,
And it ain't cheap, either—that's a myth,
One more myth of the Confederacy…
Seems like she's calmer—

JOHN: Honey, just lay back.

SYLVESTER: Entranced and uncommunicative…

MASHA: LEMME DO THE HULA FOR YOU, BABY.

SYLVESTER: … She's fainted.

JOHN: Doctor, why is her *voice* like that —

SYLVESTER: She's coming out of the physical part of it now.
     We're entering the most important phase,
     The crucial phase, the psychological —
     Some say psychic—phase, when certain
     Uh uh uh most curious behaviors uh
     Will tend to manifest themselves.
     I mentioned this. Predictions, uh uh uh
     Prognostications, uh uh *sooth*saying—

BILL JENKS: Soothsaying? Buddy, what the hell is *sooth*?

SYLVESTER: We'll see a period of trance-like, "twilight
     Semi-consciousness" we uh uh uh
     Physicians like to call it, during which
     —Does anybody have a racing form?
     —I happen to have a racing form myself!
     —I'm going to whisper names and races so
     Our patient hears them in her twilight state
     And then I think you'll uh uh be *intrigued* —
     Intrigued, I say—all right, we've got the fifth
     At Manor Downs. A lovely uh uh uh —

Outside of Austin there. They'll go the mile.
THE FIFTH AT MANOR DOWNS. THE FIFTH. "Luke's Luck."
"Blue Streak," "Destroyer," "Dark Delight," "Shazam."

MASHA: IDIOT OF AGES!

SYLVESTER: "Idiot —"
    Uh, no, the Six: "Shazam." "Shazam," in fact,
    Is Six, and number Five is actually —

MASHA: IDIOT IDIOT IDIOT! THIS ONE HEALS!

SYLVESTER: Settle down and pick me out a winner —

JOHN: This is William Jennings Bryant Jenks...

SYLVESTER: Jenks! The Shameful Shaman! Travelling?
    I do enjoy a Greyhound trip myself.
    It's magical. You get to *see* the country.

BILL JENKS: Who are you?

SYLVESTER: I asked you first.

BILL JENKS: I didn't hear you ask.

MASHA: SYLVESTER...

BILL JENKS: Oh! Sylvester! —

SYLVESTER: Uuh uh uh —

BILL JENKS: Sylvester's Big-As-Texas Topless Lounge!

SYLVESTER: Back off!—*Who is it now addresses me?*

MASHA: YOU KNOW ME.

SYLVESTER: *Give me now predictions three.*

MASHA: NOTHING FOR YOU.

SYLVESTER: Nothing? Uh. Huh. Huh —

MASHA: YOU'VE LET HER GO, YOU FOOL. SHE'S FOUND THE
               HEALER.

SYLVESTER: This guy? uh uh uh—this guy's a fraud.
               Predictions three...

MASHA: GET RID OF HIM.

SYLVESTER: *Give me now predictions three.*

MASHA: GET RID OF HIM, OR I ABIDE IN SILENCE.

SYLVESTER: Aw, come on, demon! Gimme couple *races*!
     Look at the odds on uh uh "Dark Destroyer!"
     ... We're getting nothing here. [*To BJ:*] You'll have to leave.
     Now, please. You'll have to uh uh uh to leave —

BILL JENKS: Sucker, I been trying to leave all day.
               You put me on a bus, I'll disappear.

JOHN: This is a *demon*, brother! You can *heal* her.

SYLVESTER: You are jinxin' my routine! Now blow!

GRANNY BLACK *wakes*.

GRANNY BLACK: Hot! Hot! Why do they say it's air-conditioned?
     Who do they think is the idiot around here?
     I believe it's worse this June than last.
     I feel the climate changing—global warming!
     Whatever happened to global cooling? Remember
     When it was global cooling to worry about?

BILL JENKS: I wish I could nap as sound as you, young lady.

CLERK: Go grubbing on a grave all night;
     Gnaw the dirt above a killer's corpse
     While Huntsville lies in bed. Next day you'll nap.

GRANNY BLACK: I never grubbed on a grave! You slander me!

I think you're addled by the heat!
I think you're positively shatterpated!

MASHA: ARLENE.

GRANNY BLACK: Lonnie?

MASHA: ARLENE.

GRANNY BLACK: Is it...? *Lonnie...*

MASHA: I'LL SEE YOU TONIGHT.

GRANNY BLACK: Lonnie...,

MASHA: SLEEP, SLEEP, ARLENE. I'LL SEE YOU TONIGHT.

GRANNY BLACK: All right, Lonnie. Yes, my love...

SYLVESTER: My Lord.
    I've never seen her do like that. Uh... Uh...

BILL JENKS: DEMON!... DEMON!... DEMON! NAME
    YOURSELF!

MASHA: IN WHOSE NAME DO YOU CAST ME OUT, HEALER?

SYLVESTER: That's a damn good question. Who exactly
    Asked you to the party, anyway?
    In whose name do you cast out demons?

BILL JENKS: I cast out demons in my own damn name.

JOHN: That ain't gonna work.

BILL JENKS: You'll watch it work!

SYLVESTER: Now uh uh this disturbed young gal and I
    Have got a sort of system up and running,
    And your insertion of uh uh yourself
    Is absolutely unacceptable.

BILL JENKS: NAME YOURSELF!

SYLVESTER: JACKHAMMER!

BILL JENKS: … What?
    I beg your pardon? Demon name yourself?

SYLVESTER: JACKHAMMER JAKE! I BATTER THIS MAN'S THROAT.

SYLVESTER *howls and shakes.*

BILL JENKS: To tell the truth, I wasn't expecting this.
    Hold him down, John.—Don't let go of *her*!—
    Pry them jaws. Wider… Jackhammer Jake!

BJ spits on his finger and touches it to SYLVESTER'S *tongue.*

SYLVESTER: Uh uh uh uh uh uh uh uh

BILL JENKS: Jackhammer Jake!
    Unloose the string on this man's tongue! Begone!
[SYLVESTER *calms.*]
    … Now tell me, what did Peter Piper pick?

SYLVESTER: He picked your nose, you meddling piss, and I'd
    Pay money to see him shove it up your hole…
    Peter Piper picked a peck of pickled
    Rubber baby buggy bumpers—wow.
    This Mumble-Stumb's red-dogged my vocalize
    From minute one. I had full-on, obscene
    Tourette's till mama whipped it out of me.
    But let's just stop this tent-revival here —
    Before you get me past the point of cure
    And on into the tongues and rattle-snakes.
    You gotcher cookies. Come, girl, let's go home.

BILL JENKS: DEMON! NAME YOURSELF! *NOW*!

MASHA: "DARK DELIGHT."
    "DARK DELIGHT" AT MANOR DOWNS. FIFTH RACE!

SYLVESTER: One down! All right, now, where's my sheet—

Back off now. Give her room. Give me my sheet!
I've lost my light—Don't you turn the lights on?

CLERK: Once in a while. But I never like what I see.

BILL JENKS: Let me do my work.

SYLVESTER: I need that demon!

MASHA quakes at BJ's approach.

JOHN: You can't expel a demon in the name
Of nothing but yourself—it's blasphemy.

BILL JENKS: Just let me take a whack at it. You'll see.

JOHN: It's blasphemy. The Bible's clear on that.
Mark says, "In *my* name cast out devils."

BILL JENKS: Your good ole brother Mark?

JOHN: Come on!

BILL JENKS: All right, I will. I'll call on old JC…
Jesus Christ, they crucified you, huh?
Holy Jesus, they crucified you good.
Jesus Christ, they threw you in the pit
And fed you meals of Spam and Wonderbread…
But the crucifiers never ride the Greyhound.
Jesus Christ…
[*He falls to his knees*]
                              It's Bill Jenks, fresh from prison.
Been out half a day, and my report
Says, Lord, it's still the world they killed you in.
Says, Lord, the world is desperate and mean.
Lord, come on now, turn an ear to me.
Your Catholic priests are pederastic homos.
Your preachers are sluts. They clutch your Book
In one hand green from moneybags and poke
Your Word with fingers reasty from young cunts.
The sonsabitches crucify
Occasionally a savior while revering

Prophets their fathers lynched. The motherfuckers
Live unchallenged, prosper, die unpunished.
God, I hate them. Jesus hated them, too.
Don't dispute me—Jesus Christ reviled them.
He saw who held the hammer and the nails.
He recognized who would and wouldn't hurt him,
And so he palled around with dwarfs and whores,
People everybody hated—tax collectors,
Lepers, urchins, strangers, widows, dummies…
Come on now, Jesus, turn an ear to me.
Jesus Christ, I am a criminal.
I am a tax collector, whore, and midget:
You have nothing to fear from the likes of me,
And nobody else in here is gonna hurt you,
For the crucifiers never ride the Greyhound.
Jesus Christ, I beg you for the power.
I beg you for the power and cry… DEMON!
[*He lays hands on* MASHA; *she writhes and screams.*]
     DEMON, I BANISH YOU TO—

MASHA: HEAR ME, HEALER!
    … SPARE ME BANISHMENT TO THE PIT OF HELL,
    BUT LEAVE ME TO THE WORLD OF THINGS AND MEN,
    AND I WILL GRANT YOU PROPHECIES THREE.

SYLVESTER: YOU WHORE!

BILL JENKS: What became of Prophecies "One" and "Two?"
    I think I saw "Prophecy One." But they just called it
    "Prophecy—"

JOHN: Something good will come of this!

SYLVESTER: Masha—demon—buddy—talk to me —

MASHA: ONLY SPARE ME THE PIT, AND I WILL FLEE.
    SPARE ME THE PIT, AND I WILL PROPHECY…

BILL JENKS: … OK, I'll take the deal. No pit of Hell.

MASHA: HAND ON THE CROSS.

BILL JENKS: Hand on the cross. No pit.
    Prophecy away, and walk the world
    As long as men and things inhabit here.

SYLVESTER: He's got my damn predictions! I'm a pauper!

MASHA: HEAR ME, WILLIAM JENNINGS BRYANT JENKS:
    I PROPHECY THAT YOU SHALL MEET YOUR MIRROR.
    I PROPHECY THAT YOU SHALL RAISE THE DEAD.
    I PROPHECY ONE MORE: THAT LIKE ALL MEN
    WILLIAM JENNINGS BRYANT JENKS SHALL DIE,
    AND ON HIS DEATH AN INNOCENT SHALL BE KILLED.
[*BJ lays his hands on* MASHA.]
    I FLEE! ...

JOHN: ... She's limp. That thing is gone.

SYLVESTER: Three predictions? That's your total score?
    Three predictions worth exactly zero?
    ... Son of a bitch. She could've made you wealthy
    Ten times over. What a rube you are.
[*A SIREN; pulsing red and blue light that continues until BLACKOUT.*)
    Here comes the ambulance to the whore-hospital.

BILL JENKS: I shall meet my mirror? I keep clear
    Of mirrors. I don't like their face.
    I guarantee I'll never raise the dead.
    And naturally I'll die. But all the rest
    Is nonsense. Let me see your racing form.
    Maybe she's just handicapping horses.

CLERK [*holding radio*]: Hey there—John Cassandra—on the news:
    They set your mother's date an hour ago.
    Isabel Cassandra: Death by poison!

JOHN wails.

Lights narrow: GRANNY, *the cross, the sign: SURPLUS STORE.*

HT sings as he enters from Surplus Store.

HT: If you ever get to Houston

Boy you better walk right
You better not gamble
And you better not fight

… What's all the fuss? Where'd everybody go?

GRANNY *wakes to see HT standing before the cross.*

GRANNY BLACK: Whose ghost are you? Which one? Which
　　murdered angel?

HT: Do I look like a ghost? I'm not a ghost.
　　(Am I ghost?… I don't remember dying…)

GRANNY BLACK: Harold Thomas Watson! I see you!
　　I feel your fangs sinking into my soul!
　　I didn't tell him to! Nobody told him!
　　Demons sent and fetched him, slapped him, rocked him —
　　Everybody knew he'd kill somebody.
　　I'm the one he should have killed—he loved me!
　　I'm the one he should have killed—I loved him!
　　I swear I'm leaving town. I'm bound for Dallas.
　　I won't be here among your children nor
　　Your children's children on the Huntsville streets—
　　They'll never have to look at me again!
　　Leave this poor old woman to the black
　　And miserable damnation love has earned her.

Her wailing blends with ambulance's SIREN.

BLACKOUT

TALKING FICTION:
WHAT IS RUSSIAN *SKAZ*?

by VAL VINOKUROV

WHEN WE THINK of Russian literature, what come to mind are serious and meaty, long and sober novels. I want to showcase a possible counter-tradition: *skaz*, the Russian term for "speakerly texts" written in a voice that is markedly other—less literate, more oral, quirky and colloquial—than that of the author. The development of skaz (and its non-Russian kin across other national literatures) is linked with the rise of the modern age, a response to modernity's tendency to view "Language" as written language, and spoken language as ethnographic fodder or worse. Skaz tales are not the stylized "transcripts" common in pre-industrial literature; dutifully modernist, they are about transcription itself, about writing paying attention to its poor (though often more vibrant) spoken cousin. And unlike the great Russian novels, the classics of Russian skaz tend to be short, electric, funny, and even fun.

Is skaz a literary movement? "The Russian Novel" evokes a distinct tradition, and the history of Russian literature is full of -isms (Symbolism, Futurism, Acmeism, Socialist Realism, Conceptualism) vying for public attention. It is difficult to say the same thing about Russian skaz. Although a cluster of important literary theorists have argued about the significance and the characteristics of skaz, it is not as if the dozen major writers who used it hung out in cafés, polishing each other's manifestos. Skaz writers include "Realists" such as Gogol and Leskov, "Ornamentalists" such as Babel and Zoshchenko, and post-Soviet feminists such as Liudmilla Petrushevskaya. And yet, from the earliest skaz of the 1830's to its heyday in the 1920's, these writers have been bound by an affection for "low-class" speech, for voice, and for merriment (even in the midst of moral darkness). We are not dealing with an avowed movement but with a stylistically coherent skill, a certain narrative modality that behaves like a genre.

The word *skaz* in Russian is a root—one finds it in *rasskaz* (story), *rasskazat'* (to tell), *rasskazyvat'* (to relate), *skazat'* (to say) and *skazka* (fairy tale). Originally, skaz was a kind of folkloristic catchall term, a bin for narratives that didn't quite fit the requirements of a specific oral genre. In its appealing and evocative vagueness, the word was soon stolen by such writers as Nikolai Leskov, who titled his best-known piece "The Skaz About Cross-Eyed Lefty from Tula and the Steal Flea" (1881). Thus skaz fiction—for all its oral connotations—is not speech. It is writing par excellence—writing based on an artificial (literary) reinterpretation of real (unliterary) speech patterns. The mere notion of skaz readjusts and clarifies our idea of prose fiction.

Gogol's Ukrainian Tales of the 1830's are probably the earliest and clearest examples of this genre. In "How Ivan Ivanovich Quarreled with Ivan Nikiforovich," Gogol's narrator displays the form's basic qualities: dialect, improper narrative emphasis, misplaced assumptions, and an energetic style of storytelling that turns the reader into a listener. Here, for example, is the opening paragraph:

> You have got to see Ivan Ivanovich's glorious fur jacket! It's absolutely fantastic! The fleece, oh what fleece! God, I can't stand it! Dove gray and frosty white! I'll bet you all the beer in China you can't find me somebody who's got anything like it! Take a look at it, for God's sake, especially if he's standing around talking to someone, look at it from the side: eat it up! You can't even describe it: velvet! silver! fire! Oh good God! Oh Holy Nicholas the Wonder-Worker, why haven't I got a jacket like that! He made the thing way back before Agafya Fedoseevna went off to Kiev. You know Agafya Fedoseevna, right? The same one who bit off the assessor's ear?
>
> *{trans. Vinokurov}*

Although English-language readers may not have ever heard of skaz, they may find Gogol's style at least somewhat familiar. Sholom Aleichem's Tevye, Mark Twain's Huck, I.B. Singer's Gimpel, Anthony Burgess's Alex, Sapphire's Precious: any reader of nineteenth- and twentieth-century literature knows something about the use of sub-literary narrative masks. (Such writers as Patrick Chamoiseau, Irvine Welsh and Jonathan Safran Foer also come to mind.) What is less known is the fact that this high ventriloquism has illustrious Russian literary and critical origins, a history that begins with Gogol and includes Isaac Babel and that drew the attention of the big guns of Russian criticism (Bakhtin, Eikhenbaum, Tynyanov), who saw skaz as a breath of fresh literary air—irreverent, linguistically striking and original. Simply put, skaz is where writing loathes itself and, by this self-loathing, renews itself.

Gogol is perhaps the founder of literary—as opposed to folkloristic—skaz, because his narrative mask is parodic and not just romantically ethnographic. He is not trying to accurately replicate the authentic speech patterns of a marginal group, but instead using these speech patterns for his own literary ends. Gogol wrote at a time when Russian culture was struggling to create its own prose forms (not to mention its own political forms, as the failed Decembrist uprising of 1825 attests), and his "Ukrainian Tales" reflect this embryonic chaos. These early stories capitalized on the vogue for regionalism—for the manners of the "little Russians"—among Petersburg's literary aristocrats, and they made their author justly famous. Gogol's experiments with skaz personae led him to one of his best-known narrators: Poprishchin in "The Diary of a Madman." While Poprishchin's Russian is proper, his progressive insanity—and especially his uncanny ability to read and transcribe the correspondence of certain well-placed lapdogs named Fidèle and Medji—evokes the idiosyncrasy of skaz: "Dogs are smart folk, they know all the political relations."

It is, however, with Nikolai Leskov that 19th-century skaz reaches its apogee. Leskov's literary career began after the emancipation of the serfs in 1861, a period during which aristocratic intellectuals were quick to idealize the Russian peasant. Leskov, whose own origins were mixed and provincial, wanted to present a truer and more vivid depiction of the rural and small-town life he had encountered than was found in most fiction of his day. Lacking confidence in his ability to write long realist novels, Leskov instead took advantage of his remarkable talent for verbal and narrative ingenuity. His work is full of the brilliant malapropisms that characterize skaz, as we see when his protagonist, Lefty, explains the mating customs of his native province:

> In our country, when a man wants to reveal a circumstantial intention with regard to a girl, he sends over a conversational woman, and when she has made a preposition, they politely go to the house together and look over the girl without concealment, and in front of all the relationships. {trans. William Edgerton}

In Leskov's world a microscope is a "tinyscope," and someone might receive the gift of an "alarmed clock" and may be promised a "roundy-view" with a local girl. Leskov's virtuosity came to be appreciated shortly after his death by modernists who were looking for new linguistic and narrative forms.

Politically, Leskov was neither a radical nor a reactionary; and the polarized literary establishment of the day did not reward such non-conformism. And yet much of the subtlety and power of his skaz stories comes from his post-ideological, pragmatic ambivalence. Leskov found Russia and her people fascinating and dear, as well as exasperating and repulsive. The narrator of "Lefty," the tale included here, channels these feelings in a way that only skaz makes possible. The narrator is an uneducated provincial, a conservative type who has little patience for anything foreign, much less for liberal intellectualism—and his language reflects this felicitous impatience. In the his rustic simplicity, the narrator respects homegrown authority (the Church and the Czar); his respect may be clumsy and hilarious, but it is nominally sincere. But in the end, things end badly for his hero Lefty, the clever gunsmith from Tula, and the story concludes with an estranged indictment of the wanton cruelty and injustice of official society, indeed of "the Russian way of doing things," an indictment made all the more powerful in its respectful naiveté.

Isaac Babel's skaz tends to have a very different moral orientation. There are a handful of skaz stories included in *Red Cavalry*, Babel's semi-autobiographical collection of tales about his season with Budyenny's horsemen in their failed campaign to capture Poland for the newborn Soviet Union. Babel was a short, chubby, near-sighted, humanist Jewish intellectual; his quixotic decision to ride with the Red Cossacks (under the exceedingly Russian *nom de guerre* of Kirill Liutov, literally Cyril Savage) was akin to a lamb attaching itself to a pack of wolves. And for the most part, the skaz voices in *Red Cavalry* belong to the people of the sword: Babel's comrades, the "wild beasts with principles," as he called them in his 1920 Diary. This strategy is an interesting choice, because Babel could have just as easily used his keen ear to create dialect narratives in the voices of war-ravaged Polish Jews or Catholics. Although the latter voices are heard within the stories told by Liutov, they never generate their own full-fledged skaz tales. Only the Cossacks, and typically the more brutal ones among them, are showcased as skaz narrators in *Red Cavalry*. And their stories tend to be hilarious, lyrical, casually gruesome, and morally obtuse— the "gangsta rap" of early Soviet literature.

Babel's Cossacks sound like peasants who have just been given a new linguistic implement—Communist newspeak. One tale, "Salt," takes the form of a letter to the editor of The Red Cavalryman (a broadsheet that happened to employ Babel) by Nikita Balmashev, "Soldier of the Revolution." "Dear Comrade Editor," the missive begins. "I would like to write to you about the unsensing women who are up to no good for our cause.... I am only going to write about what my eyes have seen with their own hands." Balmashev goes on to describe his murder of a defenseless woman for her brazen and "counterrevolutionary" act of salt smuggling. And yet, in the course of the letter, Balmashev seems to borrow the lyricism so typical of Liutov's prose:

> And the nice little night pitched its tent. And in that tent there were star-lanterns. And the men remembered the Kuban night and the green Kuban star. And a tune flew up like a bird. While the wheels clattered and clattered... Time passed, and when the night changed its guard and the red drummers welcomed the dawn on their red drums,... I got up from my resting place where sleep had run off like a wolf from a pack of nasty hounds.
>
> *{trans. Vinokurov}*

By lending Balmashev such eloquence, Babel implicates his own aestheticism in this depraved skaz tale. It is as though the author, while entertaining and educating his reader, also wants to draw attention to the ethical perils of oral performance, namely the desire to shock at the expense of good taste and kindness. For all of its campfire warmth, the pre-literate community is by no means necessarily kinder than the educated establishment.

Babel's Ukrainian-born friend and contemporary Mikhail Zoshchenko (1895-1958) was the writer whose name was synonymous with 20th-century Russian skaz—a true master of the form and among its key practitioners. Zoshchenko came to prominence in the mass circulation satirical press of the 1920's, and was more popular with the Russian public than were many of his peers, such as Pasternak, Babel, Akhmatova and Solzhenitsyn, who were better-known than he in the West. (His selected works, published, shortly after his death, in 1959 and 1960, sold 300,000 copies; and according to one estimate, Zoshchenko sold a total of 100 million books and satirical pamphlets during the 1920's and '30's, when he was still tolerated by the Kremlin.) Like Babel's skaz, Zoshchenko's depicts the linguistic collision between the new Soviet regime and its half-comprehending subjects. But where Babel's skaz narrators are brutal Cossacks, Zoshchenko's hero is typically a hapless schmuck—the object of both mockery and sympathy—earnestly coping with the absurdities of post-Revolutionary Russia. In a plot that anticipates "Seinfeld" by many decades, the narrator of "A Lousy Custom" (1924) offers up his testimonial on behalf of the campaign to eradicate tipping in the new Communist economy. I offer my translation of this brief sketch in its entirety:

> Last February, I got sick, fellas.
>
> I set myself up in the city hospital. And so there I was in the city hospital, see, getting better and taking it easy. It was all peace and quiet, a land of milk and honey. So clean and orderly, you almost felt bad creasing the bed. If you want to spit, there's a spittoon. Want to sit, there's a chair, but if you needed to blow your nose, then do it on your sleeve and God forbid not on the sheets. That's definitely not protocol, as they say.
>
> Anyway, you get used to it.
>
> And it's hard not to get used to it. They put so much care into everything, treat you so nice, that you couldn't dream up any better. Just imagine, some scabby little man is lying over there, and they come along with his lunch, make his bed, and put a thermometer

under his arm, shove an enema into him with their own hands, and even take an interest in his health.

And who is it that takes an interest? Important, forward-thinking people – physicians, doctors, sisters of mercy, and of course Ivan Ivanovich, the medical orderly.

And I felt such gratitude for all the personnel that I decided to express this gratitude materially.

They can't all get something, I thought, I'm not going to go that far. I'll give it to one of them. But who? I started watching them real close.

And I saw that it had to be none other than the medical orderly, Ivan Ivanovich. I could see that the man was a prominent and impressive figure who really put more effort into his job than anyone else, he was practically bursting out of his skin.

Fine, I'll give it to him. So then I had to come up with a way to slip him a little something without showing disrespect and possibly getting my face redecorated.

The right moment was soon presented.

The orderly comes up to my bed. He says hello.

"Hello," he says, "how are we feeling? Have we had a stool this morning?"

Right, I says to myself, now's my chance.

"What do you mean, sure we had a stool," I says, "but some other patient took it. But if you'd like to sit down for a minute, you can park it at the foot of my bed and we can chat.

So the orderly sits down on my bed, and so there he is, sitting there.

"Well then," I says to him, "what's doing, what's in the papers, how's the pay around here?"

"The pay here," he says, "it's not so great, but your more civilized patients, even if they're on their last legs, still manage to slip a contribution."

"Allow me," I says, "though I'm not on my last legs, I don't object to making a contribution. In fact, I've been thinking about it for a while now."

I take out the money and give it to him. And he accepted it so graciously, he even made a little curtsy with his arm.

The next day is when it all started.

I was lying there all nice and quiet, and no one had ever bothered me before, when suddenly Ivan Ivanovich went completely off his rocker because of my material thanks. He must've run over to my bed ten or fifteen times in one day. First he's straightening my pillow, then he's dragging me off for a bath, now he's offering to stick me with an enema. He drove me nuts just with the thermometer, the damn bastard. Before, he'd give me the thermometer once a day, twice max, that was it. But now it was more like fifteen times. Before, the bath used to be chilly and I liked it that way, but now he boils you alive even if you scream like the devil.

I couldn't take it anymore. I gave him more money, the asshole— just leave me alone, for God's sake. But this just bent him over backwards and he went at it even harder.

A week goes by and I realize that I won't survive this much longer.

I had sweated off fifteen pounds, I was all skinny and couldn't eat.

But there's the orderly, still trying his best.

One time he nearly cooked me in a tub of boiling water, the moron. Swear to God, the bastard made the bath so hot it popped a corn on my foot and the skin came off.

I says to him:

"What do you think you're doing, you damn jerk, boiling people like potatoes? You'll get no more material thanks from this corner!"

So then he says:

"Oh yeah? Who needs you! You can go ahead and croak, and don't count on the help of trained scientific professionals."

And he went away.

So now everything's back to normal, like before: they take my temperature once a day, I get an enema only when necessary. The bath is nice and cool again, and nobody bothers me.

It's not for nothing, this campaign going on against tipping. It's no joke, fellas, believe you me!

{trans. Vinokurov}

Zoshchenko was able to get away with his irreverent take on Soviet reality because his skaz stories ostensibly mock the petty-bourgeois sensibilities—selfishness, small-mindedness, ignorance—that Communist society was meant to reform and overcome. This was the ideological space that permitted satire in a brave new world that was otherwise officially beyond reproach. (Of course, the story above—full of exaggerated praise for municipal hospitals and their cold baths— also gently pokes fun at the regime's efforts to create this new world.)

Though he did briefly fight with the Red Army (if only out of a distaste for the more reactionary elements among the Whites), Zoshchenko was not a Party member—an ambiguous status that would eventually spell death or oblivion for any popular Soviet writer as Stalin's purges got into full swing. In a personal manifesto, Zoshchenko describes his "ideology" in the same sneaky, colloquial manner that characterize many of his stories: "I don't hate anybody—that's my precise ideology.... Well, in their general swing the Bolsheviks are closer to me than anybody else. And so I'm willing to bolshevik around with them... But I'm not a Communist (or rather, not a Marxist), and I think I never will be." Still, Zoshchenko's satirical skaz was sincere in its desire to evoke a new kind of vibrant and aesthetically compelling, working-class literary voice. In an article published in 1927, he claimed that he was a "temporary substitute" who was "parodying the sort of imaginary but genuine proletarian writer who might exist in the present-day environment." An incredible formula—Zoshchenko's narrator is "imaginary but geniune," a "temporary substitute" for someone who might already exist! Such ambiguity perfectly captures the spirit of skaz. This form of parody was tolerated until 1946, when Zhdanov, the Party's culture pitbull, passed a Resolution attacking Zoshchenko as an "unprincipled literary hoodlum." The same strikingly-worded document also condemned Anna Akhmatova as "half-whore, half-nun"—maybe its author knew something about being a literary hoodlum himself. Zoshchenko's personal history, like that of many other comic figures, was less than sunny: he had been gassed as a soldier in World War I and as a result suffered chronic pain and depression for the rest of his life; and Zhdanov's pronouncement cast him into a kind of public twilight and private heartbreak that lasted until his death in 1958.

Years later, as Soviet Russia began to disintegrate, Liudmilla Petrushevskaya used skaz to comment on the peculiar uncertainties and hardships of the 1980's and 1990's. Anna, the narrator of Petrushevskaya's novella *The Time: Night* runs a dysfunctional matriarchy out of her cramped Moscow apartment. While her journal—full of abuse, contradictory rants, awful poetry, and painfully funny tales of poverty, poor judgment and bad luck—is itself a form of skaz, it also includes the torrid diary (with running commentary) of Anna's congenitally pregnant daughter Alyona. Petrushevskaya's work shows that skaz fiction is alive and well on its native soil.

Skaz tends to flower when a culture and its literary language are especially unstable and undergoing change—although this may be an odd thing to note, since it's difficult to say for certain when any culture or literary language is truly stable. Still, an oral narrative mask sometimes provides a clever (and politically ambivalent) cover for experimentation and for portraying social distortions. Skaz perhaps also offers an immediate means of depicting a contemporary reality that is changing too quickly to be easily fixed by a more detached and analytical voice. The five writers mentioned here represent four different periods of historical and literary instability in Russia: the cultural chaos of the post-Decembrist 1830's (Gogol), the post-emancipation period of the 1880's (Leskov), the post-Revolutionary 1920's (Babel and Zoshchenko), and the post-Soviet 1990's (Petrushevskaya). Of the five, Gogol and Babel are the best known outside Russia, although the stories mentioned here are less familiar than "The Overcoat" and "The Story of My Dovecote." Leskov and Zoshchenko have received much less attention outside of Russia, precisely because the bulk of their work is skaz and because it has often been difficult to convey its charms in translation. Petrushevskaya is a contemporary writer whose work transcends the cold postmodern conceptualism that currently predominates in Russian literature, which is still pre-occupied with mocking any cultural artifact that was respected during Soviet times—including the 19th-century novel. Indeed, few classic works have escaped the taint of oppressive times. Sometimes it seems that Russian postmodernists view the very practice of story-telling as a little more than a tool with which "the authorities" encourage proper sentiments among the public. Given this climate, it is little wonder that so few voices from the post-Soviet literary scene (apart from the justifiably ubiquitous Victor Pelevin) have been translated into English. Perhaps a bit of international attention to Russia's still-vibrant skaz tradition might adjust our sense of this often inaccessible new generation.

For years, scholars of Russian culture have been predicting the internationalization of skaz as a literary term. But despite everything this term has going for it, such predictions have had limited success. Perhaps this has something to do with the fact that skaz and any attempts at translating skaz have unforgiving margins of error. Folksiness is not enough. Nor are ethnographic curiosity and linguistic playfulness. These qualities must be justified by a higher concern: what makes a skaz story good fiction? The very artificial nature of the genre makes skaz all the more vital. In good skaz, the reader perceives the subtlety of the relation of the author to the narrator—a relation characterized by an ambivalent blend of mockery, sympathy, and envy. And it is this mixture that places the classics of Russian skaz—in all their entertaining depth—among the root texts of modern world literature.

Though the form which Russians call skaz is familiar to English-language readers, we have not accepted it as a coherent concept, and that's unfortunate. This critical incoherence has resulted in the persistence of a wretched debate, in some quarters, about literature and "authenticity"—a quarrel fed by multiculturalism and its counter-spasms. In one camp lie those who insist on writing "what you know" in a voice that you know, and in the other are those for whom literature is a fabulous realm of research and narrative make-believe where a white man can write like a geisha. Of course, many otherwise intelligent people are actually in both camps, since the very terms of this debate are unproductive, simplistic, confusing and deceptive. At what point does "research" become "knowledge"? And how is anyone supposed to determine when "authentic" subjectivity is, in fact, objectively false? The very idea of skaz fiction, on the other hand, affirms that literature strives for both truth and artifice, and that the balance between them is a delicate mix of ethical and aesthetic considerations. When someone cannot fake authenticity, that is an aesthetic failure; and when one fakes it for transparently unappealing reasons, that is a moral failure. Having skaz around as a term—much in the same way we refer to "magical realism" or "stream-of-consciousness"—will help English-language writers and readers think more elegantly about all these issues that have infused a variety of awkward quibbles about voice, dialect, and authenticity.

SALT

by ISAAC BABEL

FROM *RED CAVALRY*
(TRANSLATED BY VAL VINOKUROV)

"DEAR COMRADE EDITOR. I want to write to you about some unsensing women who are up to no good for our cause. I put my hopes in you, that you who's traveled around our nation's fronts, which you have taken due note of, have not overlooked the far-flung station of Fastov, that lies a million thousand leagues away, in a such and such a district in a distant land, I was there of course, drank home-brewed beer, only wet my whiskers not my lips. There's a lot you can write regarding this aforementioned station, but as they say in our humble abode — you can shovel all you want, but the master's crap heap will still be there in the morning. That's why I am only going to write about what my eyes seen with their own hands.

It was a quiet glorious little night seven days ago, when our well-deserved Red Cavalry transport train stopped there, loaded with fighters. All of us were burning to promote the common cause and were headed to Berdichev. Only thing is, we notice that our train can't manage to get a move on, our Gavrilka can't seem to get rolling, and the fighters became all doubtful and asking each other, "Why we stopping here now?" And indeed, the stop turned out to be a huge deal in terms of the common cause, on account of the peddlers, those nasty villains among whom there was a countless force of the female sex, who were carrying on in an obnoxious manner with the railroad authorities.

Recklessly they grabbed the handrails, the nasty villains, they scampered over the metal roofs, frolicked, made trouble, and in each hand they were dragging contraband salt, up to five poods per sack. But the triumph of peddlerist capital did not last long. The initiative of the fighters who crept out of the train made it possible for the dishonored authority of the railroad personnel to breathe easy. Only those of the female sex with their bags of salt remained on the premises. Taking pity, the fighters let some of the women inside the heated cars, but others they didn't. That's how in our own railroad car of the 2nd Platoon two girls cropped up, and then after the first bell here comes this impressive woman with a baby and says:

"Let me in, my gentle Cossack lads, the whole war I've been suffering at these train stations with a baby at my breast and now I just want to go and meet my husband, but because of the railroads you can't get anywhere these days, don't I deserve a bit of help from you, my Cossack lads?"

"As a matter of fact, woman," I say to her, "whatever the platoon agrees, that will be your fate." And, turning to the platoon, I prove to them that here is a woman who wishes travel to meet her husband at an appointed place and that she in fact does have a child in her possession and so what's the decision then—should we let her in or not?

"Let her in," the boys yell. "Once we're done, she won't be wanting her husband no more...."

"No," I say to the boys rather politely, "I beg your pardon, platoon, but I am surprised to hear such horse talk. Recall, platoon, your old lives and how you too were once babes in your mothers' arms, and so it seems to me that it won't do to talk that way...."

And the Cossacks, having talked it through among themselves, started saying how persuasive our Balmashev was, and so they let the woman onto the rail car, and she climbs aboard with gratitude. And every last one of them, each one swearing by the truth of my words, tumble all over each other to make room for her, saying:

"Please sit down, woman, and be sweet to your baby the way mothers are, no one will touch you in that corner, and you will arrive untouched to your husband, just as you wish, and we depend on your conscience to raise a change of guard for us, because what's old gets old and it looks like youth is in short supply. We've seen our share of grief, woman, both when we got drafted and then later in the extra service, we were crushed by hunger and burned by cold. But you, good woman, please sit here and don't worry about a thing...."

The third bell rang and the train shoved off. And the nice little night pitched its tent. And in that tent there were star-lanterns. And the men remembered the Kuban night and the green Kuban star. And a tune flew up like a bird. While the wheels clattered and clattered...

Time passed, and when the night changed its guard and the red drummers welcomed the dawn on their red drums, then the Cossacks came up to me, seeing I was sitting there sleepless and not pleased in the least.

"Balmashev," the Cossacks say to me, "why are you so displeased and sitting sleepless?"

"I beg your most gracious pardon, fellow fighters, and I do apologize, but if I could just speak a few words with this citizen here...."

And quivering head to toe, I got up from my resting place where sleep had run off like a wolf from a pack of nasty hounds, and I walk up to her and take the baby out of her arms and rip off his diapers and rags, and in the diapers I see a nice fat forty-pound bag of salt.

"Well here's an *inter*-resting kind of kid, comrades, it don't ask for titty and it don't wet your lap and it don't bother people when they sleep...."

"Forgive me, gentle Cossacks," the woman cut into our conversation rather cold-bloodily, "wasn't me that tricked you, it was my troubles."

"Balmashev will forgive your troubles for you," I tell the woman. "That doesn't cost Balmashev much, Balmashev sells the goods for same price he paid for them. But address yourself to the Cossacks, woman, the Cossacks who elevated you as a hard-working mother of the republic. Address yourself to these two girls who are crying at present for having suffered under us through last night. Address yourself to our wives on the wheat fields of the Kuban, who are wearing out their womanly strength without their husbands, and to the husbands, who are lonely too and who are wickedly forced against their will to have their way with the girls crossing their path... But you they didn't touch, even though, as a matter of fact, that's all you're good for. Address yourself to Russia, crushed by pain...."

And she says to me:

"I've lost my salt as it is, so I'm not afraid of dishing out a bit of truth. Don't give me that about saving Russia, it's those yids Lenin and Trotsky that you're saving...."

This conversation isn't about yids, you despicable citizen. The yids don't enter into it. And by the way, I don't know about Lenin, but Trotsky is the dashing son of the Governor of Tambov, who turned his back on where he came from and joined the working class. Like prisoners sentenced to hard labor, they're dragging us out, Lenin and Trotsky are, to the free road of life, while you, foul citizen, are a worse counterrevolutionary than that White general waving his sharpest saber at us from his thousand-ruble horse. At least him you can see, that general there, from every road, and the working man has only one little dream – to cut him up. But you, dishonest citizen, with your *inter*-resting kids who don't ask for bread and don't catch cold, you we can't see, just like a flea, and so you chew on us, you chew and chew...

And I frankly do admit that I threw that citizen off the moving train and derailed her, but she, hefty as she was, sat up, shook out her skirts and went on her nasty way. And seeing this unharmed woman, with all Russia around her suffering untold and the peasant fields without an ear of grain, and the girls all dishonored, and the comrades, many of whom go to the front and few of whom return, I wanted to jump off the train and finish her off or die trying. But the Cossacks took pity on me and said:

"Just use the rifle."

So I took the trusty rifle down from the wall and washed that disgrace from the face of the working land and the republic.

And we, the fighters of the Second Platoon, swear before you, dear Comrade Editor, and before all of you, dear comrades of the editorial office, that we will deal mercilessly with all the traitors who are dragging us into the ditch and want to turn back the stream and cover Russia with corpses and dead grass.

In the name of all the fighters of the Second Platoon—Nikita Balmashev, Soldier of the Revolution."

The Complete Works of Isaac Babel, edited by Nathalie Babel, translated by Peter Constantine, with an introduction by Cynthia Ozick (Norton 2001), is available in stores and online.

A LONG BLOODLESS CUT

by DOUG DORST

IT IS PAST MIDNIGHT. The kid is tired after a long day of marching and slashing through undergrowth and dodging ambushes, but he has been forbidden to sleep. He would like to swim in the cool ocean, but he has been forbidden to swim or dip or even wade. Nor may he remove his boots to wrinkle his burning toes in the spent waves that bubble over the sand. He has been forbidden even to sit. He has strict orders, from the general himself. He must stand and guard Sergio's head.

The kid does not understand why the head must be guarded. Who would want it? It is a dead thing, caked in blood, with a sour, meaty stink that the ocean breeze cannot carry away. Flies buzz dizzily around it, then alight and prowl its terrain.

The head rests in the dry sand, well above the tide's reach. The kid nudges it with his boot, rolls it face-down. He finds its weight disconcerting. He tamps it solidly so it will not roll back. The flies settle upon the head again as soon as he takes his foot away.

The kid looks out to the ocean. He reaches into the pocket of his worn canvas pants and with a finger traces the scalloped edge of the photograph of Alvaro's *novia*. He smiles; the photograph now belongs to him. He does not take it out to admire it because the night is dark, moonless. And even if he could see the image, he cannot afford to be caught with his attention on anything but the head. Still, the image of the woman blazes in his mind, feels like something rare and vital. He has been running through forests with the rebels since his voice was high and thin; he has never tasted a secret kiss in the shadow of a giant yucca, or peeled off a blouse steeped in cool floral sweat after a climb up the volcano, or raised a skirt in the salty dark under the wharf.

He touches himself through a hole in his pocket and is pleased to encounter his own warmth. He handles himself tenderly, with slow, deliberate strokes of his thumb and forefinger, keeping his arm still so that anyone watching him will see only a soldier attentively performing his duty. In the water, creatures phosphoresce, wink.

Farther up the beach, Alvaro lies open-eyed on his plastic tarp, which crinkles beneath him as he rolls over and back, over and back. He cannot sleep. His feet are covered in sores and blisters and fungus. The sand fleas are biting. The saraguate monkeys are howling in the forest. Most of all, he is angry about the photograph. He is unaccustomed to losing. He is a gambler who leaves little to chance.

Earlier that evening, after the general had given the order and Alvaro had swung his bolo knife on a group-chanted ten-count, all the men had clustered around the two pieces of Sergio. They watched the blood winding through the sand toward the ocean. They placed bets on how far the blood would run.

He knows he should not have risked the photograph, but he could not resist. The other men had guessed so badly, planting their sticks high up on the beach, not understanding how much blood there is in a man. By betting the photograph, Alvaro forced them all to search their packs and pockets for things of greater value, and the stakes tripled. Then he calculated the coagulation time, the slope of the beach, the absorbency of the black volcanic sand, even the speed of the wind off the ocean, and he drove in his stick at the water's edge.

He should have won. Something was wrong with Sergio's blood.

The kid took away quite a haul: dozens of cigars, a pocket watch, a kilogram of foot powder, many grenades and bananas, a pewter crucifix, a necklace of polished monkey teeth, and the photograph. The kid! So young he can hardly keep his hands off himself! Alvaro knows he must retrieve the photograph soon. It is only a matter of time before the kid soils it.

Around him, a hundred dark lumps on plastic tarps taunt him with their snoring.

In his tent, the general drinks. He can afford to be giddy, even though ammunition is scarce and trench foot has taken its toll. His power has grown immeasurably since he eliminated Sergio. It will grow even more when he delivers the head to his enemy, the Queen. He imagines catapulting it over the castle walls into the garden while the Queen is entertaining guests. He laughs as he imagines a startled servant spilling a tray of canapés into her royal lap.

The general holds out his flask so he can see his reflection in the polished steel, angles it back and forth, regards himself up and down. Though his belly lolls over the waistband of his shorts, though wiry black hairs sprout from his shoulders and knuckles and ears, though he suffers innumerable tics and twitches, though his nose is but a cone of tin secured by leather straps, he knows that the men all recognize him as a commander of the highest caliber.

He takes a final drink, emptying the flask. He unbuckles his nose and places it in the leather case that also holds his teakwood chessmen. He stretches out and closes his eyes and fine-tunes his battle plan for when they reach the capital: if they surprise the Queen, a swift fianchetto akin to the Catalan Opening; if not, a frontal thrust he likens to the Falkbeer Counter Gambit. He imagines the Queen at his feet, defeated. He takes his stiffening cock in his hand and begins to pump furiously. Most nights, it is the only way he can fall asleep.

In the photograph, the woman is knee-deep in the ocean, caught in a posture of surprise as a cold wave slaps against her bottom. Her back is arched and her eyes are wide, thin brows raised high. Her elbows are tight against her sides, and her hands are at her face in a girlish half-clench. Her lips are puckered in a tiny perfect O. Splashes of sea foam blur in the air around her. Her swimsuit reveals more thigh than the kid has ever seen. Her nipples jut, pressing against taut fabric. The photograph is sepia-toned, and she is the color of honey.

Nothing in the picture shows scale. No swimmers, no birds, no trawlers or tankers or banana boats, just a blurred horizon, dimly streaked light and dark. The kid wonders if she is taller than he is. He must meet her. He believes he will, someday, believes that she will receive him, that his possession of the photograph connects them in some way they both will honor, if not fully understand. Such mysteries, he believes, are the very workings of love.

There is a curved shadow of a finger creeping in from the left border. The kid imagines the finger is his own, that he is the one who snapped the picture. He imagines he can feel the cold water winding around his calves, tickling and numbing. He imagines a softly tugging undertow.

Alvaro, fully cocooned in his tarp, feels another sand flea bite his ear. He is being eaten alive. He unrolls himself and dances in the sand, a furious chorea of swatting and scratching. A man lying nearby sleepily calls out *shut up!* and Alvaro tromps toward him and steps on his neck. The man sputters; his legs wheel, his arms flail, his fingers clutch. Alvaro leans harder, feels his bare sole grinding against cartilage, and then releases. *Next time*, he says through his teeth, *I will snap it.* The man holds his throat and begins to weep, softly.

Alvaro sees the kid faintly outlined in the dark and slips over the dunes toward him. Lessons must be taught. The gambler is not a man to be trifled with.

In his tent, the general dreams. He is younger, not yet so thick around the middle. He wears his medals, bright reminders of all he has done in the Queen's service. Night. A whispered, vespertine invitation unfurled in the royal arbor. Tight shadows hiding pearly ankles. Clover and bougainvillaea, creeping ivies, the fragrance of honeysuckle. Later, a surreptitious climb to her chambers. His legs wobble. His meaty lips quiver. His nose—still years away from being torn off by a bullet— itches. (His nose! What a glorious nose it was, long and full, with an amiable bulb at the tip!) He tries the knob, and it turns. Hinges creak. Then silence: a long, swollen moment. The scrape and hiss of a match, and one by one, three candles light. The Queen lifts the white sheet, inviting. She is wonderful to discover. He is forced to twist his neck. Vague sensations of galloping and trotting, advancing and encircling. She spins, a slippery diagonal glide, playing herself like the Ponziani Opening. She thrusts out. He tries not to gasp but does. The moment scares him, because he knows what will come next, what comes next every night, what comes next in the dream and in the memory from which it steals—her serrated, mocking laugh as she grasps him by the throat, nails sharp in his flesh. *With one word, with one wave of my wrist, she says, you will have nothing. You will walk along the wharves at midnight, in rags, alone, longing. And you will come to like it there, where the air reeks of waste and rotting shellfish, and where the only girls are toothless whores who beg for needles full of grace and then flick open knives, go straight for the pockets, and say 'Surprise' as they slit your throat.* She climbs off him, and he lies there, discarded, shrinking, and helpless, listening to threads popping as she tears the medals from his tunic.

The general awakens long enough to wonder if the traitorous Sergio had similar dreams in the nights before his head came off. It is said that all those who have loved the Queen are fated to dream of her.

Sergio remains silent, caught, as he was, on the wrong side of the bolo knife.

The head. The sand. The sea glowing yellow-green. Monkeys howling in the dark.

"You were not paying attention, kid," Alvaro says. "I could have stolen the head easily."

"I heard the sand moving under your feet. You're lucky I didn't shoot."

"If you lose the head, you will die. The general will demand it."

"I would expect nothing less. This is my duty to the cause."

"Listen closely, kid: there is no cause. This whole war is about the general's cock. The war would end in a moment if the Queen offered him another stint in her bed. Do you even know why Sergio was killed, why it is *his* head upon which your life depends?"

The wind picks up, and palm trees rustle, urgent. The kid mumbles no. He had not thought to ask.

"The general believes Sergio was the Queen's lover," Alvaro says, "which is absurd. Think. When could it have happened? Sergio was with us from the beginning, spent every night sleeping beside us on beaches and mountains, in jungles and swamps. It is about as likely that *you* have fucked the Queen. No, the general is not just fighting the Queen's army; he imagines enemies, rivals, traitors, all around him. Today it was Sergio. Tomorrow it could be you."

When the kid speaks, his voice flutters. "The general is a great leader," he protests.

From inside the tent, a moan escapes the general's throat. It drones softly on the swift salt breeze.

"The general's mind was carried off along with his nose," Alvaro says. "Listen. Do you hear? That is him, huffing and puffing and yanking his cock. You have never heard it before? Every night, three, four, five times. Someday it will break off in his hand. And you speak of greatness!"

"If this is true, then why are you here? Why do you fight?"

"I enjoy killing," Alvaro says. "I enjoy it greatly."

Heavy waves bully the shoreline. The kid is silent. He cannot think of any words.

Alvaro smiles. Faith, he knows, is so easily stolen, and so rarely recovered. His hand shoots out to pluck the photograph from the kid's pocket. He is surprised when the kid blocks him, holds fast to his thick wrist with long, strong fingers.

"It's mine," the kid says.

"I do not like you dreaming about my girl," Alvaro says, and drives his knee into the kid's groin.

The kid drops, gasps. He rolls in the sand and finds himself looking into Sergio's wide and dead and fly-spotted eyes. The pain, the sight, the stench, all unbearable.

"I could just take her from you, if I wanted," Alvaro says over him, "but I want to win her back, because I am a sportsman. I will flip a coin. If I win, you give her to me."

"If I win," the kid coughs, "you tell me her name, and where she lives."

"Agreed," Alvaro says happily. "Heads or castles?"

The kid staggers to his feet and steps away from Sergio. "Castles. I've had enough of heads for one night."

The coin is in the air, spinning. Even if there were moonlight, the kid would not have noticed that Alvaro had two coins in his hand, flipping one while tucking the other behind the fleshy mound near his thumb. Even if there were moonlight, the kid would not notice that the coin is spinning from head to head, creating a blurred and fluttering but uninterrupted image of the Queen. Even if there were moonlight, the kid would not notice Alvaro producing the second coin to show him a head and a castle, to show him that everything was fair. And because there is no moon, the kid cannot see Alvaro's *novia* one last time.

"I hope you have kept the picture clean. I was concerned you would soil her."

Already the kid's image of her is coming apart. He can recall a length of thigh, eyelashes, nipples, a glistening forehead, a mouth cooing to him in a language composed solely of O sounds, but he cannot put them all together to make a woman.

"I'll win her back," the kid says. "Someday."

"Enough. I am tired, and you and Sergio have a long night ahead."

The kid's tears fall, a hot bath of shame. "The flies," he says. "The smell."

Alvaro drapes his arm around the kid's narrow shoulders. "The head will not smell so bad if you rinse it in the ocean."

"I don't want to touch it."

"I will carry it for you. As a favor. Come."

Together they walk toward the ocean, the kid kicking through the dark sand, Alvaro buoyantly swinging the head by its long, stringy hair. At the water's edge, before the kid can grasp what is happening, Alvaro winds up and hurls the head mightily over the waves. The kid hears a faraway splash. He scans the ocean, hoping to spot the head floating in the flickering, luminous water. Hoping even to see ripples. But the head is gone, swept away by a riptide.

Gone.

"*Adios*, kid. It would be best if you started running now," Alvaro says. A warm satisfaction floods him. Victories are rarely so complete.

The kid turns slowly in circles, as if considering a direction to run, as if the high humid forest were not his only option. A sound comes from his throat, and it reminds Alvaro of a baby chinchilla crying for milk. Then, after a few stutter-steps in the sand, the kid sprints up the beach, taking a wide arc around the sleeping army.

Once the kid has disappeared into the trees, Alvaro strolls back to his tarp and settles down to sleep with the photograph buttoned safely inside his shirt pocket. Tomorrow he can go back to selling glimpses of his girl to the men for cupfuls of foot powder, and he can get some relief for his goddamned ruined feet.

In his tent, the general awakens to the soft light of dawn. He buckles on his nose and goes out to greet the men. The morning sky is pink and gray. A barnacled black crab scuttles past his feet. Woodsmoke tickles his sinuses. The pack of men rise as one and drift zombielike toward the fire, lining up for coffee with tin cups dangling from crooked fingers. The general takes a stick of salt-cured meat from his pack, bites into it, and chews contentedly, feeling kingly. *Alvaro is a bad bishop in an extreme sense*, he thinks with adminration, *and these men are my strong pawn center.*

He looks for the kid and the head, and he sees neither. His eyes whirl out of focus. He bites his lip until he tastes blood. Is there no one he can trust? Has everyone been witched by the Queen? How many heads will he have to take? Where will he keep them? His armies will be slowed, so loaded down with heads will they be! There will be a great volley of heads over the castle walls! He will need many more catapults!

He shouts Alvaro's name, demands answers. A wet shred of meat falls from his mouth into the sand. He bends to retrieve it, puts it back in his mouth just as Alvaro arrives.

"I am shocked," Alvaro says. "I thought the kid was one of us."

Bits of sand grind the general's teeth, but he continues to chew, loudly, adamantly. "Find him," he says.

"You will have his head by noon," Alvaro says, saluting crisply.

The general returns the salute and watches as Alvaro walks among the men, choosing his tracking party. Over the years, Alvaro's clothes have gone from clean olive to deep rusty brown. The general is happy to have a man like this at his right hand, a man who has been flecked, spattered, daubed, smeared, and soaked with the blood of thousands. A man who can be believed in.

Summoning calm as only a seasoned commander can, the general gathers the rest of the men around him. He methodically draws the day's troop movements in the sand with a stick, pointing out each of the moves the Queen's army might make in response. Afterward, he kicks the sand clean, leaving no trace of his strategy.

Alvaro leads three other men through the forest, all of them wiry and mustachioed, eyes red-rimmed and gleaming. His pounding feet feel strong and new; he is only dimly aware of the burst blisters oozing in his boots. He stops and scans the forest around him. The kid is good, better than Alvaro expected—he has left no trail, no footprints in the wet black soil, no broken twigs, no trampled paths through fields of borracho ferns and St. Humbert's thistles. Alvaro follows his instinct, plunging through dense thickets and snarls of diablo vine and buzzing clumps of hungry insects. Razor-leafed branches slap his face, raising welts and thin, stinging cuts. He races on. This is the part he likes best.

The kid comes to the edge of the trees, many miles north of the rebel camp. He hears voices, and he stops, crouches, tries to breathe softly though his lungs howl for air. Through the branches he can see a beach. The yellow sand is bright and unfamiliar. Playing in the waves are four young women in frilly pink suits. The water level is at their chests; when waves come, up to their necks. They laugh and splash and toss an inflated ball.

He assumes these girls have been taught to fear the rebels. He knows he must look feral and dangerous, his skin torn, his clothes heavy with black jungle muck, and he knows he must radiate the stink of war and fear and desperation.

He watches them. They bob in harmony with each lap of wave.

Would he be in danger if he shed his cover? Are the women guard-ed by men hidden nearby, fathers and brothers and husbands armed with guns and knives and scythes and mauls and mattocks? And yet, he knows he is already being hunted. To stay in the jungle alone is to be tracked relentlessly by Alvaro, a man who knows the odds, a man who *shapes* the odds, a man who shakes fate in his fist as if it were a pair of weighted dice. Play long enough, and you will lose.

He parts the branches for a better view of the girls. He reaches into his pants. Fear has stiffened him.

On the beach, ready to decamp, the general regards his men, who stand before him in a sloppy, imprecise line. Only the ones who have filled their boots with precious foot powder are standing still; the others hop from one foot to another, their toes and heels and arches all in a misery of burn and itch. *Soon*, the general promises, *there will be powder for all. My friends, there shall be enough foot powder for you and all your loved ones!*

Friends? Loved ones? some whisper in confusion. *¿Qué son?*

He looks over his men's heads and watches, transfixed with won-der, as the southern sky fills with orbs of color: olive and gunmetal and the white of bones. Thin cords extend from each orb, and from each set of cords hangs a man, and together the orbs and their men drift down-ward and sideward and downward through the blue with the unhur-ried grace of jellyfish in the deep. Attached to each man is a gun. The general takes them to be angels, heavenly reinforcements delivered to him by a higher power whose existence he has never considered. The angels are beautiful, and their firepower much needed, though he won-ders, briefly, if a heaven-sent fighting force can be as ruthless as he needs them to be.

His men shout, but he does not hear. They break for the jungle, scattering as they run. Sand flies in lovely rooster-tails from beneath the flapping soles of their boots, many of which were (and will be again) stripped from the feet of corpses.

Only when he is alone and the gun-toting angels have shed their deflated orbs and are rushing into the jungle and across the beach toward him does his paretic mind absorb the truth. *Puta de muelle!* he barks, cursing the Queen. *Wharf whore!* It is her army! Pinning him into a corner with the rarely-used but potent Karagoosian Onslaught! A savvy endgame modeled on The Boerboom Mate! He understands his position: he is in trouble, is faced with the zugzwang to end all zugzwangs. He unholsters his sidearm and races toward the nearest thing he can kill, wishing he had never let Alvaro go after the kid. Alvaro would have seen this coming. Alvaro would have orchestrated a defense.

The battle is a rout. The men are slaughtered, chased by the Queen's army through the jungle—over fallen limbs, across rivulets and swamps, through gauntlets of tree-dwelling, poison-fanged snakes—before one by one they are fallen upon and butchered like boars. The jungle echoes with truncated, blood-choked cries of *mamá, mamá, mamá.*

The general is taken prisoner, bound at the wrists and ankles with barbed wire that has rusted in the jungle dampness. The Queen's general approaches him with a shining knife, each serration polished to high gleam. *My orders*, the Queen's general says, and the general nods, and his ears are sawn off. *My orders*, the Queen's general says, and the general nods, and his eyes are carved out. *My orders*, the Queen's general says, and the general nods, and a grenade is forced into his mouth. The pin protrudes like a pacifier. Shards of the general's broken teeth litter the black sand, at home among the pebbles and the shells and the yellowed remains of small crustaceans. His tin nose is unbuckled, taken for a trophy.

His head is yanked as the pin is pulled, the metallic *snick* reverberating in his skull. The sand-spray of fleeing feet stings his lips and his raw eye sockets. He does not become a reflective man in his final moments. He does not reminisce about the pet espada monkey that he, as a boy, trained to accompany him on guiro while he played marimba. He does not contemplate the futility of war and pillage and politics. He does not even count down the precious seconds he has left with his head in place. All he thinks about is the Queen and her latest rook, mating mating mating mating

* * *

And what of Sergio's head? It is several miles offshore, carried by the southeast current that each spring deposits many tons of flotsam on the white-sand beaches of a small island known as Ahogado Cay. The picked-clean skull will end up on the shore of the cay amid a pile of fish carcasses, vacant carapaces of murdered sea turtles, and sour-smelling kelp, all of which will be coated in a slick, rainbow-hued slurry of diesel fuel.

Years ago, Sergio might have been saved and resurrected by friendly Nereids. A trio of them might have recovered the head and spirited it away to a shimmering grotto, where they would have conjured a new body—complete with an implanted underwater breathing apparatus—and returned life to him, all the while fondling him gloriously, and he would thereafter have lived with them in benthic bliss. Alas, the Nereids are all gone, scooped up by the trawlers, pressed and vacuum-packed in their own oil.

Instead, the head is feasted upon by marine creatures. Hagfish rasp away pieces of the saltwater-softened flesh and suck them up. Chunks are stolen by the pincers of hungry crabs. Dagger-eels chase each other through the lank weeds of black hair.

Alvaro hears the explosion. It is but a tiny pop in the distance, filtered through thick layers of vegetation, but Alvaro knows. "The general is dead," he tells the tracking party. "We shall need a new one." He points to a thin man tugging at the hair of his mustache. "Flaco," he says, "you are now the general."

"Not you?" Flaco asks. Age-browned scars are crosshatched into both his cheeks, severe reminders of an earlier war.

Alvaro shakes his head. He has no interest in titles, in the burdens of formal command.

"I would like a hat," Flaco says. "Something with a plume. I would have respected our general more if he had worn a hat with a plume."

"We will find you a hat," Alvaro promises. "With a plume. I will hunt the bird myself, once our mission is complete."

Flaco stands straighter as the power takes hold. "A brightly colored bird," he orders.

"The most beautiful bird on the island."

"And also, as I am the general, I demand a peek at your *novia*."

Alvaro smiles. "This time, it is a gift from me," he says, unbuttoning his shirt pocket with one swift flick of wrist. "But a good general knows he cannot just take. Like the other men, he must pay, or he must bet."

The new general nods quickly, comes to him, takes possession of the photograph with greedy fingers and greedy eyes. He angles it back and forth in the sunlight that drains through the trees, as if he is trying to catch a glimpse of the girl from behind, as if he does not understand the laws of two dimensions.

Looking over the general's shoulder, Alvaro sees a flaw on the surface of the photograph. A spot where the image has no gloss, does not shine in the weak sunlight. A spot in the upper-right-hand corner. A daub of what might be the kid's dried spunk, marring the horizon behind the wave-slapped *novia* whose name he can no longer remember. The kid! It is a shame Alvaro can kill him but once! He snatches the photograph from the general's hands. "Enough," he says. "We have a mission."

"We have a mission," the general echoes.

Alvaro runs his thumb along his knife to test the blade, opening a perfect, thin, shallow cut from which no blood leaks. And then they run.

The kid steps out from his hiding place and crosses the beach in a simple, slow walk, with neither stealth nor authority. He removes his shirt and boots, drops his gun in the sand. He is unashamed of his tenting trousers.

The girls spot him. Their ball falls uncaught and bobs brightly. They stare.

He wades out to them. The water is warmer than he expects. He can feel tiny fish at his feet, tasting the salt of his toes. He holds his hands above his head, open palms revealing themselves as empty. It is, he hopes, a gesture of peace. "Ladies," he says, and it is a difficult word, one that makes his tongue feel fat and parched and clumsy. "Ladies," he says again. "Please don't be afraid."

They are silent. They goggle. The tallest and fairest-skinned girl folds her sun-pinked arms across her chest, as if she must shield from his gaze not just her small, pointed breasts but the ruffled pink fabric that covers them. And yet, did not another girl, the shortest, push herself higher in the next wave so he could see more of her? Or did he imagine it?

They do not speak. He wonders if they are not local, then realizes he is the one who is far from home. Do they understand his dialect, his accent? Has his tongue failed him? Or did he forget even to say those words aloud? As he strides deeper into the water, he spies a boat moored off the tip of the cove. There are shouts from the boat—male voices. Then the sounds of an anchor pulled up, and a motor gunned.

"Are—?" he asks the girls, but gets no further. "But—" he says, trying again. Then: "I—."

The boat speeds toward them, trailing a violent wake. He tries to read the girls' faces, but he cannot; their expressions offer him nothing he can understand. Will he be turned back into the jungle? Die, bullet-riddled, here in the shallows? Taken in, fed and nursed, led to a bed? He closes his eyes and waits, listening to the motor's roar and the shouts and the waves and the girls' silence. Empty arms high in the air, he delivers himself unto them, hoping.

GATEWAY TO THE WEST

by ELLEN MOORE

"WAKE HIM UP last," my supervisor warned me about Greg, the patient in the corner room. We weren't supposed to call them "patients." They were "residents," and this one had a bad cold which threatened to become pneumonia. Pneumonia is a killer for people like Greg, so I let him sleep. This was a residential treatment facility for people with cerebral palsy and I was a nurse's aid, although I wasn't supposed to call myself that, either. I was a "care giver." Boeing had laid off a lot of workers; it was the only job I could find.

We were staying at the Motel 99 on Aurora Avenue North but we couldn't afford it much longer. We arrived in Seattle on a Sunday. By then, it was Thursday and with the weekend looming, we needed to find one or the other fast: a job or an apartment. I decided to focus on job.

"Why can't you find something?" I asked my new husband. He'd been staring at the TV all morning.

"It's easier for girls."

There was nothing easy about it. I had to admit, though, I was doing better than he was. He'd been moribund since our arrival, since Disneyland maybe, or maybe since Vegas.

* * *

The resident was coughing. He didn't look like he was choking. I guessed it was just the cold. The episode passed, but he was still shaking his head. His face was now red and turned to the side, his eyes were looking up and back, as if to indicate something behind him. He shook his head a couple of times for emphasis.

"His chart. He wants you to get his chart," Big Red called over to me from the next feeding table.

I retrieved the laminated chart that hung from the back of the resident's customized wheel chair. This resident was the 'Moon Man,' so called because his body was shaped like a crescent moon. He was tall (or would have been, if he could stand—maybe 6'3") and concentration-camp thin. His father had fashioned a special chair for him out of wood, pipe, padding, and vinyl. It was an enormous, rolling, blue letter "C"—like something out of a fantasy dance sequence on Captain Kangaroo. The blue vinyl brought out the blue in his eyes. And his hair, which was blonde and fine, was perpetually on end; electrified by his involuntary movements against the vinyl in a permanent halo around his face.

He closed his eyes and waited for me to acknowledge the gesture. "Dash," I said. He opened his eyes, nodded, and closed them again. "Dash," I said again. He looked up toward the ceiling to indicate the end of the first letter. I looked at the chart, the Morse code. "M," I said aloud, so he'd know whether I got it right.

He nodded, then blinked once, quickly and looked up. "Dot." I checked the chart again. A quick blink was a dot and a longer blink, a dash. "O," I said.

"Move?" I guessed at his intention, trying to expedite matters.

He shook his head, breathed deeply, then blinked again. He shut his eyes and held them. Then another blink and he looked up. "Dot, dash, dot. R."

"More?" I asked. He nodded enthusiastically. More what? I surveyed his choices.

"Juice?" No. "Oatmeal?" His bowl was still half full.

Blink. Blink. Blink. Look up.

S. "Sugar!"

He nodded again, smiling his crooked smile, and I piled the sugar on and watched as it melted into a luscious, brown pool.

We sat on a bench in Tomorrowland, watching our peer group – married couples from across America, obese, with kids in tow, licking ice cream cones in January. We were newlyweds. They were our future.

"I thought I loved her."

He was talking about his old girlfriend again. They had just broken up. Again. Supposedly. He spent all his savings on her most recent abortion. I didn't like this kind of talk.

"Do you still love her?" I had to ask. What else was I supposed to say? He didn't answer. He didn't seem to know anything about himself, nothing he'd admit to anyway. We let it drop.

Then again, near Carmel. We'd taken the scenic route but the coast was in fog. I did all the driving. He didn't have a license, being from New York City and all. The winding road had worn me out, that and the realization that one false turn could be my last. I pulled over at one of those turnouts, scenic overlooks on sunny days. You could feel the cliff drop off and hear the waves crash on the rocks below, but all you could see was cotton candy, enveloping the car, closing in on us.

"We should have had that kid."

I turned toward the window, resting my forehead on the cool tempered glass. I wanted to tell him to shut up about her, it was my honeymoon, I'm the one who married him, I'm the one who helped him escape from all that, the so-called friends we left behind. I wanted to tell him to get out of the car; the car I'd purchased with my savings while he spent all his money on her. But I also wanted to keep him talking because I knew it was his thoughts, not his words, that were the enemy. It wasn't really that he still loved her, if he did. That wasn't the problem. That would have been too simple. I wasn't even jealous of her, really. She was a benign figure in a hospital gown 3,000 miles away.

I got the job based on my experience in the medical field: summers as a home health aid, work in a medical library, a research lab, and assistant to the chief of surgery at Albany Med Center. I was supposed to be a doctor. That's what I thought anyway, it's what everybody thought. That was the plan. My grandfather had been a doctor and I was to pick up his mantle and prevail. The chief of surgery was poised to write me a letter of recommendation. I was a shoo-in for med school.

Then I met him. He was trouble, exactly the kind of trouble that could help me escape the plan.

"You know he was a doctor."

"What?"

"Chekhov. He was a doctor first, a writer second."

That's what he told me when I told him the plan. I knew about Chekhov the playwright, of course; I loved theater, I was studying "The Seagull." But Chekhov, the doctor, was an unknown quantity. Who cares he was a doctor, I reasoned. It was his avocation, his characters, his words that mattered, not the peasant's cough he treated in the middle of the night a hundred years past. The peasant was dead, the cough was silent, the doctor was gone, but the words were here.

"No longer do the cranes wake and cry in the meadows, and in the linden groves the hum of beetles is no longer heard."

Treplev wrote those words for his beloved, Nina, to recite in his play within Chekhov's play, "The Seagull." Treplev wanted to prove to Nina, to his mother, and ultimately, to his rival, Trigorin, that he had both talent and soul. Because it's Chekhov and because his theme, first and foremost, is unrequited love, Nina ignores Treplev and falls instead for the aloof and unobtainable Trigorin, following him to Moscow.

"I've made up my mind; the die is cast; I am going on the stage. I'm leaving behind my father and everything. Like you, I'm going to Moscow," Nina tells Trigorin. And like Nina, I soon abandoned family and home, a reasonable boyfriend, a secure future in a familiar place, determined to pursue a career onstage in a distant town renowned for its theater. Or so I thought. What I'd really done, as Nina had before me, was something as common as chase a man.

I found us an apartment in a converted motel. It was behind a gas station on Queen Anne Avenue. When they came to refill the gas tanks, you had to quickly shove your window shut or suffer the nauseating consequences.

Next door was a family—a mother, a sometime father, and a little girl. "He's not really my daddy," she confided in me once. She was seven or eight with long, dark hair. Christine. I liked to have her over for cookies and milk. We'd play cards. It was almost like being home again, playing cards with my sister, letting her win. Letting other people win was my specialty.

"Where's your dad?" she asked me.

"He's not my dad," I explained, "he's my husband." She didn't seem to buy it. "He's at work."

By then, he'd found a job as a directory assistance operator at the phone company. With our newfound prosperity, we'd acquired a few trimmings—a waterbed, kitchen table and chairs, and a stereo system; turntable, receiver, and amplifier in a cherry-veneer cabinet. It was a monument to our success in an otherwise empty living room. On Saturday nights, we liked to play records. My husband thought playing music over the speakers would attract too much attention, so he'd use the headphones. He'd bounce around the living room, dancing to the music, attached to the stereo by a long cord, like some crazy monkey on a string. I liked to watch, sitting on the floor by the open cabinet door. The green and red amplifier lights reflected on the glass; if I relaxed my gaze, they'd multiply, like cars on the highway, as I listened to his music bleed.

"Listen," I turned down the volume. They were fighting again next door.

My husband taught me that trick he learned in Boy Scouts: you take a glass and hold it up to the wall so you can hear what's being said on the other side. It didn't really work. They were shouting but I couldn't tell what. Then there was a thud, like a body hitting the wall.

"Should we call the cops?" I asked.

"No. They'll come interview us and he'll know who called. It might make things worse. He might take it out on them or come after us."

Mind your own business. New Yorkers engrave it on their hearts.

"But what about Christine?"

"What about her? He's not fighting with her. She's probably in bed. Anyway, you shouldn't bring her over here anymore. We shouldn't get involved."

Involved, from the Latin, *volvere*: to roll, to wrap, to entwine. Like a big ball of string tying me to Christine; Christine to her sometimes dad; her sometimes dad to her all-the-time mom; me to my husband; him to his ex; his ex to the child she lost and the friends we left behind.

I didn't want the hassle either, though, so I shut up.

After breakfast, many of the residents left for a daily work detail. It involved bulk mailings. They gathered at the front door and were loaded into handicap vans. Some resisted participating and would feign illness to avoid it. Others, like the Moon Man, were exempt. The Moon Man didn't even have to live at the facility. He had the singular distinction of being the only resident to self-admit. The rest had been transferred from other facilities or were there because their families couldn't care for them at home. The Moon Man's family wanted him home, but he wanted to strike out, to make his way in the world. He and I were the same age, an age of definition, and he had defined himself as a writer.

"You're a writer and I'm an actress," Nina told Treplev when she sneaked back to see him, after her affair with Trigorin had disintegrated, after Trigorin lost interest in her and returned to his former love, Arkadina, Treplev's mother. "We've been drawn into the whirlpool, both of us."

The whirlpool Nina referred to is that spinning place where art is made, where all things seem possible, where doubt and faith slide side by side. That dangerous place in the heart where hope wrestles with despair, where beauty may prevail and art may result, unless, of course, the artist drowns in the process. The Moon Man, it seemed, had hopped on that carousel, hoping to be transported.

You're a writer and I'm an actress, I thought, as I wheeled him back from breakfast and set him up at his electric typewriter. He wore a special hat—another invention of his father's—it consisted of a leather strap—a belt really, which fastened around his head. There was another strap that overarched the crown of his head and kept the strap from slipping down. In the front of the hat, a long dowel had been attached, with a rubber tip at the end. This is how the Moon Man typed. With some considerable effort, he aimed the point of his hat at the desired key.

"In n theeeeee foreeeeeeeest arre many treees." His story began.

"And in the linden groves, the hum of beetles is no longer heard." I practiced my monologue in my head. I had an audition after work. I pulled the photocopy out of my pocket, to check my lines. The Moon Man looked over at me, raising his eyebrows.

"I have an audition."

That excited him. He grinned; rocking, and snorting in a way I didn't care for.

"It's not so great. It's just an audition. I'm an actress. Trying to be."

He started blinking. I didn't really want to converse. "Show me," is what he said.

"No, I can't. I'm not prepared." It was a false modesty. Although I barely knew my lines, I believed deep down that my incredible talent would carry me.

"I'm not really a nurse's aid. I mean… I took this job because it gets off early. That way, I can still audition."

I was treading on thin ice. My supervisor had warned me, "Be sensitive to their feelings, don't exacerbate their sense of deprivation, rubbing your freedom in their face." But I wasn't free, at least I didn't feel that way. He was limited by a physical disability, but I was limited, too. An actress has many limitations—her looks, her age, her speech. So does a bride.

"Break leg," he blinked.

"I didn't know what to do with my hands. I couldn't even stand properly on stage or control my voice. You have no idea what it's like to know you're acting badly." That's what Nina tells Treplev in the final scene of the play.

"How was the audition?" my husband asked over dinner.

I didn't answer. He waited.

"Not good."

"What do you mean?"

"What I said."

We ate in silence.

"When do you find out?"

"There's nothing to find out. I was bad. I wasn't prepared."

"Why?"

"Why what? Why was I bad? Or why wasn't I prepared?"

"Nevermind," he murmured.

I got up to start dishes.

"Well, better luck next time," he said to my back.

Christine sat on top of the dryer. She liked it there, to feel its warmth beneath her while the clothes spun lazily dry. We'd moved our meetings to the laundry room, neutral territory. When the washer started spinning, she switched, clambering over on top of it. She liked the powerful spin, what it did to her voice.

"Uh…uh…uh…uh…uh…uh… Go…oh…oh…oh…oh…oh… Fi…ii…ii…ii…ii..sh!"

I reached into the discard pile.

Big Red carried the Moon Man, wrapped in a towel, fresh from the shower. He laid him on the bed and asked if I could take over. I usually did the women and left the men to him, but we were behind, there were still two residents lined up, waiting back in the shower room. I greeted the Moon Man, but without the code board handy, I didn't really expect a reply. His cold was better. He waited patiently. I grabbed a fresh towel and started to dry his limbs, leaving the other towel to protect his modesty and his bedding. His long, useless arms cramped up as I tried to lift from the elbow and swab at his underarms. His chest was sunken and ribbed like a washboard and I gently toweled it dry. Once, when I worked as a home health aid, a patient complained that I scrubbed her too vigorously. I think, embarrassed at the intimacy of my task, cleaning her crotch, I had inadvertently rubbed too hard. Now I was being careful, not wanting to hurt the Moon Man, or appear uncomfortable. Perhaps I was too gentle; when I pulled back the towel to dry his crotch, his penis was stiff. I made a cursory attempt to dab at it and reached to dry the skin between his testicles and his leg. It's very important in non-ambulatory patients to protect their skin from bedsores, drying them thoroughly and applying powder to absorb excess moisture. I sprinkled the Moon Man with powder and spread some in the folds of his groin. All the while, the Moon Man was red-faced and his eyes looked up and away, toward the head of his bed.

I struggled to dress him, first, in a pair of briefs. Then I gently reached under his shoulder blades and lifted his torso. Sitting behind him, I reached around and put his arms through the sleeves of a shirt, then buttoned it closed. I laid him back down, put his pants on and fastened them. I gave him socks and shoes. I combed his hair and showed him the result in a mirror. He was ready to go back into his chair so I excused myself, ostensibly to find someone to assist with the transfer. Instead, I hid in the staff bathroom.

Was I ashamed? I didn't know. I didn't feel exploited, but I didn't feel innocent either. I wasn't attracted, but I was pained. I wished I could give the Moon Man more, or that someone could. I didn't want him to die a virgin but knew he probably would. I was confused. Was I mother, friend, lover? 'You're a writer, and I'm an actress' and now I'm an actress playing the part of the lover you will never have. And now you're an actor too. You're a man, just home from work, exhausted; you flop on the bed, soaking wet from your shower. Your lover bends to dry you, to tease and comfort you. She wants you to get dressed and take her out. But first....

We saw the glow on the horizon for maybe a hundred miles. It seemed the sun would rise at midnight. Then, when we cruised over the last dune, there it was; sprawled out below, exposed, like a fistful of diamonds on velvet. Las Vegas. We knew what it meant, for us anyway, a test of our resolve. It was in St. Louis, at the Gateway to the West, that the tide had shifted. In the day and night since, I'd thought of little else.

We arrived in St. Louis at three in the morning, with one objective: find the Gateway to the West. Without that magic portal, it seemed the East would continue forever, spreading out in front of the car, behind us, on all sides; nothing would ever change; no one would ever escape; no place would be different than the place we left behind. The arch would change all that. We didn't know it yet. So far, it was just something to do on a cold night in late December. We parked and got out of the car. The wind was bitter, ripping across the river and up the hill. The arch loomed ahead—magnificent, black against a blacker night, a perfect form, an elegant bridge between old and new, East and

West, high and low, the humble and the grand. We walked toward it slowly, purposefully. Then, suddenly, we joined hands and began to run. We ran under and through, and by God, it was different on the other side, we were different, we were Westerners, explorers, conquerors even. The arch had made us new. We laughed and jumped and spun like children, hand in hand, until we fell, dizzy, on the ground. We kissed and held each other there, in the dark, on the frozen grass, alongside the Mississippi, in the West. "Marry me," he whispered.

It made sense. It still does. It was worth a try. Old alliances would break down, families would recede, teenage troubles would be over, adulthood would commence. I was ready for a new set of troubles, or so I thought.

"Let's do it," I answered.

New Year's Day, 1978. The bride wore blue corduroy pants and a pink peasant smock.

"An idea struck me for a short story: a young girl like you, has lived all her life by a lake. She loves it the way a seagull does; she's happy and free like a seagull. But a man comes and sees her and because he has nothing better to do he destroys her like this bird."

When it becomes painfully obvious to Treplev that Nina is rejecting him in favor of the older, more accomplished, more sophisticated Trigorin, he is driven to distraction. He wanders down to the lake and shoots a seagull, presenting the dead bird to his ladylove in a desperate gesture intended to either win her back or at least demonstrate to her the depth of his feelings, the magnitude of his loss. It backfires.

"You're so irritable lately," she says, "you talk in symbols. This is a symbol too. I'm sorry but I don't understand it. I'm afraid I'm too simple to understand you."

Whether it's her simplicity or her cunning that causes her to misconstrue is unclear. What is clear is that she's over him, she's set her sights on new game. What she doesn't realize is that she is the game, that Trigorin will destroy her.

Trigorin comes across the dead seagull. He jots down a note. "What are you writing?" Nina asks, already obsessed with him, already abandoning her will.

"An idea struck me for a short story," he answers. She's mesmerized.

- / .... / . / .-. / . .. / ... -.-. / —– / -. / -.-. / . / .-. / -
"There is concert."
... / . / .- / - / - / .-.. / . ... / -..- / —– / .—. / .... / —– / -. / -.—
"Seattle Symphony."
.. / -. .—. / .- / .-. / -.- .-.. / .-. / . / . —– / —– / —.. / .- / .-. / -
"In park. Free. Mozart."
.—– / —– / ..- / .-.. / -.. -.—– / —– / ..- .-.. / .. / .-.- / . -/ —– —. / —–
"Would you like to go?"

That's how he asked me. It took some time. It probably took some courage too. It was almost like he was asking me for a date but it was also like he was asking me for a favor.

I knew that if I didn't agree, he probably couldn't go. How he knew about the concert, I have no idea. But Mozart was his favorite. He listened to him when he wrote.

It wouldn't be easy. It would involve lifting him from the chair and somehow securing him in the seat of my Chevy Malibu. Then somehow lifting the unwieldy chair into my trunk. It would stick out, so I'd have to find a way to tie it down. But I could get help with all of that from someone at the facility. I'd take back roads and drive very slowly. I'd plan my route, maybe practice it. We'd get to the park and I'd have to reverse the process, but without help, transferring him alone, back into the chair. Maybe a passerby would help me. There might be grass and fields and hills to contend with. The wheels of his chair were small, like those on a dolly. They'd probably get stuck in the soft ground and the whole chair might tip over. It might rain. Once we reached the concert site, I suppose I'd have to transfer him to a blanket and lay the chair on its side. Otherwise we'd block views and be far too conspicuous and he'd be high and I'd be low and we couldn't communicate. There'd be stares certainly, and he'd probably get hungry and need to eat something, maybe even need to use the bathroom.

I thought I could do it. I wanted to try.

"What? Are you crazy?" My husband was stunned.

I explained my plan, how it wouldn't be easy but it would be possible and how I thought it'd be worthwhile.

"No." He said.

No? Was he my boss? Was I asking permission?

"Why not?"

"Well, first of all, we don't have insurance for that kind of thing."

Do you need special insurance to take an already bent and broken man on an outing? Can you get that kind of policy? Does it exist?

Maybe my husband was threatened by the fact that I'd be taking another man out. I realized that could be an issue even though I didn't think my husband considered the Moon Man a threat. He wasn't a threat. I enjoyed what I perceived as the Moon Man's attentions and felt they were sincere. But, I was far too much like Nina to be content with such simple admiration. I wanted to be shot through the heart. It was my destiny. Since I was little, I didn't want an easy life, I wanted a hard one, more of a challenge.

"You could go too," I offered, knowing he wouldn't accept, but offering in order to appear innocent.

"I don't want to go and you shouldn't either."

He knew what I should want; even I didn't know that.

"Besides, it's not your car." That was news to me. My car had died and his brother had given us this Malibu to replace it. I registered and insured it in my name since I was the only one who drove. "It's my family's car."

He was pulling rank, redefining property, coming down on the side of his family, a family I knew he both despised and revered. He went further.

"I forbid it."

"You 'forbid' it? What are you saying?"

He shrugged.

"You're saying you don't want me to go just because something might happen, even though nothing will. And that I shouldn't do this small thing for someone, which would mean a lot to him, wouldn't be much trouble for me, would be no trouble for you, and all because... what? I'm not your family or he's not your family or we're not all somehow in your special family?"

"However you want to put it."

There was nothing more to say, and to prove it, he put on his head-phones.

When I got to his room, he had the stick hat on and was typing. I turned down the music so he could hear me. I got the chart from the back of his chair and angled him so I could see his eyes. Then I perched on the bed opposite.

"You know that concert you asked me about?"

He nodded.

"Well, I'd like to go, I really would. I love Mozart."

He nodded again and smiled in an effort to be encouraging.

"But I can't take you. I'm sorry."

He stuck out his lower lip, shut his eyes, and shook his head, as if to say, no big deal.

"There's a problem with my car. I need to have fixed."

He turned his face back toward the corner with the typewriter, indicating his desire to get back to work. I took the out and rolled him back around.

"I hope you can still go," I said, as I hung the chart on the handle of his chair.

When Nina comes to visit Treplev, towards the end of the play, after several years in Moscow, she is distraught and distracted. No longer the girl who grew up by the lake and "loved it the way a seagull does," the beautiful, young, petulant actress who starred in Treplev's summer theatrical at the opening of the play. Nina relates the story of her relationship with Trigorin and its desperate deterioration.

"He always laughed at my dreams, until after a while, I stopped believing in them myself."

But who was responsible? Nina's trajectory made for good drama, but was it for me?

My grandfather, the one I was to emulate, was a country doctor like Chekhov. He didn't like it much. In fact, he hated it. Whether that's what led to his suicide, I don't know.

* * *

When I walked past the apartment next door, the curtains were pulled back. I'd never seen inside. They'd always been closed. The apartment looked tiny with nothing in it, nothing on the walls, no furniture, nothing. I knocked on the door. The window was ajar and I called through the aluminum casement.

"Christine?"

She was gone. One day I had a little sister, the next day she was gone. My family was disbanding.

I was still dazed when I entered my apartment. At first I didn't notice the pile of fish cards on the carpet. She must have stuffed them under the door. Flat, numbered fish, a school of them, staring up at me with their unblinking eyes. I bent to collect them, but it wasn't easy with feathers for fingers and a gunshot wound to the heart.

I got what I wanted; a tragic story, an obstacle course, feathers on the floor. It served me once, but not anymore.

YOUR NEW BEST FRIEND

PART ONE OF A LONGER WORK CONCERNING CLIMBING MOUNT KAILASH,
BELIEVED BY MILLIONS TO BE THE MOST SACRED MOUNTAIN ON EARTH.

by JEFF GREENWALD

LESSON ONE

"Tibetans have a saying they take with them to Mount Kailash," Ian
Baker advises me as we day-hike up the slopes of Nagarjun Peak, a
thickly forested hill overlooking Nepal's Kathmandu Valley. "It goes
like this: *Kha zher, lam khyer*. The translation, literally, is this:
'Whatever happens… whatever arises… bring it to the path.'"

"That's because the meaning of pilgrimage, at least in the Asian
sense is 'a journey beyond preferences.' Especially when we're talking
about Kailash—the holiest of Asia's mountains. You have to be completely open, ready to accept whatever comes up, rather than seeking a
specific objective. That's the only way to fulfill the highest potential of
pilgrimage—which is a clear awakening of our Buddha Nature."

Baker—an explorer and Buddhist scholar—has lived in Nepal near-
ly twenty years. He made international headlines in 1998, when he led
a National Geographic-funded expedition into the gorges of China's
Tsangpo River, and discovered the Hidden Falls of the Brahmaputra.
I'm tapping his wisdom before my own departure for Kailash—a trip
I've wanted to make for ten years.

We follow a red clay trail through dense patches of ferns and sal
trees, passing an army garrison. Pants dry on the barbed wire fence.

The soldiers, in camouflage shirts and boxer shorts, wave to us in relief. Kathmandu has been in a state of emergency for months, facing the threat of an armed coup by *maobadis*: Maoist guerrillas. The rebels already control a quarter of Nepal's 75 districts, and are rumored to be taking strategy and terror lessons from Shining Path, Khmer Rouge and Tamil Tiger veterans. Since its inception, in 1996, the war has claimed nearly 5,000 lives.

The hike up Nagarjun is itself a mini-pilgrimage. Legend has it that eons ago, when the Kathmandu Valley was a vast inland lake inhabited by a race of noble snake gods, a visitor named Bipaswi—the first of all the human buddhas—trekked to the peak of this hill. Standing atop the summit, he threw a seed into the water. The seed bloomed into a radiant lotus, blazing with diamonds and rubies. The sight attracted gawkers from all over Asia, including a sword-wielding saint named Manjushri. Manjushri surveyed the broad lake, raised his sword, and sliced a deep gorge. The waters drained out (forcing the snake gods to relocate), and the Kathmandu Valley became Asia's most desirable real estate.

About forty minutes into our walk, raindrops begin to fall. The trail up Nagarjun is fine when dry; soak it down, and it's like a greased chute. The rain might also bring out the season's first, voracious leeches; a profound personal terror. I watch the foliage for any sign of them, and check my shoes often.

It takes us an hour to reach the flat meadow that sits about two-thirds of the way up Nagarjun's flank. Two thousand feet below, the bricks and timbers of Kathmandu spread across the valley like a pixelated quilt. We're peeling our oranges when we hear a strange sound—as if the surrounding forest is applauding politely. The noise grows louder.

"Look north," Ian says. A huge storm cloud is crawling over the hillside, pounding the trees with rain. "It's coming this way." A few heavy drops strike my pants, and crater the dirt around us.

I shrug on my daypack and follow Ian, who is already jogging down the trail. Within minutes it's pouring. The ground is as slick as a mango pit. Ian breaks into a gallop, pushing his limits. I try to keep up, thumping along in stiff new boots.

The trail gets steeper, and the switchbacks sharper. I misjudge a corner... and the next thing I know I'm off the trail, briefly airborne before plunging down a precipitous hillside covered with leafy bushes and trees. I catapult down the hill, head over heels, dimly aware of two things: (1) at any instant I might break my neck, and (2) my entire body, much like a lint roller, is acting as a magnet for leeches. A tree looms in front of me; I throw out my arm in self-defense, bracing for impact. Plant and human slam together—and an instant later I'm on my feet, brushing myself off frantically. Ian rushes to my side. There are no leeches—but I've hurt my wrist pretty badly. A few mobility tests seem to indicate that it isn't actually broken, but it's going to ache for weeks. Bad luck: I'm leaving for Kailash tomorrow.

Later that night, Ian pours me a whiskey. My wrist is swollen. "An unfortunate, but very timely, event," he says, over-pleased with the day's moral lesson. "It's exactly when you anticipate difficulties, and begin wishing things were different than what they are, that you run into trouble."

"You have to admit the fact that I was pretty intuitive," I say. "I *knew* the rain would be a problem. We should have turned back."

"On the contrary," Ian says. "You fell *because* you saw the rain as an obstacle; because you weren't ready to accept things as they were."

"I fell," I answer, "because I was running after *you*."

We leave it at that.

Jewel of the Snows

In a world whose inhabitants rarely see eye to eye, it's astounding that at least two billion humans agree on at least one thing: the most sacred mountain on Earth is a rounded, white-shouldered peak of average height, rising from the trans-Himalayan range of western Tibet.

For at least two thousand years, Mount Kailash has been the spiritual and geographical focus for Asia's two greatest religions. Hindus see the mountain as an earthly manifestation of Mount Meru, the *axis mundi* around which the entire universe revolves. It's also the home of Shiva, the God of Creation and Destruction. Shiva has a fiery third eye, and a serious temper if you invade his privacy: two good reasons no one climbs this mountain. If you interrupt one of the god's frequent liaisons with Uma—his gorgeous consort—he'll burn you to a crisp.

Buddhists also revere Kailash as Meru. But for the Tibetans especially, the mountain has always been attractive to gods, saints and demons. The story goes that the great poet-saint Milarepa, a reformed mass murderer who mastered the arts of black and white magic, won the mountain in a series of fantastic wagers with the previous tenant. The evidence of their contests, in the form of hand-prints, head-prints and miraculously-placed stones, cover the Kailash slopes.

Every spring, on the full moon of May, a meadow near the southern flank of Kailash hosts a festival called Saga Dawa. Hindus and Buddhists from every corner of Asia converge on the site to celebrate the enlightenment of the Buddha. A tall pole is raised, prayers are shouted, and hundreds of pilgrims begin the 35-mile *kora*, or devotional circuit, around the base of the sacred mountain.

Tibet's form of Buddhism, known as *mahayana*, is a lot like pinball. The idea is to rack up karmic merit, and cut down on the future lifetimes that all beings must endure on the long and arduous road to liberation. The scoring system is Byzantine, multi-layered with free plays and jackpots. This year (2129, by the Tibetan calendar) is the Year of the Horse, the most auspicious of the twelve astrological signs. Circling Mount Kailash just once in a Horse year is equal to thirteen koras performed at any other time. Being there for Saga Dawa, of course, wins even bigger bonuses.

But this year is unusual for another reason as well. During the last Horse year—1990—Nepal was recovering from a bloody, pro-democracy revolution, and China was just emerging on the world economic scene. By the next one, 2014, Nepal might well be embroiled in a civil war. Beijing may have completed an airport near the mountain, changing its character forever. Most significant of all, the beloved Dalai Lama—the silent focus of every Tibetan prayer—might no longer be among us.

It seems quite possible that this year's Saga Dawa celebration will be last in which either Nepal or Tibet exist—at least as we have known them.

The journey to Kailash (which Tibetans call *Kang Rinpoche*, "Precious Jewel of the Snows") is considered the most dangerous and difficult an individual can attempt: not just physically, but in every sense. Just the *desire* to go to Kailash can generate problems. In 1994, I traveled halfway around the world—without airplanes—in hopes of making the pilgrimage. By the time I arrived in Kathmandu, after five months on the road, it was too late: my partner had bailed, my gear had been stolen, and I was literally fainting from exhaustion. Despite that introduction, I never lost my craving for the mountain.

There are any number of ways to get to Kailash. Before the 1950s Tibetans typically made the trip by horse, or on foot. Some still approach Kailash in the most reverent way possible: creeping toward the mountain over a period of months, doing full-body prostrations every three steps. No matter how they traveled, bandits lurked everywhere; and if that didn't stop them, the violent storms that rage across the Tibetan plateau might.

Today, for most pilgrims, jeeps and trucks have replaced yak trains and knee-pads. But the trip remains brutal. Reaching Kailash involves a week-long drive from Lhasa, grinding along roads so dusty and pitted that a factory-fresh Land Cruiser is quickly transformed into a stuffy, brain-jarring Tinkertoy.

There is one alternative. An hour's flight southwest of Kathmandu lies Nepalganj, a crowded city on the Nepal/India border. From Nepalganj one flies due north, on Yeti Airlines, to the airstrip at Simikot: a Himalayan village 9,400 feet high.

Once you reach Simikot, it's a six-day trek to the Nepal/Tibet border. With advance planning, a jeep can drive out from Lhasa and meet you there. From that point it's a relatively painless, day-long drive to Mount Kailash. But the trek from Simikot is not without its perils. That part of Nepal—Humla—is controlled by *maobadis*: the young Maoist rebels, locked in a futile struggle to "liberate" Nepal from its necrotic government. When their struggle began, in 1996, the rebels enjoyed a wave of popular support. By 2001, though, their tactics turned to torture, extortion and execution. Though no Western travelers have yet been harmed by these insurgents, they're still a pain in the ass. For the past year, Maoist cells have been routinely looting trekkers, demanding money (as well as cameras and portable CD players) for their struggle against the counter-revolutionary regime. The pattern is so predictable that trekkers to Kailash—those approaching through Humla—are told in advance how much they'll be robbed of.

A Slight Problem

At 2 p.m. on the 16th of May, a taxi pulls up in front of my Kathmandu flat. Tsering, the Tibetan owner of Sunny Treks and Tours, helps load my duffel bag into the car. We emerge from my compound and begin navigating the Kathmandu roads, bound for the domestic terminal at Tribhuvan International Airport. I gaze out the window, fascinated, as always, by the city's street life. Naked kids chase a hoop down an alley; a cow noses through a pile of vegetable trimmings. Brilliant orange saris dry on a grassy incline, and a thin *saddhu*, a Hindu ascetic, rattles the door of a tailor's shop. Glass bangles gleam on a roadside stand; next door, severed goat heads peer out behind a thin gauze fly-screen.

Due to the rebel activity in western Nepal, the majority of western pilgrims are approaching Mt. Kailash by road. My sole companion on this trek was to be a young Swiss man—but a week ago he had canceled. All Tsering has told me about his replacement is that she is a 51-year old German "housewife" with an interest in the spiritual. Her name is Helga. Several days earlier, at the Sunny office, I'd seen her visa application. Her mug shot reminded me of a quotation I'd read somewhere: "If you look like your passport photo, you're too ill to travel."

"Who's our guide?" I ask Tsering.

"His name is Padma. My cousin. He is from Humla—the place you are going."

"He's how old?"

"Twenty-three."

Tsering turns his head slightly, squinting sheepishly. "I think there is something I should tell you."

"Oh? What's that?"

Tsering licks his lips. "A slight problem. Maybe some little trouble between Helga and your guide."

"Eh?" I'm baffled. "How do they know each other?" Our driver swerves to avoid a push cart stacked with plastic tricycles. "What's the deal? Are they fighting about something?"

Tsering throws his head back, and laughs with real mirth. "No no no no no. Not that kind of trouble. When Tibetans say 'trouble,' they mean love. Love trouble. Love *is* trouble."

"I still don't understand."

"Last September also, Helga went on a trek to Kailash. A big one: thirty-five clients. Padma was the guide. She fell in love with him, and came back to make this trek."

"Tsering," I say slowly, "let's get this straight. You're telling me that I'm spending the next three weeks with a pair of lovers—a married, middle-aged German woman, and our 23-year-old Sherpa guide?"

"Relax," Tsering assures me. "Padma is very professional. And Helga herself is very excited to go to Kailash again." He grins at me. "I promise: you'll have a wonderful time."

During the past ten years, the waiting area at the international arm of Kathmandu's airport has been given a multi-million dollar facelift, courtesy of the Australian government. Not so the domestic lounge, which still smells vaguely of ozone and urine. Tsering walks me through security, and runs off to put out a few logistical fires.

There are a few other Kailash-bound westerners in the departure lounge, all waiting for the Buddha Air flight to Nepalganj. The first ones I meet, inevitably, are an American couple: Brad and Lois, from Santa Fe. Brad is a retired rafting guide, mountain climber and sailor, a clear-eyed outdoorsman with a flat, Medici nose broken by a baseball when he was thirteen. Lois, his companion, is also a river guide; she's fair and athletic, but a little too slim; it seems she's been battling her share of micro-organisms. Both are deeply committed Buddhist practitioners. They're sitting in plastic chairs, fingering *malla* beads and intoning prayers to Tara, the Buddhist Goddess of Compassion.

It's surprising I wasn't grouped up with them. But they're on their own trip: a customized itinerary that includes more time at Kailash, and long breaks for prayer and meditation. Not my thing; though I respect Tibetan Buddhism, its trimmings are a bit too rococo for my tastes. The visualization of multiple gods, worship of bejeweled idols, and prostrations to high lamas conflict fundamentally with my own cultural conditioning—which featured an unseeable God, kosher gelatin, and a long tradition of heroes who would rather die than bow.

Tsering returns from his negotiations, and leads me toward a corner of the waiting area. A dark-haired woman sits alone, listening to a portable CD player and mouthing subaudible lyrics. "Jeff, meet Helga," he announces. Helga removes her headphones. We shake hands, smile, and make a bit of small talk.

"So where are you from?"

"Munich. It is in the south."

"I've been there. It's a lovely city."

"Yes, it's okay."

Helga, on first impression, brings to mind the Grinch: not Jim Carrey, but the actual Grinch, as drawn by Dr. Seuss. Despite her smile, there is a sourness in her eyes, an air of bitter disappointment. Her greeting is devoid of warmth. She glances repeatedly at the ticket counter, where a wiry man in a salmon-pink GoreTex expedition monkey suit is sorting through a handful of passports.

"Tsering tells me that you've been on this trek before."

"Yes. Last September."

"They say it's quite difficult. You must really enjoy the mountains to return so soon."

But Helga has stopped listening; the man in the monkey suit is approaching. This, as I'd suspected, is Padma.

"Hello, Sir!" He greets me with enthusiasm, pumps my hand, and smiles, showing a thousand white teeth. He's fit and handsome, with a square jaw and a compact frame.

The moment Tsering has departed, Padma sits beside Helga. She envelopes him like a vine, throwing her arms around his neck and her leg over his thigh. I have ceased to exist. Her eyes gaze into his. I cough; she casts me a defiant look. A cold flash grips my spine, like the sudden realization that I'm on the wrong train.

Tsering, I realize, has made an empty promise. The obstacles on this pilgrimage will be very different from anything I had envisioned. "I hadn't been aware," I remark casually, "that you two are involved in a relationship."

Helga smiles thinly, tightening her grip on Padma. "Now you know," she says.

BATIKA BORDERLAND BLUES

Nepalganj is one mile from the border with India. This part of Nepal, the Terai lowlands, is as flat and brown as a *chapati*. Even from the airplane it looks griddle-hot, the ground iridescent with heat shimmer. Two Maruti jeeps, Indian-made, meet us at the airport. We careen toward the Batika Hotel down the center of the main road, our driver blasting his horn at the streams of bicycles, trucks, bullock carts and pedestrians. There's a school on our right. The crosswalk "yield" sign—a white triangle, bordered in red—shows the silhouetted figures of two schoolgirls, clutching their books and running for their lives.

Nepalganj feels more like India than Nepal—narrow stooped men with gray beards and white *dhotis*, humped Brahmin bulls pulling wooden carts piled with hay, cheek-to-jowl shops festooned with brightly painted signs: DEEP GUEST HOUSE, BUDDHA PHOTO, SHITALL COMMUNICATIONS.

The Batika itself is basic, but serviceable. The last two keys are given to Brad and Lois, and me. Helga and Padma move to a nearby hotel; they don't tell me which. I climb the stairs, and flop onto my bed. The room is tolerable while the fans are spinning, but when the electricity fails—and it fails a dozen times that first afternoon—the heat is stupefying.

Despite clear skies in Nepalganj, the weather in northwestern Nepal is bleak: black clouds and thunderstorms. There have been no flights to Simikot for two days. More than a dozen Spanish trekkers are stranded at the Batika, filling their days with Tuborg beer and Star TV's Arnold Schwarzenegger marathon.

My attempts to engage Padma in conversation have been fruitless. His English, muttered in strings of disconnected words, is incomprehensible. Our exchanges are greeted with naked hostility by Helga. She glares at me, pulling on Padma's pink GoreTex sleeve as I ask him to repeat himself, to please speak up, trying with all my might to make sense of sentences like, "Coming time, soon tomorrow, airplane, we see possible, I think."

Up in the room, for lack of anything else to do, I dump out my duffel bag and rearrange the contents. It is amazing how much crap I've brought. The chocolate truffles have melted, coating the cover of an Oscar Wilde omnibus. Here is a plug-in mosquito destroyer, and a box of instant oatmeal. Somehow, I've packed a tie. At the bottom of the heap is the mountain gear: expedition-weight long johns, fleece gloves and glove liners, thick wool socks, a GoreTex parka. Just looking at this stuff makes me sweat. But Kailash is high, and the air is thin. Though it seems inconceivable, I'll be grateful for those long johns someday. With any luck, I might need them tomorrow.

Lois joins me for dinner. She laughs easily, her thin frame tented in a light cotton dress that I envy in this heat. She's been to Kailash three times; this is Brad's first visit. The trip is a spiritual experiment for the couple, who have guided together on the Colorado River for years. Though Lois is a veteran Buddhist, Brad took his vows only a year ago. Having spoken with him during lunch, I know something Lois doesn't. Brad plans to propose to her atop the Drolma La: a dizzying, 18,600' pass at the midpoint of the Kailash kora.

We wake up at five, congregate in the hotel lobby, and pile into a bus bound for the airport. The Spanish travelers, who arrived at the terminal even earlier, have gone nowhere. I watch with bloodshot eyes as the sun rises over the Ganges Plain, sucking every molecule of dew out of the dun-colored grasses. Word arrives two hours later: all flights to Simikot are canceled, for the third day in a row. We file miserably onto the bus, arriving back at the Batika by nine.

Kam zher, lam khyer: Bring it to the path.

The second most comfortable spot at the Batika, aside from the algae-coated swimming pool, is the dining room, where a row of ceiling fans twist the air into an asthmatic breeze. Waiting for lunch, I read the personal notices in the *Times of India*:

> *My Dearest Meenakshi, you are my everything. I am nothing without your friendship. You will be in my heart forever, even if you hate me.*—Harish

> *Dearest Priyanka, I love you a lot. And I mean it. But I know you won't ever love me. That's why I am going to Puna forever. I will miss you a lot. Bye and love you*—Arshad

And so the hours pass: rationing my novel, watching *True Lies*, sleeping, watching *Judgment Day*, commiserating with Brad and Lois, and drinking liter after liter of "Good" brand drinking water.

The flights to Simikot are grounded a fourth consecutive day. A pilot at the airport shakes his head; the weather system seems rooted in place. There may be no flights for quite a while.

It's getting serious. The Saga Dawa festival is happening as sched-uled, whether we make it or not. Even if we fly tomorrow, our week-long trek to the Tibetan border will have to be made in five days. The good news is Helga, Padma and I will now be camping at the same sites as Brad and Lois. But if the plane doesn't fly, our only alternative is to backtrack to Kathmandu, and drive. Before we leave the airport, I corner Padma in the men's room.

"Padma, we need to discuss our options. What we can do if the plane is canceled tomorrow."

He nods. "I think maybe sometime coming after telephone—but listen tomorrow, sir. "

"Pardon?" A strident honking erupts in the background. "That's the bus. Listen, can the three of us talk about this over lunch?"

"Okay, sir."

Lunch is served at one. Brad and Lois join me, then disappear into their room for the two o'clock showing of *Predator*.

Helga and Padma wander in fifteen minutes later, and head for the far end of the room. They see me, but make no sign of greeting. I give them time to settle in, then move to join them.

They're arranged side by side. I sit across the table, and fold my hands. "Hi, guys. Food's pretty good here, no?" There is no response; I bulldoze ahead. "So. What are we thinking about tomorrow?"

There is a long and icy silence. Helga ignores me completely; Padma glances guiltily up from his food, his gaze reaching as high as my neck.

"Well," I begin, "I'd like to talk about…"

"Leave us alone," Helga snaps. "Can't you see we're eating?"

"I'm sorry if this is bad timing, but it's our only chance to talk about these plans."

"There is nothing to discuss. Padma is on vacation. With *me*."

"Pardon me?"

"When I pay to Tsering, I tell him I want a three week trek with Padma—*alone*. This is our vacation. You had better take care for yourself."

This is clearly the moment to confront our resident hellcat and inform her, in lively terms, that I, too, have paid for an equal share of our guide's attention. Or to pick up the phone, call Tsering in Kathmandu, and inform him that Padma and Helga are becoming… *troublesome*. But Helga's remark has stunned me like a cattle prod, and I find myself mute with anger and anxiety. My mind snaps back to that brief Tibetan maxim, offered by Ian on the slopes of Nagarjun: *Whatever happens… whatever arises… bring it to the path.*

For better or worse, this situation is my karma; my challenge; my fate. The most beneficial thing I can do is remain calm, and accept the fact that my journey to Kailash will be a solitary one.

I hold my peace, rise silently, and walk from the room.

A LEECH NAMED RAMBO

Mountain weather is calmest in the early morning. We stagger down to the dining room at 4:30 a.m., eat pale toast, and bus to the airport before dawn. The clouds hold steady, and we take off just after sunrise. Our altitude is never more that a few thousand feet above the ground. We leave the flatlands and enter the middle hills, flying level with terraced hillsides. Rivers shine below us; thin trails uncoil between scattered villages like tapeworms. The hills become sharper—the Himalayas are growing almost as fast as the elements can erode them—and snow appears on the peaks. A few minutes later we bank west, and descend into a carpeted valley toward Simikot. We have traveled, in less than an hour, from nearly sea level to 9,500' altitude.

I step off the plane. The air is crystalline, and snow-covered peaks gleam almost painfully against the sky. Cows graze alongside the dirt runway. There's a storybook quality to the scene. But the dark side tips its hand, as well. Uniformed soldiers holding automatic rifles stand at every corner of the airstrip. We are deep in Maoist country.

How quickly it all comes back. The agony, first. The slow, panting ascent on protesting legs; the throbbing in the temples, as the brain sputters along on a fraction of its usual oxygen; the kids with their necklaces and nose rings, whining for pens or sweets or *one rupee*. And then there's a pass: white prayer flags flap above a cairn of mantra-etched *mani* stones, and mountains foam on the horizon.

This is not designer hiking. The trails are rocky and ungroomed, with long descents down slippery gravel and longer ascents on splintery scree. The villages are ramshackle, like shanty towns, with few outward signs of worship or celebration. Locals stare at me as I pass; their children wear filthy, tattered clothing, or nothing at all. It is difficult to see where even a penny of forty years' worth of aid money—millions of dollars from nearly every developed nation—has gone.

The rebels, with their own perspective on the poverty and corruption, have tightened their grip on the Humla region. I hear more from Ramraj, a young schoolteacher who is walking back to his village from Simikot.

"The Maoists are big trouble," he admits.

"Have they bothered you personally?"

"Of course. They are taking from each schoolteacher one half of our salary!"

The annual salary for teachers like Ramraj—who also has a wife and child to support—is less than $200.

Mid-afternoon we arrive at Dharapuri, a one-horse village along a tributary of the Karnali, and wait for our gear. It's been a short day, but we need to acclimate to the altitude. I unpack my laptop, and sit down to make a few notes.

Jigme, the sharp and articulate guide assigned to Brad and Lois, is assembling a tent in the broad corral reserved for trekking groups. He sees me working, and hurries toward my bench. "Better if you wait," he whispers. "The *maobadis* will come to this village as soon as they know we are here. They want mostly money—but if they see this machine, they may take it also."

It's good counsel. I stow the laptop—along with my cameras, cash and Clif Bars—in the foot of my mummy bag.

They move into the village in the late afternoon, reaching a force of about eight by twilight. They're boys, really, ranging in age between 15 and 20, armed with locally-made rifles, daggers, and a lot of attitude. Wearing Nikes and jeans, they're far better dressed than any of the other locals.

The requisite "donation," they inform us, has been raised; it's now $100 per person. Padma and Jigme will have to pony up 7,000 rupees ($90), and our Nepalese cook 5,500. Even our barefoot porters will part with 150 rupees each; an extortionate sum in a country where the average monthly income is less than $25.

Brad, Lois and I combine our stashes. Setting aside the suggested tips for our guides and staff, we come up with a total of $180—not two-thirds of what the rebel bandits have demanded.

I ask to speak with their leader. My plan is simple and brilliant: I'll inform him that we just don't have enough money to pay. Jigme reluctantly agrees to act as translator, and brings the man over. We squat outside my tent, a few feet from the edge of an unprotected drop onto the trail, a good twenty feet below. The Maoist deputy, who calls himself Rambo, perches on the edge, a bayoneted rifle slung loosely over his left shoulder. It occurs to me that, with a slight nudge, I could bump him right off the cliff. I can't say I'm not tempted.

We banter for nearly an hour, Jigme addressing Rambo in grave and respectful tones. He tells him that I am a journalist, and that publicity for the Maoist ideals might be more valuable than money.

"You would be far better off," I add, relying on his lack of Yiddish, "to let me write a story, and tell the whole world what *schmucks* you are."

Rambo nods. He moves off to confer with his superior, and returns after ten minutes. Jigme translates.

"He says that he agrees, but that this is the most difficult time in the peoples' struggle. Everyone—even we Nepalese—must pay the full amount. No exceptions."

"And if we just don't have the cash?" Even here, confronted by armed rebels, I resist paying retail.

Jigme looks at the ground and mutters the question to Rambo, who replies curtly. "He says they will take travelers' checks."

My mind races. Suppose I confront Rambo directly, flatly refusing to pay? What would he do? When locals give the Maoists trouble their legs are shattered, or they're skinned alive. But no foreigners have ever been harmed by the rebels. Even the *maobadis* are clever enough to realize that, long live the revolution, tourism will be a crucial source of revenue for many years to come. Would Rambo dare to harm a Western trekker? No, he would not... but he'd have few qualms about venting his frustration on our staff.

I fork over the $50 I'd set aside for staff tips, and Brad and Lois dig out $150 in American Express travelers' checks. They realize, with glee, that since the money is being stolen from us at gunpoint, American Express will be obliged to refund the checks. No such luck for me. I'm left with just 500 rupees—less than $7—for the next two weeks.

The good news is, I get a receipt. Rambo pulls a smart little booklet out of his satchel, and proceeds to write me up: "Your name, please?" The docket, illustrated with tiny pictures of Lenin, Marx, Trotsky, Mao and Stalin—Stalin!—is handsomely printed on glossy stock. Why the receipt? Simple. If any other armed rebels ambush me during the next twelve months, Rambo explains, simply show them this. I'd be free to go!

Nodding earnestly, I examine the receipt by the light of my headlamp. The production values are high; but in typical Nepali fashion, there's a marvelous spelling flaw, repeated endlessly in the back-pattern of the receipt. I'm now an official patron of Nepal's "Moism" party.

KARMIC DEBT

The Karnali is the texture of elephant hide, a boiling gray river that looks fully capable of cutting the gorge it thunders through—of cutting it another thousand feet. I trek along the base of a high cliff braided with waterfalls. They sluice down from invisible heights and join the main torrent, which receives their ablutions with barely a wrinkle.

Days pass. I walk alone. Brad and Lois are on their own schedule, walking at an easy pace, stopping frequently to meditate and recite Tibetan prayers. We connect at the campsites, in the mornings and evenings. I'm self-conscious about invading their privacy, but they—convinced that my plight has been choreographed by higher powers—accept my company as their own karmic debt. They invite me into their tent for dinner, laugh at my jokes and share their Snickers bars, none of which will make it any easier to part ways with them at the foot of Kailash.

In stark contrast stand Helga and our guide. Padma sets up my tent, but otherwise we have no contact. Helga refuses to even look at me; if I pass her at a rest stop she turns away from me, or buries her face in Padma's shoulder. The whole experience makes me feel loathsome, leprous.

It's common knowledge that she has forbidden Padma to speak with me. One morning, though, when she disappears into the toilet tent, Padma approaches me like a sad puppy. He is dressed in his perennial outfit, the salmon-pink GoreTex expedition monkey suit given to him by Helga.

"I am sorry, sir," he whimpers. Away from his succubus, he's surprisingly articulate. "I want to speak with you. But she gets so angry if I talk to you for even one minute! She will take back these clothes, and everything. What to do?"

Padma stands before me, his eyes wide. For the first time, I see him as he is: a desperately confused 23-year-old, caught between duty and opportunity. There's no point warning him about losing his job; the one thing every young Nepali man wants, aside from a date with Manisha Koirala, is to get out of Nepal. The American Embassy in Kathmandu receives an average of 1,500 visa applications a day, but grants just 10 percent of them. Helga has promised him a ticket to Germany, paid housing, and an education—so long as he continues to obey.

"It's all right, Padma," I say. "I can take care of myself." I'm neither bitter nor resigned; it's a proactive statement. Brad and Lois are right: viewed in the context of pilgrimage, my dilemma makes a crazy kind of sense. I'm doing this trip alone.

The cooking staff, sympathetic to my bizarre situation, attends to my comfort with a persistence that borders on parody. Afternoon tea, during which they arrive at my tent door with a tray of biscuits and beverages, is a Nepalese version of "Who's on First?"

"Tea, Sir?"

"Hot chocolate, please." I spoon sweetened Cadbury's into my cup, and the boy pours hot milk from an aluminum kettle. I stir.

"Take sugar?"

"No, thank you."

"Black tea?"

"I have a full cup of chocolate."

"Milk, Sir?"

"No, I have plenty of milk."

"Coffee?"

"No thank you; I'm drinking chocolate."

"Have a biscuit?"

"Please."

"Have another?"

"Thank you."

"Another?"

"Thank you."

"Another?"

"That's enough."

"Tea, Sir?"

"I'm still drinking chocolate."

"Coffee?"

"I think not."

"We like you, sir."

"And why is that?"

"You speak Nepali very well."

"I barely speak at all."

"You are our man, sir."

"Thank you."

"Black tea?"

I dream that night of death: my own death, in various tableaux. Falling off a smooth rock overhanging a huge drop, possibly over the Karnali River. Groping desperately for purchase, then experiencing that final moment, the awareness that death is only a thought away. My body falling through space, landing on the rocks below. All such thoughts—including my fantasies of violence against the Maoists, and repressed anger about Helga—seem part of a pre-Kailash purification, sort of like the Dolby system. My most fearsome and negative aspects will swell in volume, roaring with high-pitched static, before they are expunged by the Jewel of the Snows.

HEAVEN'S DOOR

The trail is littered with round black pellets: sheep shit. Even now, sheep are used as pack animals in the Himalaya, carrying pillow-sized bags to Purang, over the border in occupied Tibet. There, the bags will be filled with coarse white salt. The salt will be carried back to Humla, and traded for rice. We pass through the village of Muchuu. No need to stop at the checkpost; it's a pile of blackened stones, burned months ago by the Maoists.

We're above treeline now; there's nothing but lichen, shrubs, and stunted juniper. The trail shines bright as moondust. It looks like stratified clay; the dried-up mud of an ancient seabed. The path here is level, and very wide. Kathmandu-based bureaucrats—few of which, if any, have even set foot in this district—have approved a road through Humla. The motorway would link Simikot with the Chinese town of Purang, an hour's drive from the border. When finished, it will put countless nomads and traders out of work.

"Don't hold your breath," Brad assures me. "Despite the grading, they've got a long way to go." The main obstacles to completing the project (besides landslides, the monsoon and generally suspect engineering) are the rebels, who have vowed to attack the road as soon as it becomes operational.

Some distance beyond lies the settlement of Tharo Dunga: site of a natural "pillar stone" that once marked the border between Nepal and Tibet. The riverside meadows served as a trading post as well, where merchants from north and south could meet and exchange their salt and rice.

Approaching Tharo Dunga the hills are bare, striped with veins of mineral and patches of snow, immense beyond comprehension. To the south rises a pyramidal peak, home of the goddess who swallows the sun and creates eclipses.

It's a spectacular trail, 14,000' high, winding far above the tree line. No one else is in sight. Clouds swirl over my head like sentient wraiths, assuming sacred shapes, and the air rings like a bell. I feel an overwhelming sense that I've entered one of those phenomenal spots where the lines are open, where the landscape gets holy, and spooky; where one might speak directly to God.

It's been the toughest day of our trek, climbing more than 3,000 vertical feet. Tomorrow we ascend another thousand feet, then drop to the border towns of Hilsa (in Nepal) and Zher (Tibet).

Brad, who has a sharp eye for detail, witnessed a remarkable sight this afternoon: a yak, dropping dead from heat exhaustion. For generations, yaks have been used to ply these salt and rice trading routes. By the late 1990s, though, the temperature had warmed so dramatically that yaks could no longer tolerate the heat. Mules and sheep are now the pack animals of choice. No one knows why the weather has altered this way, or where the climate is going. So far, the locals have been able to adapt; it will take the yaks a few thousand years longer.

It hardly matters. Ten years from now, this area of Nepal will be unrecognizable. Yaks and mules will be obsolete. Panel trucks will grunt along the newly completed road, carving ruts in the landscape and littering the hillsides with beer bottles, cigarette packets and blue plastic bags. The air will smell of diesel. By then, of course, the Chinese may have built an airport over the border in Ali, turning Mount Kailash itself into an easily accessible tourist haven—something they've already achieved with the Potala Palace, in Lhasa.

We climb uphill from Tharo Dunga, through dry grass speckled with wildflowers. The sky is a lapis blue you see only in Marvel comics. At this elevation, our eyes play tricks on us; it's all tied in with the oxygen. Back home, closer to sea level, we look at a hill and know, in our brain and body, how high it is. We know how much effort it will take to carry ourselves to the top. A boulder perched twenty yards up the trail looks close—but try reaching it. It seems to recede with every step, like the finish line in Zeno's Paradox.

Crossing the Nara La, the 14,620' saddle separating Nepal and Tibet, is a victory of the spirit; the pass seemed impossibly distant even when it was 100 feet away. The view from that aerie was the textbook image of Tibet: a barren and ancient sea floor, uplifted three miles into the air.

The most brutal part of the day is not the uphill to the pass, nor the downhill to the river, but the climb from Hilsa to the army encampment at Zher. Heat waves shimmered from the trail, a Sisyphan ladder of sand. By the time I reached the checkpost, my face felt like seared ahi tuna.

For some reason, no one ever searches me. The teenage soldiers at Zher glance briefly at my gear, and move on with trusting smiles. Brad and Lois, arriving an hour later, are not as lucky. Can the Chinese smell American Buddhists? Their duffels are ransacked. The process turns absurd when the soldiers, who are looking for pictures of the Dalai Lama—his image is banned in Tibet—stumble upon Lois's stash of cassettes. Suspecting subversive messages from the exiled Tibetan leader, they demand the tapes be played. Brad's Walkman is produced—it has a built-in speaker—and the first recording inserted. The squadron commander squints at the unit, and pushes the "play" button.

"Start me up!"

The soldiers pull out a sack packed with underwear, and fish between the socks and panties.

"Start me up! Start me up! I'll never stop..."

They find Lois's journal, flip intently through the pages, and peer suspiciously through her binoculars.

"You make a grown man cry..."

One soldier tastes her bottle of contact lens solution, while another examines her jog bra with hesitant curiosity, like the ape confronting the monolith in *2001: A Space Odyssey.*

"You make a grown man cry..."

DEMON'S LAKE

I'm introduced to Tashi, our local guide: a stocky, strong-willed, English-speaking Tibetan with a chronic cough. Tashi hones in immediately on the monkey business between Padma and Helga, and snorts in disgust. He's seen this mess a dozen times or more: the lonely woman bartering sexual favors from her Sherpa guide, and calling it love.

Our vehicles await us: sturdy Toyota Land Cruisers that will serve as our steeds for the trans-Tibetan voyage. Our guides pack them to the dome lights, every cubic inch filled with camping gear, food and gasoline. We have trekked five days, and forty-five miles, to reach this point; we'll drive an equal distance in the next ninety minutes.

A rock-strewn, washboard road takes us from the hellhole of Zher to the shithole of Purang, a once-proud Tibetan trading village now controlled by the Chinese army. The town looks like a defunct factory yard, shortly after the Apocalypse. No Tibetan architecture remains; just row after row of anonymous blockhouse shops.

"These days, so many Chinese prostitutes," Tashi laments, surveying the ramshackle doorways. "They are even showing prawn movies."

Our guesthouse, a bare official edifice, could as easily be a prison. The beds are comfortable, though, a welcome relief after four nights in a tent. I'm bunked with Brad and Lois in a two-room suite.

Padma pokes his head in long enough to drop off my bag. We exchange a few words about tomorrow's drive. Through the window, I hear Helga yelling his name and stamping her foot. Tashi runs up to her. "What's the problem?"

"Padma should be with me. I don't allow him in there."

Our Tibetan guide chuckles. "It's not for you to tell him where to be."

Helga looks at him as if he's something she's scraped off her shoe. "You don't understand," she says. "Padma is very poor."

Tashi's eyes blaze. "And you think that..."

"Padma is poor," she continues, "and my husband is very rich. I was going to help Padma, and bring him to school in Germany, and buy his clothes. Do you see what he wears? Do you know how much it costs?" She's referring, of course, to the salmon-pink GoreTex expedition monkey suit. "More than 3,000 marks! Yes. I was going to do everything for him. But now, I am not too sure."

Tashi sputters, his motherboard in flames. He's been short-circuited by the Prime Directive of guiding: never make enemies of your clients, especially the ones who can tip. As for defending Padma—there's no mileage there, either. He holds his tongue, walks toward the hotel restaurant, and orders a large beer.

That evening, Helga drinks as well. We hear her railing at her lover, her voice crackling with hysteria. Doors slam, and a bottle breaks.

Bring it to the path.

North of Purang lies a frontier so vast that the mind cannot contain it. Too bad it's China; this would be the perfect training ground for a NASA Mars mission. To our right, the diamond-bright slopes of Gurla Mandhata (25,348') rise at a low incline, like the cone of Olympus Mons.

We sight Mount Kailash soon after. It is a lone incisor, biting through the haze, barely visible beyond the waters of Raksas Tal— Demon's Lake. Small as it is, the sight is stunning, like one's first sight of Machu Picchu or the Grand Canyon. Tashi taps the driver, and we pull over onto the roadside gravel. The doors burst open and we spill out, grateful for the chance to stretch our legs.

With the engine turned off, the world is eerily quiet. Two crows cry overhead, and the wind churns the dust into dancing vortices. I take a few pictures, aware that it's a futile effort: this landscape cannot be captured.

The other Land Cruiser appears in the distance, a splotch of whirling dust. We move back toward our car. "We're coming to a checkpoint," Tashi informs us, "so we have to change seats. It's better if I sit in front. Padma, please go behind the driver. Helga and Jeff in the middle."

"I will *not*," Helga shouts. Her face is contorted with fear.

Tashi looks at her, dumbfounded.

Helga breathes rapidly. "In Germany," she says, "I have a special gift: I can read auras. You know what means this, 'aura'?"

Tashi nods.

"Yes? Good. It is the energy field around a person. It can be every different color: gold, red, purple, blue. But *he*—" She jabs a finger in my direction—"has a *black* aura. Completely black. Horrible. Dangerous. I cannot be in that energy field. Not for one second."

This is new. "Helga," I say, "You're going to have to put aside your..."

"A black aura!" She hisses. "And everything that comes out of his mouth, it is like diarrhea."

There's a long silence. Tashi looks stunned; Padma hangs his head. Our driver, grinning slightly, lights a cigarette. I take a deep breath of my own. "If I'd known this was your problem, Helga," I say, "I would have called for a helicopter, and had you medically evacuated from Nepalganj. But there's nothing to be done for it now. Let's just get in the car, sit quietly, and be good little pilgrims."

Helga brightens. "That's a good idea," she says.

"Thank you."

"No; it is good idea you go by helicopter. We call today for heli-copter. Padma... *Padma*! Please, you call for helicopter. We send him away by helicopter. Very good idea. We call from camp. You go tomor-row. By helicopter!"

With this Helga runs off, disappearing down the steep grade sur-rounding the lake. A few minutes later we see her, skipping along the edge of Raksas Tal. Padma runs off to fetch her, his pink costume glowing in the distance.

"Not good," whispers Tashi, his voice already weary. "A crazy one."

I turn to him gamely. "Which?"

The second Land Cruiser pulls up behind us. Brad rolls down his window; *Sticky Fingers* thumps from three-inch speakers. "What's up?"

Tashi explains the situation. After a brief discussion, Jigme gets out—he'll ride in my place—and Brad and Lois make room for me beside them. As I climb in, they scan me with narrowed eyes.

"All right, guys. What's the verdict?"

"You're aura-free—as far as we can tell." A pregnant pause. "But we don't have the gift."

This gets a laugh. But as we drive onward, gaining altitude, my spirits fall with the air pressure. The prospect of another ten days with Helga is intolerable.

"Lois." I try not to sound desperate. "You're a Buddhist practitioner. You've taken the vows. What strategy would you use with Helga?"

She leans back, staring upward. "That's a tough one.... Let me think."

"She's obviously unstable," I add. "So I shouldn't take this stuff personally. But she's getting under my skin. I just can't believe that I'm being forced to deal with this kind of craziness—or my own anger."

"Welcome to Kailash," Lois says.

"So the rumors are true." I stare out the window. "It really is a crucible."

"Absolutely. And the first thing you have to realize is, this is not about Helga. It's about you. And if *I* were you.... Well, I'd be upset, of course, but I'd also be grateful."

"You're kidding."

"I'm not. According to the Dalai Lama—and not just him—the people who cause us the most grief are our greatest teachers. They provide priceless opportunities to control our anger, and deconstruct our egos."

"What are you suggesting?"

"Every time Helga hassles you, thank her. Graciously and sincerely."

At first, the suggestion seems absurd. But maybe Lois is right; there's a definite attraction in the thought of taking the spiritual high ground. And the devil, on my other shoulder, likes the idea as well. Because if I were in Helga's position, and someone started thanking *me*, it would send me through the roof.

"I'll try it," I say.

FLIES AND BUDDHAS

We spend a night by the edge of Manasarovar, an expansive, gem-blue lake just east of Raksas Tal. Of the two lakes, Manasarovar is by far the holier site, revered by Hindu pilgrims as an emanation of the Mind of Brahma. A sip of its waters, the old texts say, absolves the sins of a hundred lifetimes. Our cook boils a pot—liberating millions of amoebas from their humble incarnation—and we mix holy water with powdered chocolate.

Early the next morning I walk to the shore with an empty plastic bottle. Water from Manasarovar is highly prized, and I will take some back to Kathmandu. But the lake's surface is frozen solid; if I want this blessing, I must break the ice with my fist. On the way back to camp I'm spied by Helga, who ducks back into her tent. I suck my scraped knuckles, tasting a metaphor.

At least thirty Land Cruisers leave Manasarovar within minutes of each other. We drive, half-blinded, across the surface of a hostile alien planet whose atmosphere consists entirely of dust. I will myself into a state of suspended animation. Ten minutes or three years later, the air clears. Just ahead lies Darchen, our final pre-kora destination. We scan the horizon—but Kailash, which should be visible from this vantage, is hidden behind clouds.

As the gateway city to Asia's holiest mountain, Darchen leaves much to be desired. Before the Cultural Revolution, this was a Tibetan way-station; now it's a Chinese checkpoint. The hybrid combines the worst of the two cultures. The place is so crowded, littered, and filthy that it reminds me of the live-in dumps photographed by Sebastião Salgado. Even the dogs seem appalled, sniffing at the garbage with flaccid tails.

But there's an energy here, an atmosphere that transcends the human stain. The upper plain is an ocean of trucks and buses, festooned with prayer flags and loaded with supplies. They carry pilgrims and monks, seekers and tourists, musicians and madmen. Beyond lies a vast expanse of desert, without an end in sight. And the dust! There is dust everywhere. Trucks and Land Cruisers and hurricanes of dust, blood red dust, gyring and gusting on the infinite plateau.

We stop for two hours. Padma and Tashi bargain for gasoline and perishables. I lace up my boots. The others will drive around the mountain's flank, meet the Lha Chu River, and pitch camp near the broad meadow where the Saga Dawa pole will be erected. The site is some six miles away. Since I hope to complete the entire kora—all 35 miles of it—I stay behind, and set off on my own, from Darchen itself.

Ten minutes of walking, and the trash and bedlam are far behind. Tibetan families amble along the dirt trail, ahead of me and behind, the elders spinning copper prayer wheels filled with the mantra of Chenrezig: *om mani padme hum!* Pilgrims in heavy woolen robes take three steps, raise their joined palms, then prostrate themselves on the ground—a rhythm they will follow around the entire mountain. Thin leather pads protect their hands and knees; in a year or two, they'll discover rollerblading gear.

After two hours on a gentle upgrade, I round a bend. The clouds have cleared, and the mountain—The Mountain—explodes into view.

Like a million pilgrims before me, I stare with unabashed awe.

Each side of Kailash has a name of its own. This, the "sapphire" face, is a striped white dome, crowned by a low nipple. Seen from here, it's tempting to think of Kailash in feminine terms. But according to myth, the mountain is intensely male: the ultimate phallus, rooted in the depths and rising up to heaven. Mere humans, of course, can't see the big picture. To my eye the mountain evokes a muscled ribcage, thrust upward, defying the pilgrim to find its heart.

The trail veers north, and the landscape transforms. A river flows below. Sandstone cliffs rear up above the dramatic Lha Chu valley, its elongated floor punctuated by boulders, yaks, and countless tent camps.

The first part of the kora ends at Serchung, where a chaotic settlement has sprung up around the supine Saga Dawa pole. Smoke from powdered juniper—*trang*—pours into the air from a white, womb-shaped censer. There are hundreds of Tibetan tents, brocaded with the Eight Auspicious Symbols.

On a typical Saga Dawa, a few thousand pilgrims might converge on the "Golden Basin" of Serchung, a natural amphitheater beneath Kailash's snow-stepped southern face. This May, for the Horse Year, Serchung is packed with an estimated 45,000 pilgrims. The crowd is dense, devotional and rowdy; a cross between a Papal *benedizione* and the NBA playoffs.

It's a long walk from the meadow to my tent, which Tashi has wisely erected at the far edge of the vast encampment. Settling in, I'm mesmerized by the unobstructed view. Kailash is a dream, a gem, a palace. Recognizing this mountain as the holiest of holies was one of the many things the Asians got right. There is simply nothing like it. The shape—call it breast, phallus, or cream-covered pastry—strikes a deep chord in the collective unconscious. It seems utterly familiar; though not necessarily, I realize with a shock, from this lifetime.

A timeless moment—until an Austrian tour group parks its Land Cruisers between our camp and the mountain. I watch helplessly as they erect their toilet tent directly in my line of sight; so directly, in fact, that it seems to have been planned by geomancy, the flat khaki peak of the outhouse perfectly aligned with Kailash's signature nipple.

I recall the words of Issa, a Japanese poet/monk:

Where there are humans
You'll find flies, and Buddhas.

All night the wind buffets my tent, making it shake like a palsied cow. I dream that a deafening avalanche sweeps through the camp, carrying Helga's tent—with Helga in it—off a mile-high cliff. When I crawl out in the frigid morning, Kailash has a fresh coating of snow. A biting wind blows down the valley. I duck behind a house-sized boulder, scaring off a prairie dog. The sky is pale lavender, and the cliffs are tinged with persimmon.

Our cook tent, with its high roof and canvas walls, is the warmest place in camp. Padma makes an appearance, silently assembling his lover's meal—she'd rather crouch in her foxhole, cramped and cold, than share the space with me. I'm actually disappointed; there's been nothing to thank her for. One more hot chocolate, and a slathering of sunscreen and I join the mass migration to the Golden Meadow.

The Saga Dawa pole is immense—at least twenty feet high, with a steel trunk about two feet thick. One end touches the ground, near a deep anchor hole. The other is raised above the ground, pointing at the sun-drenched flanks of Kailash. A stocky Grand Marshal in yellow lama's garb sits astride the post, high above the ground, tying long cords of prayer flags to its shaft.

Never before have so many come to this festival. There are tens of thousands of people, with many more already on the kora. Most sit on the surrounding hillside, like picnickers at a free concert; hundreds more churn in a wide doughnut around the central tower, held at bay by Chinese police. Pilgrims from Outer Mongolia and Ootacamund mingle with Tibetans from Amdo and Kham. It's a scene from the Silk Road's heyday: a hodgepodge of silks and rags, turquoise and silver, animal hides, vinyl, leather, pink cinnabar, pearls the size of golf balls, and hat of every description, from plastic fedoras to jeweled and feathered turbans. There are faces from Samarkand's heyday, the consorts of Genghis Khan, infants at the breast, Chinese troops with battery-powered shock batons, South Indian saddhus, and Japanese tourists in Hello Kitty earmuffs.

Beseiged by so many distractions, it's easy to forget the point of this event. It isn't being staged for spectators. Tibetan Buddhism, for all its pomp and dogma, has a very simple core. The Dalai Lama sums it up elegantly: *My religion is kindness.* And the point of that kindness, whether toward oneself or toward humanity, has a single goal: the end of suffering.

With that in mind, the purpose of this ritual is clear. The pilgrims at Saga Dawa have come to shout a huge, collective prayer. They are here to save the world.

A collective roar jolts me back to the present. The pole is ready, and the auspicious moment has come. There's a shout from the Grand Marshal, and the hoisting begins.

In days gone by, the Saga Dawa pole was pulled into position by yaks. There are still plenty of them in Tibet—it's much colder than Nepal—but these days, the organizers rely on Chinese trucks. Two diesel winches, along with three strong ropes manned by scores of Tibetans, pull the column erect. Black smoke boils into the air, and the post slowly climbs toward the vertical. It wobbles, tilts to the right, and falls snugly into its anchor. The moment it's up, the crowd goes wild—and the cops can't hold them back. An enormous mob rushes the center, throwing handfuls of trang, *tsampa* (buckwheat flour), and white silk *kata* scarves. I echo their victory cry: *Ha Gyel Lo!* Minutes later, we're drowned out by a bellowing roar. A troupe of lamas parades through the crowd, bashing cymbals and blowing on Tibetan longhorns.

With the festival ending, the moment I've dreaded is at hand. Brad and Lois, who have shielded me from the full force of Helga's death ray, must now depart. They will abandon the crowds, and spend the next three days camping beside a remote monastery several miles from the Kailash kora. By the time they begin their circuit, mine will be complete.

We walk to the waiting Land Cruiser. Jigme is lashing their duffel bags to the roof rack. I wish I had a gift for him—he's far more deserving than Padma—but the "Moists" have leeched me dry. He wishes me well, clasping my hand between his.

Brad, the river guide turned lay monk, does the traditional guy-hugging, back-thumping thing. Lois's embrace is softer, and more fragile; I can feel the ribs beneath her shirt. "Have a wonderful time," she says.

"I just hope I can survive. It's going to be a tough trek without you."

"Just remember," says Brad, half-joking. "This is one of the four Great Festival Days. The karmic impact of everything you think, do or say—positive or negative—is multiplied 40,000 times."

"That's great. Do dreams count?"

"*Everything* counts."

"Of course." I sigh, and put my hands on their shoulders. "In that case, I just wish my buddies were sticking around."

Lois runs her arm around my waist, and turns me to face north. The immense face of Kailash billows against the sky.

She nods at the mountain, and gives me a look I haven't seen before. "There's your new best friend," she says. "Right there."

PACAZO

by ROY KESEY

HERE IN PIURA you must be very careful; if you are not careful enough, the pacazo will shit on your head. As you walk, you must watch for any hint of movement in the branches that intertwine above you. The pacazo is waiting. He will wait as long as it takes.

I want to be clear about something: pacazos are not birds. They are lizards five feet long. In other parts of Peru, I have heard, they live on the ground. Reynaldo tells me that here they live in trees because of the foxes that come out at night, but this cannot be true. The foxes are the size of housecats, and would stand no chance—if one were to pass too close to a pacazo on the ground, the pacazo would seize it by the head, crush its skull, and drag it up into the dark trees.

Often the pacazo here on campus is gray. Other times it is brown or black; its color depends on the light, I suspect. I have no idea what it eats. Birds' eggs, perhaps, or perhaps the birds themselves. Insects, snakes, smaller lizards. It must be carnivorous, I think, but it does not move gracefully in the trees or on the ground. It is too fat and too ugly to move gracefully anywhere. Sometimes it chooses a branch that will not hold its weight, and comes crashing down. After a moment, it steps slowly toward the nearest trunk, head up, crest erect and eyes slitted, choosing victims at random or by smell: its eyesight is poor. It steps slowly, as if it were ancient, and perhaps it is. Perhaps they never die.

Reynaldo, my friend and colleague, walks with me among the campus trees, the algarrobo, zapote, chapán. He teaches me the names of the trees, and we scan the branches for the pacazo, whose shit is nothing like bird shit. It is a pint of rancid molasses. It takes weeks to wash the smell out of your hair. Your students, all but one of them, become accustomed to sitting only in the farthest rows.

There are other smells here in Piura, of course. There is the air of offal and urine and sweat that wells up from the open drain near my house: most of the city's drains collapsed in the storms of the last El Niño, and have not yet been repaired. There is the smell of chalk and sweat in the classrooms. Of mushrooms and sweat in the brothels. Of jasmine and laurel, diamela and sweat in the streets late at night. It is always hot here. Always.

My wife smelled of mango and cypress and sage between her shoulder blades.

Reynaldo is a chemistry professor, not a botanist, but he is never wrong about the names of trees, and he warns me of what can fall on your head here in Peru. There is the pacazo shit. There are also the matacojudos. *Mata* comes from *matar*, to kill. *Cojudos* are idiots, imbeciles, and only an imbecile would stand beneath a matacojudo tree in April, which in Piura is the middle of autumn, when these trees drop their fruit. The matacojudo looks like the largest potato you have ever seen, the kind of potato that people marvel at, and save on their mantles, even in Idaho itself. They hang high and low on the tree and can weigh twenty pounds, and if one were to drop from any appreciable height and strike your cranium, it would bash through the bone. So far I have been lucky.

Matacojudos have no commercial use that I know of. Neither does pacazo shit, but it is in some ways essential: to your baby daughter you can say, "If you don't stop crying, the pacazo will come and shit on your head." According to what I have read, it's okay to say this to your baby daughter as long as you use a voice empty of agony or rage, and full of love. They only understand the tone.

Reynaldo mixes things, creates, teaches chemistry. I teach English, and mix nothing with anything else. The real professors look at me with expressions of pity and concern, though I make more money than they do. They invite me into their houses where there are parties, and women with long legs and short skirts and tight colorful blouses, and we drink and dance, and the rooms smell of rum and perfume and sweat. In some of the houses you will find a picture of the Sacred Heart of Christ: a beautiful bearded white man whose chest has been opened to bare his heart bound in thorn. If the picture is a painting rather than a poster, mounted at the bottom of the frame is a small red light bulb which is never turned off and is replaced immediately whenever it burns out. I do not know why, and do not wish to know.

My wife was a beautiful girl. Her black hair hung almost to her waist. Her eyes gathered all light. When she danced, the air went slick and sweet with her movement, and I leaned back against the wall to keep from falling. I wear gray dress shirts to work, now. Gray is one of my many colors.

In Piura, one often eats seafood for lunch, but never for dinner. When it rains hard and long, fires start and the water to your home is shut off. People wait in a careful line until the bus arrives, and then the line crushes forward and children are trampled. Everyone has porcelain figurines of puppies and rabbits and chickadees on their countertops. Do not ask why. No one knows.

Among other reasons, I came to South America because I was told that here even fat ugly men can marry beautiful, intelligent women who love to swim and dance and love, as long as the men have blue eyes and are not totally cojudo. It turns out that this is sometimes true. Pilar signed up for one of my classes not long after the pacazo shat on my head, and she sat in the front row alone. Reynaldo said that dating a student was manipulative, unethical, and repulsive, though not an uncommon phenomenon. I told him that he was right. He said she would break my heart. I did not listen.

Perhaps I would have listened if he had said, She will alter what it means to be in the world, she will go late to the market to buy mangos, she will peel them and cut them in slices, she will allow you to run the slices across her bare stomach and thighs and between her shoulder blades, the juice will become one of her many scents and flavors, and three weeks after giving birth to your child, she will be raped and strangled by a taxi driver who will abandon her fifteen miles from the highway deep in the Sechura Desert, where she will regain tortured, delirious consciousness, walk the wrong direction, and die of dehydration the following day.

Here, white people are called "colored." *Colorado*, colored, it is one of the words Peruvians use for us. In some contexts it may be translated as "reddish-brown," but here, I think, they call us colorado because we turn so many colors, and are so many colors at once. We start boll-white, and become pink when we go unethically, repulsively to the beach with the student we are dating, the student we will marry in early summer. Some time later our arms are the color of weak tea, our neck and forehead are still the pink of boiled shrimp, and the rest of our body remains boll-white. Peruvians find this remarkable.

I do not mean to imply, of course, that all Peruvians look alike. Emigrants came years ago from Eastern Europe, and their grandchildren are white, and the boys are called, like me, colorado, and the girls are called colorada. Other emigrants came from China and Japan and Korea, and their grandchildren are called *chino* or *china*. Blacks were brought as slaves and their grandchildren are called *negro* or *negra*. And the ones that look the way you once thought all Peruvians did—short of stature, dark-skinned, straight dark hair and small dark eyes—they are called *cholo* or *chola*. The Spaniards meant it as an insult. Now, like colorado and chino and negro, it is most often just a word.

I do not mean to imply, either, that all cholos look alike. And I am saying that it is not strange to be called by your color, here. It is simply what happens. The ones who call most often are the taxi drivers. There are hundreds of taxis in this small city, many more than are needed. To become a taxi driver you don't need a driver's license or insurance. You need only a car, and a taxista sticker, which is sold for ten cents in the market where you can also buy mangos, and galvanized tubs, and llama fetuses in big clear bottles.

The taxistas here are desperate for customers. They follow you down the street, honking repeatedly, begging you to need them. Asking them to stop honking does not help. Screaming at them and pounding your fat fists on their hood does not help either. They follow me slowly and shout *Colorado!* or *Mister!* "Mister" is one word they all know in English and have learned to pronounce almost correctly. Also,

"Marlon Brando" and "ten dollars." I do not know why they learn to say "ten dollars." You could cross town fifteen times for less.

That evening, Pilar tried to sneak out for fresh mangos, a surprise for me for the following morning. I caught her as I walked up the sidewalk, just back from work, from teaching the differences in pronunciation and meaning and use between "bat" and "vat," "seen" and "sin," "bread" and "breath." I caught her as she came out our front door, and I held her, and smelled the cypress of her, the sage. I asked where she was going, and she smiled and told me. She said that Mariángel, our baby daughter, was with the maid in the back bedroom. I did not need to worry about anything, she said. I could relax. Then she stopped the first taxi that passed by.

I loved and married Pilar for many reasons, and one was that she never listened to anything I said. I often say foolish things, and it made me happy that she found them amusing and ignored them. One thing I often said was, "Don't ride in front next to the driver. Ride in back, where you can get out in a hurry if you have to. You never know." I said it again that night. She laughed, mouth open, lips bright, and got in beside the driver. He was a thin, dark, brown-eyed man, like so many here. As he drove away, out of habit I glanced at the license plate. It began with "P," the first letter of her name, and ended with "22," her age.

Reynaldo walks beside me across campus and teaches me the names of the trees and asks why I do not go back to California. He would go to California if he could, he says. If they would give him a visa, he would travel to California and drink Cokes and eat hamburgers and go to Disneyland and love a tall blond woman on the beach. He would learn to speak English and play basketball, would teach chemistry at a university where the classrooms look onto the ocean and have ceiling fans that work at several speeds. He says this, and this is what I say: "What is the name of that tree over there, Reynaldo? You told me once before, but I've forgotten."

My students learn to conjugate. They learn to skim and scan. They learn to pronounce "volleyball" and to curse appropriately, to write resumes and reports and love notes, to ask favors without giving offense, all in English, as if this will help. I would like to tell them the truth, but they are too beautiful.

And this is what will happen tomorrow, or the day after tomorrow: I wake. I shower, scrubbing myself for ten or twenty minutes, because professorial body odor is the main reason students do not learn as much as they could. I feed Mariángel, dress and eat. I walk to work, and as I pass the small park not far from my house, a taxi follows me down the street, honking madly. The driver shouts *Colorado!* and I don't look up: looking up only encourages them. He pulls his cab closer to the sidewalk, says *Mister? Taxi?* and still I do not look up. I stare at the blinding sidewalk and smell the open drain. He glides away in his taxi, then decides I am worth one more try. He pulls over to the curb beneath the matacojudo tree. There he waits. Out of habit and hope, I glance at his license plate. It begins with "P" and ends with "22."

I do not move gracefully, not in trees and not on solid ground. I step slowly to his taxi, head up, eyes slitted against the sun. I look in through the window on the passenger's side, and his thin dark face is almost familiar. *It was you, wasn't it?* I say. *Mister?* he says. I open the door and drag him through and out of his taxi, I slam him against the hot hood, I reach up and pull one low fruit from the matacojudo tree, and with that fruit I strike and strike until his head bursts open.

No cars pass. It is likely that some or perhaps many of my neighbors heard and saw from their open windows. I walk back to my house and burn my bloodstained, brain-spattered clothes in the galvanized tub I bought yesterday at the market for this purpose. I gather the ashes in a paper bag. I shower and dress again. I scatter the ashes in the stagnant waters of the open drain before my house, and take a different path to work.

As I walk, of course, I suddenly remember: there are hundreds of taxis in this city. More than one license plate could well bear the same first letter, the same last two numbers. And perhaps the drivers exchange cars sometimes. There are thousands of dark-skinned, black-haired, brown-eyed men in this city. My poor eyes do not always see the differences.

I return to my house and call in sick. Reynaldo comes to see me in the evening, when the sky catches soft fire in the west, when the smells of jasmine and offal settle over me. He sits and watches as I hold the bottle of warm milk to Mariángel's lips. Reynaldo looks in my eyes, and he knows. He asks anyway.

- What happened?
- I killed him.
- The taxi driver? The one who....
- I think so.
- You're not sure?
- It is hard to be sure. I think so.
- Did anyone see you?
- I don't know.
- If anyone saw you, they will call the police, and the police will come. Not tonight, probably. Tonight they will only watch. They will come tomorrow morning.
- I know.
- I have friends in Bolivia.
- What would I do there?
- From there you could fly back to your country.
- And there? What would I do?

Reynaldo nods.

- And so?
- If no one comes, I'll be at work tomorrow afternoon.
- Would you like me to stay with you?
- No. Thank you, but no.
- Is there anything you need? Food or drink or....
- No, thank you. What I need cannot be bought.
- Perhaps you just don't know where to shop.

It is an old joke between us, and we smile weakly. Reynaldo nods again.

- Until tomorrow, then.
- Until tomorrow.

He leaves, and is back fifteen minutes later with the painting of the Sacred Heart from his house. He hangs it on an empty nail and plugs the red light into a socket. He shrugs and sits down on the couch beside me, staring up at the painting.

- Perhaps this will help.

I don't answer. Again he shrugs. He swallows and stands.

- Come by the laboratory tomorrow. I've planted a new tree beside the walkway—a lúcuma, from the Tarma Valley in Junín.

I say that I will, and watch as he walks out the door.

All this, the matacojudo and ashes and Sacred Heart, this is what will happen, tomorrow, or the next day, or the day after that. The details may differ—I have imagined it many ways—but not the results. For now, I will wait.

DOUG DORST lives in San Francisco, where he is finishing a novel, *Alive in Necropolis*, and a collection of stories, *The Surf Guru*, both of which will be published by Nan A. Talese/Doubleday.

JEFF GREENWALD'S most recent book is *Scratching the Surface: Impressions of Planet Earth, From Hollywood to Shiraz*. He lives in Oakland. For more information, visit www.jeffgreenwald.com.

A.M. HOMES's new book of stories, *Things You Should Know*, will be published by Harper Collins this September. She is the author of the novels *Music For Torching, The End of Alice, In A Country Of Mothers, Jack*, as well as the short story collection *The Safety of Objects*, and the artists' book *Appendix A:*. She is currently at work on a travelogue called *The California Project: People, Places and The Castle On The Hill*, which will be published at the very end of this year.

GABE HUDSON's story collection, *Dear Mr. President* (Knopf), will appear in September. His fiction has appeared in *McSweeney's 4* and *8*, *Black Book*, and *The New Yorker*. He lives in New York City, where he instructs alternative survival courses.

DENIS JOHNSON is the Playwrite-In-Residence at Campo Santo and Intersection for the Arts in San Francisco. He is the author of seven books (including *Angels* and *Jesus' Son*), five books of poetry (including the anthology *The Throne of the Third Heaven of the Millenium General Assembly*), and *Seek: Reports from the Edges of America and Beyond*, a collection of his international journalism.

ROY KESEY lives in Peru with his wife and daughter. This is his second story to appear in *McSweeney's*.

K. KVASHAY-BOYLE grew up in sunny Santa Barbara and recently graduated from U.S.C. This is her first published story.

NATHANIEL MINTON lives in Los Angeles. He occasionally writes for the movies. His fiction has appeared in *Zyzzyva*, and he is currently at work on his first novel about cancer.

(continued)

ELLEN MOORE is a screenwriter and playwright. She lives in San Francisco.

VAL VINOKUROV, a writer and translator, teaches literature and religious studies at Eugene Lang College in New York City. He is working on an anthology of Russian 'skaz' fiction.

WILLIAM T. VOLLMANN's most recent books include *The Royal Family* and *The Atlas*. His latest, *Argall*, is the third in his Seven Dreams series. Sometime in 2003, *McSweeney's* will publish Vollmann's *Rising Up and Rising Down*. He lives in Sacramento.